COLLARING BROOKE

CLUB ZODIAC, BOOK THREE

BECCA JAMESON

ACKNOWLEDGMENTS

Many thanks to Christa Soule for helping me get through the difficult subject of domestic violence and treating my heroine with grace and respect. Bless her for encouraging me to write this book, having the faith that I could succeed, and then assuring me it was one of my best.

Thanks to my daughter for once again proofreading for me when I was in a time crunch. Thank God she had a long break between semesters to help out her mom this year.

Kudos as usual to my cover artist, Scott Carpenter, for designing these series covers with little to no help from this very unartistic author.

ABOUT THE BOOK

Her entire world is falling apart...

Faced with losing her job and her apartment, Brooke is in crisis mode when she inadvertently stumbles into the world of BDSM. Intrigued, she learns everything she can about submission and finds she craves it.

He's not a sadist...

Carter's been watching the gorgeous redhead learn the ropes in his club. She won't meet his gaze. Her secrets will probably terrify him. And her desires run in a direction that makes him uneasy.

She needs the release only a firm sadist can provide...

Her haunting past has led her to release her stress through spankings, floggings, and whippings. She is leery about Carter's suggestion that she can get the same results from the more sensual elements of the lifestyle.

He has to let her go...

No matter how badly he would like to collar her, she must face her past head on and find herself before she can truly belong to him.

PROLOGUE

The sound was almost worse than the result. It always was. That whistling noise of leather whizzing through the air before it struck its target.

Me.

Brooke covered her ears, tucking her small body in tighter, praying it would end soon.

It wouldn't.

It never did.

Another whoosh of leather. Another slice of pain as it hit her across the back this time.

She bit her lips between her teeth to keep from screaming. Screaming was strictly forbidden. It drew attention from the neighbors. She couldn't imagine how much worse her life would be if anyone called the police.

If she could just be better.

Do better.

Not mess up so often.

It was her fault.

She shouldn't have spilled the coffee.

Her hand had been unsteady. She was hungry. Always hungry. It made her shake. Especially in the morning.

"You stupid girl." The belt hit her across the butt, shocking her with how much worse that next strike hurt.

More reprimands. Seething words hissed out in a low tone so none of the neighbors would hear. "You're nothing. You'll never amount to anything. You can't even pour a cup of coffee without spilling it."

Brooke whimpered, but stopped herself as quickly as possible, hoping she hadn't been heard. She held her breath to keep from making another sound.

"What? You're not going to cry like a big baby this time?" Another whoosh of the belt.

She could anticipate every strike from the sound. She'd been beaten so many times that she knew the timing perfectly. She spread her fingers, tucked her face in closer to the corner of the wall, and prayed it would be over soon.

"Get up."

Brooke didn't dare move. That line was often a trick.

"I said, get up." Louder this time. Closer. "Are you deaf now too?"

Her heart pounded.

"Fine. Then stay in that corner for the rest of the day. You deserve it." Footsteps moved away. The belt was tossed aside, the sound of the buckle hitting the kitchen table soothing. It signified the beating was over.

Brooke didn't allow herself to breathe easy, though. She didn't even move. She wouldn't dare move for the rest of the day.

What time was it?

Morning. Early. It would be a long day.

It had been months since the last time she'd endured a beating like this. She could feel the warm wetness of blood running down her back. It was a familiar sensation. It wasn't usually this bad, but she was used to it. She could even predict from the level of pain alone how long the welts would take to heal.

A door slammed.

Slowly, gradually, she started to breathe again. At least she was alone now. There was peace in her loneliness.

She enjoyed being alone.

No one could hurt her when she was alone.

CHAPTER 1

The first time she saw him she was hauling a bucket of cleaning supplies through the dim lighting of Club Zodiac on her way toward the private rooms that lined the hallway.

Brooke had no idea what his name was, but she assumed he was one of the owners. He had his head down, his fingers flying across the keypad of his cell phone while he sauntered toward the stairs that led to the third floor.

He didn't notice her, but then again she stood stock still watching him. He was not only significantly taller than her, but broad. Enormous. His blond hair was tousled as though he'd either run his hands through it or hadn't combed it at all.

Her heart raced for no good reason. She should not be standing there watching him move. She shouldn't even care enough to glance at him. But she did. She continued to stare after he rounded the corner completely out of sight.

A noise behind her made her spin around so quickly she nearly dropped her supplies. Her face flushed, heat rushing up her cheeks as though she'd been caught stealing or killing puppies or something.

"I'm so sorry." The woman who spoke rushed forward. "I

didn't realize anyone was here or I wouldn't have snuck up on you. I didn't mean to scare you to death. Are you okay?" The woman was blond with pale skin. She was not much taller or larger than Brooke.

When she reached for Brooke's arm to gently touch her, Brooke flinched before she could stop herself. She had to take a deep breath before she found her voice. "No worries. I should have heard you. My mind was..." Where was her mind? She had no idea how to finish that statement, so she let it hang.

The blonde held out a hand. "Faith Robbins."

Brooke stared at her hand for a moment before she realized she needed to take it. She shifted her bucket from her right hand to her left awkwardly in order to return the gesture. "Brooke Madden."

"Nice to meet you, Brooke. Are you a member of the club?" she asked innocently.

Brooke's eyes widened. "No. I, uh..." She felt utterly foolish. "I work for the company that cleans the building." She pointed at her bucket. "I was about to do the floors in the hallway." *When I got sidetracked by the giant of a man who should not have been able to penetrate my thick walls.*

Faith smiled, her face also flushing with embarrassment. Why would she feel awkward? "Ah. Then I'm in your way. I just came in to practice while the club is closed. Will it bother you if I work in the main room?" She nodded over Brooke's shoulder.

Brooke glanced behind her at the darkened room that was filled with the craziest most unimaginable equipment she had seen in her life. What the hell was Faith going to do in there to "practice"?

For weeks Brooke been cleaning this club, and only because she cleaned the entire building, including the business located on the first floor below Zodiac. The first time she'd come in, another team member from the cleaning service had been with her, and thank God because Brooke might have left the place screaming.

She realized Faith was waiting for her to respond. "Oh, no. Of course not. Do what you need to do. I'll work around you. I mean, unless that's a problem. I can come back." That wasn't entirely true. The reality was Brooke was almost done for the day. After mopping this hall, she intended to go home. Exhausted.

Faith hesitated, narrowing her eyes slightly. "You're sure you don't mind? I don't mean to traumatize anyone."

Traumatize anyone? Brooke waved her off with a forced giggle. "Don't worry about me. Do your thing. I'll mop this hallway and get out of your way."

Brooke proceeded to mop the hallway, but her curiosity got the better of her, and she continuously passed by the wide opening that dumped the hallway into the main room. Snooping. Faith turned on several lights, illuminating the large room in a way that made it seem far less ominous. The walls, ceiling, and floor were all painted black, but with a few overhead lights, the odd pieces of furniture scattered around made the place look far less intimidating.

When a loud snapping sound rent through the silence, Brooke jumped out of her skin and rushed around the corner to make sure Faith was okay.

She was still breathing heavily when she came to a halt, finding the blond woman facing a strange bench and flicking a long whip thingy through the air. Another snap came as a shock to Brooke, making her emit a sharp squeal.

She clapped her hand over her mouth, mortified at being caught as Faith turned around.

Faith rushed forward again, still holding the whip. "Shit. I'm sorry. I'm totally making your day miserable time and again." She set the whip down on a chair as she approached. "I'll wait until you're done here before I continue. I forget that most people would be horrified to watch me practice."

Brooke licked her lips. "Practice for what?" She glanced around the room, wondering what the hell actually happened in the club when it was open.

Faith smiled. "You have no knowledge of BDSM, do you?"

"BDSM?" Brooke shook her head, realizing how stupid she sounded as the acronym seeped in. "I mean, yes. I understand the gist. Bondage and stuff. What are you doing with that leather rope?" She sucked in a sharp breath. "I'm sorry. None of my business."

Faith's brows drew together.

Brooke backed up, nearly stumbling. She was supposed to clean the floors and then leave. The owners of CCS—the number one company for business cleaning in Miami—would frown on her engaging the client. Commercial Cleaning Services, Inc. Their motto was: Less is more. Clean and get out. Don't encourage conversation and give a business any reason to fire them.

"Wait." Faith stepped forward. "I'm the one who should be apologizing. It was rude of me to assume you wouldn't freak out. I forget not everyone is used to seeing someone wield a whip."

"What? Goodness no. I've seen everything," Brooke lied as she waved a hand in front of her face to blow off the strange interaction. "You would not believe what cleaning people witness. Whips. Chains. Whatever." She had no actual idea what she was talking about.

For a second, neither of them said a word, and then Faith cocked her head to the side, a slow smile forming. A moment later, she laughed.

Brooke couldn't help but join her. She laughed so hard, she bent at the waist. She couldn't remember the last time she'd laughed like that. And then she sobered as she realized she'd *never* laughed that hard.

Faith was wiping tears from her eyes as Brooke tried to control her outburst.

How mortifying. She couldn't have said anything more ridiculous. But Faith didn't seem to mind.

Finally, Faith took a deep breath and nodded behind her. "Come on. The least I can do is give you a demonstration so you don't leave here wondering."

Brooke stopped mid-breath, taking another step backward. "Oh, no. I couldn't."

"Why not?" Faith glanced around. "You're curious, right?"

Brooke nodded against her better judgment. *More like horrified, but sure.*

The next thing she knew, Faith took her mop from her hand and leaned it against the wall. "Come on," she repeated in a tone that brooked no argument. She gently took Brooke by the arm and led her across the room toward a bench. "Sit here. Don't move. Just watch."

Brooke felt extremely out of her element jumping up onto the bench thingy to sit while Faith picked up her whip again. She was intrigued. And frightened.

Faith approached, spun the handle of the whip around, and offered it to Brooke. "Here. Check it out. Best place to start. It's just leather woven together. When I fling it through the air, it makes that cracking noise you heard."

The one that made me nearly pee my pants. Brooke's hands were shaking as she examined the whip and then handed it back.

"I'm what they call a Domme."

"You mean like a Dominatrix? A woman?"

"Yep, but people don't really say Dominatrix anymore. Just Domme. I'm a female Domme. The guys don't get to have all the fun. Didn't your mom tell you that you can be anything you want?" she teased.

Brooke gulped. *Not even close...* She rocked back and forth on her butt, tucking her hands under her thighs to keep from revealing more than she wanted. Shifting her gaze to the whip, she leaned back a few inches as if she might be injured by it any second. "What are you practicing?" she asked to change the subject. She also really wanted to watch.

"Precision."

"Uh-huh."

Faith backed up several yards, swung the whip slowly through the air a few times, and then gave it a sharp yank, which recreated that same cracking noise as before.

Brooke yelped, flinching as the tail end of the whip struck a pole.

"Precision," Faith repeated as she turned around. "Don't want to hurt anyone."

"You...you...hit people with that?"

"Yes. But it's not nearly as bad as you'd think. I can alter the intensity so that I leave little to no marks." She winked. "I've been doing this a while."

Brooke's mouth was dry. "I can't imagine how that would not hurt." *I know for a fact it would hurt. Bad. It would leave a welt. Probably blood.* She cringed.

Faith turned back around, lined herself up with the pole, and whipped the tail through the air again, slower this time, with less of a crack. It still hit the pole right where she'd aimed, but not with as much force. Nevertheless, it would hurt.

Faith returned to stand next to Brooke, setting the whip behind her on the bench. "That's a bit advanced. I can show you other toys if you're interested."

Brooke was at a loss for words. Half of her was incredibly curious. The other half wanted to run from the club and never look back. "Maybe you could just explain this to me a bit?" She glanced around. "What all happens in here? People come here, get tied to these benches and things, and beaten? Why would they want to do that?"

Faith smiled. "Damn. It's been a long time since I've explained the inside of a club to a newbie."

Brooke had no idea what that meant, but she said nothing.

Faith glanced around. "Your description oversimplifies things. First of all, nothing happens in Zodiac that isn't safe, sane, and consensual. No one plays without a safeword. No one plays without reading the house rules and signing a waiver."

"Who would consent to letting someone whip them?" *Not me.*

"You'd be surprised. People have all sorts of reasons why they practice masochism." She lifted her gaze. "Masochists are people who enjoy some form of pain with their BDSM."

Brooke's heart was pounding. She glanced at the whip, memories of being struck with a similar object more times than she could count flooding her mind. The pain. The humiliation. The torture.

The strangely peaceful numbness.

As if Faith read her mind, she continued. "Many submissives say they get a release from being spanked or flogged or struck by any number of objects. Like they're absolved from some perceived wrongdoing, real or imagined. It can be freeing."

Brooke continued to stare at the whip Faith had wielded so expertly. Freeing... Something about the idea made her skin tingle. It had been so long since the last time she'd felt that kind of release.

So rarely did she step out of line, even lately. But today she had. She'd felt guilt for the last several hours. Her offense? Falling under the spell of a man. It was wrong. She knew it. And yet, she'd been unable to stop herself. The blond god who was part owner of Zodiac had tempted her.

"You okay?" Faith asked.

Brooke jerked her gaze up to meet Faith's.

"I've said too much. I'm so sorry. I get carried away when it seems like someone wants to learn. I forget not everyone wants to hear about my world. Forgive me."

Brooke slowly nodded her head. "No. Really. It's fine." She licked her dry lips. "Would you show me what it's like?"

11

Carter stood at the bottom of the stairs, peering around the corner without making a sound. He'd seen Faith at work several times, so he knew she was safe, but the woman sitting on the bench was horrified, and her terror had grown by the minute.

Still, he hated to intervene. It wasn't like Faith and the woman were engaged in a scene, but on the other hand, it sort of was.

The woman on the bench had wide green eyes he swore he could detect even from across the room. Or maybe it was her gorgeous long red hair that made him assume her eye color. A sprinkle of freckles coated her cheeks, making her look innocent and young.

For a moment he wondered if she was old enough to be inside the club at all, but then he remembered seeing that shock of red hair before and realized she was the woman he'd seen cleaning in the hallway earlier.

She's with the cleaning company? And Faith is giving her a demo?

That last question out of the redhead's mouth made him stiffen. It didn't matter that the club wasn't open right now. Faith still would need to get the woman to sign a waiver if she were going to play.

Luckily he didn't have to intervene because Faith came through for him. "I'd be happy to demonstrate anything you want, but you'll have to sign a waiver first. No one plays inside Zodiac without reading all the rules first."

"Oh, right. Of course." The redhead scooted off the bench. "Well, never mind. I really need to finish up and get out of here." She beelined for the hallway, grabbing her mop along the way. "Thank you for showing me your whip," she called over her shoulder. "It was...interesting." She smiled, and damn but that smile lit up her entire face and stopped Carter's breath.

Good grief, Carter. Stop ogling the woman. She's not even familiar with BDSM. In fact, she'd been rather horrified.

Redheads always got to him. Every time. This one was no exception.

He watched her backside as she rushed across the room. Her jeans were worn and fit loosely on her like they weren't hers. Or she'd lost weight. She was too skinny as it was. He sincerely hoped she hadn't lost weight. Her T-shirt was dark green and he'd noticed the logo of the cleaning company in the upper right corner. She had on tennis shoes. Old. Scuffed. Dirty. But then again, no one would wear nice shoes to clean a building.

As soon as she disappeared around the corner, Carter sauntered into the room as if he happened to arrive at that moment. "Hey, Faith. How's it going?"

"Good." She turned to face him. "Thanks for letting me practice before you open."

He shrugged. "Like I said, no worries. Lincoln, Rowen, and I would prefer you be completely in tune with your apparatus when you play. We don't mind you practicing any time one of us is here." He didn't think Rowen had met Faith yet, but the three of them were owners of the club, so they trusted each other to make decisions.

"Well, thanks anyway." Faith smiled. "I know we just met. It's kind of all of you."

"Your reputation precedes you." He winked and then turned toward the front of the room. "Would you like me to give your friend a waiver to look over?"

Faith chuckled, obviously realizing he'd heard at least some of their conversation. "Sure. That's a good idea. Not sure if she'll come back again, but just in case."

He inhaled slowly as he made his way to the front desk and grabbed a stapled waiver from under the counter. If nothing else, it gave him the excuse to approach the redhead and see if she was as sexy up close as she was from a distance.

When he stepped out into the hallway, she was tucking her mop bucket into the supply closet. She yelped when she turned around, a hand landing on her chest.

He stopped moving. "Shit. Sorry. Didn't mean to scare you."

She stared at the floor. "No. My fault. I was in my own world."

I'll bet. After watching Faith wield that whip, most people fall into another dimension. He took a few steps closer, holding out the waiver. "Faith asked me to give you this. Just in case."

She retreated a few feet before stopping herself and lifting her gaze enough to see what he was holding.

"It's a waiver. If you want Faith to do some demos or if you want to try anything out, you need to look over these papers first, sign them, and return them," he told the top of her head.

For a moment, he wasn't sure she would take his offering. Finally, she stepped forward, grabbed the waiver, and retreated. "Thanks. I'll think about it."

"Good idea. Never jump into anything you aren't sure about. Information is power." He reached into his back pocket and pulled out a business card. When he held it out toward her, he spoke again. "Take my card. If you have any questions, I'd be happy to help."

"Uh…" She hesitated longer this time.

Did his business card have cooties?

Finally, she reached out with her slender fingers and carefully tugged the card from his hand, making every effort to avoid touching him. "Thank you."

He was treading through unchartered territory here. He wasn't a dick, and normally women found him attractive. They didn't usually try to avoid his touch.

"I'm Carter, by the way. Carter Ellis." His name was on the card, so his introduction was superfluous, but he didn't know what else to say.

"Brooke Madden," she murmured. "Thanks again. I should get going." She spun around, grabbed a backpack he hadn't noticed from the corner of the room, and fled past him to get to the stairs that would lead to the first-floor entrance.

Somehow she managed to skirt around him without touching him or making eye contact.

He realized too late he never did get to confirm her eye color.

He'd bet anything they were green, though. And he fully intended to verify that in the near future. What days did their cleaning service come?

CHAPTER 3

The following Wednesday Carter forced himself to stay upstairs while Brooke was on the main floor. He was aware of her presence and knew she and Faith had interacted, but he'd kept himself out of sight. But the week after that, he didn't have the willpower any longer. Curiosity forced him down the stairs where he stopped at the bottom out of sight. He heard her soft, sweet voice before he saw her.

She giggled.

His heart stopped. The sound went straight to his cock.

Whoa. Where did that come from?

The memory of her shocking red curls, pale skin, and supposed gorgeous green eyes had haunted him for fourteen days. For no good reason. He didn't know her at all. But that didn't stop him from imagining all sorts of things about her.

He'd even started jerking off to her image in the shower.

At the sound of her giggle, he leaned his forehead against the wall of the stairwell and thanked God he was alone. It was wrong to eavesdrop on her and Faith, but he couldn't stop himself. And besides, who was it hurting?

He had to know what made her laugh, though, so he peeked

around the corner long enough to see Faith dancing the ends of a flogger over her forearms.

Damn. If that was the sound she made from the stroke of leather on her wrists, how would she react to the dance of a feather across her belly...or her thighs?

He jerked his head back when the women turned. And then he listened.

Faith's voice was prominent and louder than Brooke's. He got the impression Brooke was extremely shy or skittish, especially since she hadn't made eye contact with him when they met and in fact fled as quickly as possible.

For some ridiculous reason, her shyness turned him on even more.

"So, this is a spanking bench," Faith was saying, "or it can be used for anything the Domme wants."

"How do you...?" Brooke's inquisitive voice came through.

"Your knees go here, and your elbows here. Your belly rests here."

Carter didn't need to look to know where Faith was pointing. But damn, he wished he could see Brooke's reaction.

"And you strap people down?"

"Sometimes. Sometimes I expect the submissive to stay where I tell them without restraint. That can be even more of a mind fuck than actually securing their wrists and ankles."

"So, people voluntarily come to Zodiac to be spanked, or whatever." Brooke was commenting more than asking, as if she was trying to wrap her head around the concept. She was so green. Part of him wished she wasn't learning about BDSM. Or perhaps he wished he was the one teaching her. He found himself jealous of Faith.

Faith chuckled. "Yeah. I guess it's hard to understand when you've never been exposed before. You've signed the waiver now. You're welcome to come when the club is open too, you know. It might help you to watch one night. Lots of people come just to watch. There's no harm in observing. Some people even prefer it."

"Oh. No. I couldn't. I feel bad enough taking up your time. I should let you do your thing."

"Oh gosh, don't worry about it. I offered. I'm always happy to educate someone about the lifestyle. I'd rather help inform people about what BDSM is really about than have them wandering through life misinformed or mistakenly horrified."

"Okay. Well, if you're sure you don't mind." The hesitancy in her voice once again made Carter ache to round the corner and approach.

He did not.

"What is that?" she asked next. God, how he wished he could see what she was pointing at.

"It's a St. Andrew's cross. The bottom might stand facing it or facing away."

"Bottom?"

"Submissive. The person on the receiving end, you could say. The Domme is often called the top. In some cases, they switch."

"Switch?"

"Yeah. Just because someone is topping another doesn't mean they always do. They might also bottom another time."

"Oh."

After several seconds of silence, Carter couldn't resist peering around the corner again.

Brooke had her hand on one side of the X and she was smoothing her palm up the well-sanded, varnished wood. Reverently.

Fuck me. What was it with this woman?

"You want to try it?" Faith asked.

"Yes. I think I'd like that." Brooke's voice was stronger. Certain.

Carter's breath stopped. His cock jumped again. He should walk away. He should tiptoe back up the stairs and leave Faith and Brooke alone. It was wrong of him to eavesdrop like this.

But he couldn't stop himself.

～

Brooke had no idea what possessed her to agree to whatever Faith had in mind. In fact, she had no idea what it was Faith had in mind.

What she knew was she trusted Faith implicitly after only meeting her twice. Last week when she'd cleaned the club, Faith had once again been there "practicing." They had exchanged pleasantries and Brooke had silently watched Faith work for a while.

When Brooke had finished cleaning, she'd taken Faith up on the offer to stay later the following week, and here they were now.

For the past several nights Brooke had tossed and turned, wondering what it would be like to submit to someone like Faith. Someone controlled and confident. And kind. It was obvious Faith didn't strike her submissives out of anger. Quite the opposite.

A few trips to the library gave Brooke a better understanding of the lifestyle. She had spent several hours reading everything she could find about BDSM. She had no idea why she found herself so intrigued, but here she was.

And now she was taking things even further than she'd anticipated. Why would she set herself up to be struck by someone? She had to be crazy.

"Face the cross," Faith began. "Step closer and lift your arms up the sides of the X."

Brooke did as she was told, noticing how Faith's voice had changed, her tone dropping, her words somehow soothing while demanding at the same time. Hypnotizing in a way.

Brooke flinched when Faith tapped a peg into the cross near her hand, the sound echoing through the room. "Grab the peg. Wrap your fingers around it."

Easy enough, though she jerked again when Faith did the same on the other side.

A gentle hand landed on Brooke's shoulder. "Relax. I'm not going to do anything that will harm you. I'm just giving you a small taste of what it's like to bottom for someone. Concentrate on how it makes you feel. Mentally. It's a head space. Don't think about anything else right now."

Faith's hand on Brooke's shoulder and then back helped calm her. For a moment she wondered if Faith always worked with women. Maybe she was a lesbian. She hadn't gotten that impression at any point, but then what did she know? "Do you always top women?" she asked boldly.

"No. I top whoever wants me to. It's not sexual at all. It's simply something that gives people a release they need."

"Sexual?" she asked before she could stop herself. She bit her lip and closed her eyes. *What could possibly be sexual about this?* She had done enough research to realize many aspects of BDSM were sexual in nature, but surely not the type Faith participated in. How could flogging and whipping people be sexual?

"Let me amend what I said. BDSM can certainly be sexual. It often is. Many people get off on being restrained or even flogged or whipped. Many Doms also get off on that power play. But it's not always like that. Some people just like the release from a flogging or a spanking or even something harder like a whip, crop, or cane.

"Think of it as sort of a pressure valve. It relieves anxiety and stress for some without being sexual at all. And when I'm dominating someone, it doesn't make me aroused. I can't control the reactions of my submissives, of course. Some of them may get aroused from my actions, but I don't sleep with them."

"Oh." Brooke would have to process that more later. She couldn't wrap her head around it. At the moment she couldn't conceive of being voluntarily beaten for any reason, sexual or otherwise, so she was at a total loss to internalize either explanation.

Except you can imagine it...

She shuddered. The word *penance* popped into her head. Like an atonement for wrongdoing. Like religious people going to confession or something. Interesting that her brain would go there. Perhaps if she let Faith strike her, she might find herself exonerated of some perceived wrongdoing.

She knew exactly what she had to atone for—her stupid interest in the club's owner, Carter Ellis. Thoughts of the man had haunted her day and night for the past two weeks. Even though she hadn't seen him since the night he'd given her his card and the waiver, she hadn't been able to purge him from her mind.

She could feel herself relaxing at the idea of releasing pent-up stress through whatever Faith was going to do to her next.

"That's it. Just relax. Lean your forehead on the cross if you want. You can close your eyes or keep them open. I'm not going to restrain you. You're too new to the lifestyle for that. But I want you to hold on to the pegs on your own, because I've told you to do so."

Brooke sucked in a breath and gripped the pegs tighter, feeling the command so deeply that the end result caused her to practically sense her wrists strapped to the cross.

Faith's fingers trailed up Brooke's arm until she wrapped them around her wrists, imitating exactly what Brooke was thinking. She was good. "I'm going to use a flogger on you. It will be so gentle at first, you won't feel much of anything. As I pick up the intensity, you'll feel like you're getting a massage."

That seemed impossible, but Brooke nodded.

"Before I start, you need a safeword. Never play with anyone without negotiating a safeword first. And never play for one more second with anyone who doesn't take that safeword seriously. For most clubs, the universal safeword is *red. Yellow* if you need a moment to slow down and regroup. *Red* means stop altogether and end the scene."

Brooke nodded. She had read about safewords.

"Tell me your safeword."

"Red."

"Good. If it gets too intense, use it. I'll stop immediately. If you need me to slow down, use *yellow*," she repeated.

"Got it. Red. Yellow." She took a few deep breaths, worrying what it would feel like to have Faith swing that flogger at her and craving it at the same time. She had truly lost her marbles.

"Deep breaths. Lean against the cross if you want." Faith's hand trailed down Brooke's back again before disappearing.

A few seconds later, the flogger whooshed through the air and landed on Brooke's shoulder blade. Brooke flinched, sucking in a sharp breath before realizing it didn't hurt at all. In fact, she hardly felt it. Just as Faith had told her.

Another strike landed on her other shoulder blade, and Brooke relaxed. Lowering onto her heels and blowing out a breath.

"You okay?"

"Yes."

"More?"

"Okay. Yes."

When Faith moved around behind her more fully, she set up a rhythm, swinging the flogger through the air in what Brooke knew from observing earlier was a figure-eight pattern. Each soft blow landed on Brooke's back, working down toward her butt and then thighs before inching back toward her shoulders.

There was no doubt it was soothing. Relaxing. Exactly like the massage Faith had intimated. With every strike, Brooke relaxed more, going into her head and absorbing the pressure from the strips of leather.

Faith paused again, stepped to the side, and spoke close to Brooke's ear. "You doing okay?"

"Yes."

"You're slipping into a subspace. Pretty incredible for someone's first foray into submission." Brooke could hear the smile in Faith's voice. "You sure you haven't been flogged before?"

"I'm sure." She smiled back. "But I might like to do it again."

When had she gotten so bold?

"You want me to increase the pressure?"

"Um, sure. Yes, okay. Let's try that." She could feel the stress leaving her body with every strike to her back.

"Okay. Don't forget to stop me if you need to with your safeword."

"I will." She wouldn't. She knew instinctively she wouldn't use a safeword with Faith. She trusted her. And she sensed she could like this lifestyle if she let herself. It was indeed as freeing as Faith insinuated.

Every muscle in her body relaxed when Faith resumed flogging her. As the strikes grew closer together and landed with more force, Brooke felt herself going deeper into her head. It didn't hurt, but her skin heated beneath her T-shirt and jeans. The warmth was welcoming.

It seemed like only moments passed before Faith set the flogger aside and came to Brooke's ear again, her palm smoothing up and down Brooke's back. "You're a natural."

Brooke said nothing. What did it say about her that she was a natural? She tensed for a moment, wondering if Faith could tell she had been beaten before.

Beaten, she reminded herself. Nothing like the flogging she'd gotten from Faith. Beaten. Hard.

A part of her wanted that now. She wanted Faith to continue, hitting her harder, but she couldn't bring herself to ask. *What's wrong with me? Why would I want someone to intentionally hit me?*

"Deep breaths," Faith whispered. "Come back to me."

From where? *I'm right here.*

"That's it. Open your eyes. Look at me."

Brooke blinked her eyes open, facing Faith.

23

Faith smiled. "That's it. You're in subspace."

"What's subspace?"

"It's a place some people can go in their mind when they scene like this. Escape. Release." Faith wrapped her hand around one of Brooke's. "Let go of the pegs. Your fingers are going to be sore. You're gripping the pegs too tight."

Brooke released the pegs and lowered her arms. She was sore and stiff just as Faith suggested.

"Come sit down. You need water." Faith guided her over to a leather loveseat and opened a bottle of water for her before handing it over. "Rest a minute. Breathe."

Brooke drank about half the bottle before shaking herself back into the present as if she'd been far away. "Wow. That was... powerful." She met Faith's gaze.

Faith was smiling. "Yes. You slide into subspace very easily. Keep that in mind when you play with someone else. You should tell them. Most Doms won't expect it."

Brooke flinched. "I'm not doing something like this with someone else." The idea had never crossed her mind. She had come here to see what all the hype was about. Nothing else. Now she knew. Right?

Faith nodded, not at all condescendingly. "Okay. But if you change your mind, it's important to let whoever tops you know how easily you slide into your head. Not every Dom is as knowledgeable as others about handling a submissive who goes in deep like that. It's difficult to continue to consent when you're in subspace. Someone might strike you too hard."

Brooke nodded slowly. Half of her wondered what it would feel like to be hit harder. In a controlled environment like this. With her permission. While the person doing so was not angry.

She shuddered, lowering her gaze to the floor.

Faith surprised her with her next words. "I know you wanted more, but it wasn't prudent this first time. You need to process what we did for a few days before trying again. If you really want me to use another tool and strike you hard enough to actually hurt or raise welts, we can discuss it another time."

Heat rushed up Brooke's face as she continued to stare at the floor. She couldn't even nod. She was still trying to process what it said about her to crave something like this.

She finally glanced around the room. The entire club existed for people to play like she just did with Faith. So there were others like her. And others like Faith. She was not alone.

Was she a masochist?

And did all masochists have a history like hers?

CHAPTER 4

Carter made sure he was at the front desk pretending to organize papers and tidy up the entrance an hour later when Brooke and Faith were leaving.

Faith lifted her face to smile at Carter. Brooke kept her gaze toward the floor, allowing her red curls to hide her expression. She was either shy, she hated men, or she was intimidated by him, in particular. None of those things made him happy.

Nevertheless, he greeted them. "Hey, ladies. I thought I heard voices down here."

While Brooke took a step behind Faith, Faith spoke. "Giving Brooke an introduction to the lifestyle. Do you mind if we use a private room Saturday afternoon before the club opens?"

"Sure." Though he wasn't sure what difference it would make when no one else was around and the club wasn't open. *Except you were around.* He winced, wondering if the women had sensed him watching.

Faith shrugged. "I just think it might be easier for Brooke to relax in a smaller space. The wide-open main room can be intimidating even when the club is closed."

"I understand. Use whichever room you'd like. You can lock the door and close the blinds too. Just be safe." Was he making a mistake? He hoped not. He knew Faith well enough to trust her judgment. She was an amazing Domme who had recently switched her membership to Zodiac from Breeze. The owner of Breeze had nothing but wonderful things to say about her.

But what about Brooke? She was the most skittish person Carter had ever seen. She tugged at his heart strings from behind Faith. He knew so little about her, and yet he was intrigued.

Watching her submit to Faith had stopped his breath in his lungs. It hadn't taken long for her to slide into a subspace many people were never able to achieve. As her shoulders relaxed and her head slumped forward, his dick had stiffened painfully.

Not only was she gorgeous, but she appeared to be naturally submissive in a way that piqued his interest even further. Ever since the first night he met her, he'd imagined her in positions of submission, but he'd had no proof his daydreams were anything but just that—dreams—until today. Damn, she was fantastic. If only he could somehow get her to work with him instead of Faith. But no way could he suggest that yet. She was new. If she wanted to bond with Faith, he needed to step back and let her.

He decided to engage her, or least attempt to. "You signed the waiver, right, Brooke?" He leaned around Faith a few inches in attempt to put Brooke more fully in his line of sight. He knew she'd signed everything, but what else could he say to force her to speak to him?

"Yes," she murmured, still facing the floor.

"And you read it thoroughly? No questions?"

"No." She shook her head, lifting her gaze to approximately his chest. He was not the tallest man alive, but he towered over Brooke. She couldn't have been more than about five two. She cleared her throat. "I only had a few questions. Faith answered them."

"Okay." *Shit*. He wanted to engage her more, but he couldn't think of a damn thing to say. "Well, if you ever need anything, you still have my card, right?"

"Yes." She licked her lips, took a deep breath, and then turned toward the stairs that led down to the exit. "I've gotta get going. I'll see you next week, Faith." And just like that, she was gone.

Faith sighed, setting her elbows on the counter. "Nice try." She smiled.

"What?"

She rolled her eyes. "Don't be coy with me. You were practically drooling over her."

Carter shrugged. "She's cute."

"She's a hot mess."

"I can see that." He didn't want to pry. It would be wrong to ask Faith to break any confidence she had with Brooke.

Faith sighed again. "I don't even know what her deal is, or I would ask for advice. All I know is she's genuinely submissive and eager to learn. So, I'll do my best to help her find herself. But she's wound up tight, and there's no way she's going to let her guard down fully in the main room."

Carter wasn't sure what Faith meant by that since he'd been on the stairwell for nearly the entire scene and from his vantage point, Brooke had slipped easily into subspace. Not only that, but she had absorbed the flogging like a seasoned submissive, and he would bet money she would have asked for more.

He also knew Faith wouldn't have let Brooke go further this early in her exploration. Faith knew what she was doing. She would not take risks.

"If there's anything I can do..."

She blew out a breath. "Maybe someday. For now, all I can do is ensure she's playing safe. She's eager to learn, as if the entire lifestyle had been foreign to her until now and suddenly she realizes it's exactly what she craves."

"That's usually how it happens. People get a peek and then can't stop."

She nodded. "She has some deep stuff buried inside her. If I had to guess, I'd bet it involves a man. Or perhaps more than one man."

Carter winced. He would have guessed that too, but damn, he didn't like to hear it out loud. "You think she's been abused?"

"Maybe. It's hard to tell. She won't open up about it, and I don't want to push her too hard. But she closed off completely when I suggested she come to the club while it's open. And she nearly lost her shit when I asked if she'd like to work with someone else."

He hated to point out his next thought, but... "Do you think she's into *you*?"

Faith shook her head. "No. I thought of that, but I don't think so. She pays close attention to the apparatus and the toys when I show her new things. Not me. She's never come on to me or even gotten in my space. I think it's the lifestyle she's curious about, and she trusts me."

That was promising. "Then perhaps your assumption is correct. Maybe she's been abused by a man, and she trusts you because you're a woman." That was *not* promising as far as Carter's interests were concerned.

"Could be. In any case, she's made it clear she'd like to explore rougher play, so I'll cautiously give her that in a private setting." Faith tapped the counter and shoved off. "I need to get going. I'll see you again soon." She waved as she made her way toward the stairs.

Carter's heart beat faster as he stood alone in the silence. He wanted to approach Brooke and straight out proposition her. Ask her on a date or something. He was attracted to her physically. He was also attracted to her shyness. He had a history of dating women who were more introverted and quiet. Loud, obnoxious women with agendas always turned him off.

On the other hand, he had concerns about this particular sexy redhead. If *she* had a history of dating abusive men, he had no idea how to handle that. His own upbringing did not include witnessing abuse. He was peripherally aware of club members or outside friends who were victims of abuse or abusers, but he could only imagine the challenges they faced.

Another red flag was her apparent desire to experience something rougher with Faith. What did that mean? He knew Faith was talented with a whip, a crop, a paddle, nearly any tool. But what did Brooke desire? Welts? Blood?

He shuddered. He was a Dom in every sense of the word. Hell, he was part owner of this club with Lincoln and Rowen. He and Rowen had bought into the business with Lincoln three years ago.

Carter had joined his first club when he was eighteen, even before he'd joined the army and served eight years. He and Rowen had enlisted in the army at the same time and became close friends in boot camp—a friendship that never faltered. It was Carter who educated Rowen on the specifics of BDSM after realizing they had a shared interest.

But no matter how long he'd been in the lifestyle or how knowledgeable he was, Carter wasn't a sadist by any stretch of the imagination. He enjoyed the Dominant/submissive side of things. He liked to be with a woman who submitted to him sexually, especially in the bedroom, but he didn't have a desire to inflict pain on anyone.

He was educated in all aspects of the lifestyle, enough to ensure safety inside the club he partially owned, but his personal tastes did not run toward sadism. If Brooke ended up looking for a Dom or Domme who would fulfill some sort of masochistic need, Carter would never be that man.

Lincoln was the sadist of the three owners. If it came down to it, he might be able to help Brooke or find someone else to help her.

Carter winced. The thought of some other man handling her made his skin crawl.

Finally, he shook thoughts of Brooke from his mind and headed back upstairs to finish some paperwork. There was no reason to create problems that didn't exist. Maybe Brooke was experimenting and she would eventually find herself to be someone he could dominate.

If she ever looked him in the eye.

The truth was, there were a lot of unknowns about Brooke, and a few of them were pretty important. No matter how physically attracted to her Carter found himself, it was what was inside that mattered. Only time would reveal how compatible she might be with him.

Brooke flopped down on her mattress later that night, pulled the blanket over her body, and stared at the ceiling. She had sold the bedroom set months ago, keeping only the mattress which wouldn't have been easy to sell anyway.

Her clothes—what few she owned—were in boxes in the corner. The rest of the apartment was as sparsely furnished as the bedroom. She had kept the kitchen table and two chairs only because they too weren't worth more than a few dollars. But the living room was empty by now. She'd sold the television and sofa with the bedroom furniture.

Closing her eyes, she took a breath and fought the tears that escaped to run down her face. She was out of money. Her job didn't pay enough to even cover the rent alone. CCS would only permit her to work thirty hours a week so they wouldn't have to cover health insurance, which also meant she didn't *have* health insurance.

This wasn't something new. She'd never had health insurance

in her life. Thank God she'd never broken a bone or needed stitches in her twenty-two years. Although even if she had needed medical care, she wouldn't have gotten it. She had become a pro at hiding her injuries and pretending nothing had happened at all. Doing so kept things from spiraling into darker places she didn't want to go.

She shuddered. The tears fell in earnest now. Most nights she didn't allow herself the luxury of crying. It wasn't worth it.

She wiped the tears away with the back of her hand and tried to come up with a plan. She had no skills other than cleaning. No education. No friends. No relatives. She hadn't paid her rent in two months. It wouldn't be long before the building manager kicked her out. He'd left her several notices, sliding them under the door or taping them to the outside. It was only a matter of time. Talking to him wouldn't do any good. She didn't have the rent. Period.

Every dime she made needed to go into maintaining her car, and it was holding up by a thread and a prayer. She wasn't a religious person—in fact, she'd never been inside a church—but she wasn't above praying on the off chance it helped. So far she had seen no evidence in her life that it did a bit of good. But then again, maybe she would have been homeless before now without it.

The fifteen-year-old Pontiac Grand Prix was her most valuable possession. So far it still ran well, and she managed to keep the bare minimum of insurance on it. At least she wasn't breaking any laws.

She needed the car. Selling it wasn't an option. Everything else had been sold off first, because she'd known for months it would be her home eventually. Wandering the streets of Miami didn't appeal to her at all. As long as she worked for barely above minimum wage for thirty hours a week, she could afford to keep the car and live in it. It wasn't ideal, but not one moment of her life had been ideal.

Brooke rolled onto her side and drew her knees up, curling into a ball. Thank God she'd never needed to run the heat in her apartment because there was no way she would have been able to afford that luxury, but some nights she got chilled anyway. The temperature in Miami rarely got cold enough for most people to heat their homes, but most people weren't as skinny as Brooke.

Her stomach grumbled and she ignored it. She'd eaten a peanut butter sandwich when she got home. It would have to do until tomorrow because she'd used the last two slices of bread and scraped the jar of peanut butter clean. She knew she would easily qualify for food assistance from a local food bank, but she'd never had the guts to enter one. Perhaps that decision hadn't been wise. Now that she was close to eviction, it occurred to her that a bit less pride over the last six months might have provided her with enough money to pay the rent a little longer.

The place was a shithole anyway. The walls were paper thin. She could hear the neighbors to the left arguing day and night. The people above her must have been running a dance studio out of their living room, and the old man living to her right snored so loudly she had to cover her head with her pillow at night.

The manager rarely repaired anything until the fifth request, and then only begrudgingly in a manner that usually involved duct tape. The place hadn't been painted in all the years she'd lived in it, so there was little chance she would get back any security deposit—if one had ever been paid in the first place.

Yeah, her shitty life was about to get shittier.

The only bright light in her world was the woman she'd accidentally met at Club Zodiac several weeks ago. Faith Robbins. The blonde had no idea she was Brooke's only friend in the world.

At first, the reason Brooke had agreed to let Faith introduce her to the lifestyle was to interact with a human and avoid boredom. Brooke had not suspected she would find any aspect of the lifestyle remotely to her liking, but then she'd proven herself wrong.

From the first moment she'd watched Faith wielding her whip, she'd seen things through a new lens. Tonight was the first time she'd let Faith flog her, but she'd immediately craved more. It felt amazing. In her warped world, she knew she would relax and some of her stress would lighten if Faith used that whip or the crop on her. She'd seen Faith practice swinging both.

Brooke had no idea how to ask for what she wanted, nor did she have the balls to do so, but indirectly she knew she'd gotten the point communicated earlier because Faith had suggested they use a private room on Saturday.

Three days from now. She had only ever been to Zodiac on Wednesdays—the day she cleaned—and she'd started leaving Zodiac for last, partly by design because it gave her the freedom to stick around when she was done working. It gave her hope. A reason to keep going through the motions.

She knew it wouldn't last. Nothing ever did. But for now, she had one thing to look forward to, and maybe Saturday Faith would use the whip on her. Would Faith be willing to strike her hard enough to draw blood?

Laundry was a constant problem. She had enough clothes to get through the week each week except for the work T-shirts. She only had two of them, and she washed them out in the sink and hung them to dry after work every day. That way each shirt had more than a full day to dry before she needed it again. She was poor, but she never left the house dirty.

There was a superstore only two blocks from her apartment. She used the store brand of soap and shampoo and every other thing she needed. In the six months since she'd found herself alone, she had never left the house without a shower and clean clothes. It was the first change she'd made the moment she was on her own.

She had no idea how she was going to manage when she lost the apartment, but she would find a way somehow.

Her stomach growled again, and she closed her eyes and willed herself to sleep. She had to be up at seven to get to work by eight. Most nights that wasn't a problem. After all, she only worked six hours a day. She had her afternoons free. But, lately she'd been struggling to concentrate very long on anything. If she were completely honest, the real struggle was getting the owner of Zodiac out of her mind.

Carter Ellis. She had his card. She'd flipped it around in her hands for so long the edges were worn. His number was committed to memory. Not that she'd ever use it, but she'd somehow memorized it anyway.

Even though she'd never made direct eye contact with him, she knew exactly what he looked like. He was blond and tan and built like a body builder. According to his card, he worked in construction when he wasn't at Zodiac. Not surprising considering how fit he was. He surely spent every spare hour at the gym.

She had no business thinking about him at all, but nevertheless, thoughts of him filtered into her psyche often. A gentle giant to her diminutive stature. Every time he'd spoken to her, he'd used a soft tone that made her skin tingle. In her limited experience, men didn't speak so calmly.

She had absolutely no reason to trust him, nor *did* she trust him, but he made her heart beat faster both times she'd seen him, and he'd awoken something inside her she should not be examining. Even giving him real estate in her brain was dangerous. She knew better than to let herself be captivated by a man. Nothing good could come of it. She needed to shake him from her mind and avoid him at all costs.

That could be difficult since he always seemed to be at the club when she was there. Was it a coincidence? Surely the man didn't come in because she was there. That was absurd. Unless he didn't trust her, and he thought he needed to be there to make sure she didn't steal anything. That was far more likely.

It also infuriated her. She'd never once stolen anything in her life. Not even when she was hungry. Never. She knew she was poor and had nothing of value in her world, but she was a good employee. She did her job well and had never broken anything at any business or taken so much as a paper clip.

Calm down, Brooke. You're making this stuff up. No one accused you of stealing.

Another matter crept into her mind. Faith had asked her if she wanted to do a scene when the club was open. Brooke had declined for several reasons. For one, she was not a social person. Large crowds made her nervous. Her heart raced and her blood pressure rose. She had no ability to make conversation with people, and she hated when someone addressed her directly.

For another thing, it would embarrass her for anyone to know she was even considering a role in the lifestyle. It was one thing to communicate her needs to Faith, but opening that up to other people wasn't on her radar.

Thirdly, she had no money. She knew the club dues were way out of her price range. If she had that kind of money, she would pay the rent. She hadn't mentioned it to Faith yet, but she felt like she was already crossing the line by letting the woman work with her after she finished cleaning because she was not officially a member. Chances were, this thing she had going with Faith wouldn't last much longer. Faith would grow bored of helping her, and eventually the financial aspects would catch up with her.

And lastly, there was Carter. It was one thing to run into him when she was there cleaning, but it was another thing entirely to have to converse with him in a social setting or greet him at the door. *Never going to happen.*

She wished the flogging earlier would have purged him from her system. A warning of sorts that she needed to get her head straight. Men were trouble. But Carter was still occupying her mind. Perhaps if Faith had struck her harder or whipped her, Brooke would have been able to shake images of him.

Maybe next week…

The idea of taking things further made her body warm.

Flopping onto her back, she blinked at the ceiling again. Her foray into BDSM was a lucky break that fell into her lap by coincidence and had a finite lifespan. All she could do was soak up everything Faith offered and wait for the bubble to burst.

CHAPTER 5

For the next few weeks, Carter forced himself to stay out of Faith's arrangement with Brooke. He didn't say a word when he noticed that Faith silently paid a membership fee for Brooke, although he suspected Brooke knew nothing about it.

In truth, he never would have asked for the fees. For one thing, he didn't get the impression Brooke would ever come to the club when it was open, so the point was moot. For another thing, he suspected she wasn't exactly rolling in cash.

Either Faith simply felt better about covering Brooke since they were using the club in off hours, or Faith planned to lure Brooke into coming when the club was open. Either way, Carter kept his mouth shut and added Brooke to the books.

So, it was an incredible surprise when Carter looked up one Wednesday night to find Brooke entering the club. He nearly tripped over himself as he stammered a greeting. "Hey." He forced himself to keep his words to a minimum, not wanting to scare her any more than she already appeared to be.

She nodded without fully lifting her gaze, as usual. She was wringing her fingers together as she stepped closer to him. "Um,

Faith suggested I come in when the club is open and watch. That's okay?"

"Of course. You're welcome here any time. You have full membership privileges. You can watch or participate any time you want. Would you like me to give you a quick tour?"

She hesitated a moment, considering his proposition as if he'd suggested they go fuck in one of the private rooms. She even took a step back.

He wanted to kick himself for not keeping his sentences brief.

Finally, she nodded. "That would be nice. Thanks. Is Faith here?"

He shook his head, and then realized she couldn't see him, so he cleared his throat. "No. Not tonight." No way in hell was he going to tell her where he thought Faith was tonight. If she wasn't freaked out already, she would be if she found out what Carter suspected—that Faith was with Rowen.

Carter was a good judge of people. He spent enough time watching the members come and go from the club that he could read most people in a heartbeat. He would bet anything Faith was not simply a Domme. Not that she wasn't good at it. She was one of the best he'd ever watched. The entire club came to a halt to watch her perform. But Carter suspected she was either a switch or lying to herself.

He'd seen her leave the club with Rowen the previous Saturday, her entire demeanor demure and submissive. Not a trace of dominance. He wouldn't call Rowen out on it, but Carter believed Rowen was dominating Faith in secret.

If that was the case, and if Faith decided to commit to Rowen, where would that leave Brooke? Carter shuddered to consider the implications.

The important thing was that Brooke had just agreed to allow Carter to give her a tour, and he had no intention of squandering the opportunity. After a quick glance around, Carter spotted his employee Aaron nearby. "Hey, can you watch the front for a bit?"

"Of course." Aaron didn't say another word as he took Carter's spot at the top of the stairs, manning the entrance to the club.

Carter wiped his hands on his blue jeans and forced himself not to touch Brooke anywhere as he pointed toward the entrance to the main room. "After you."

Shocking him, Brooke spoke again. "Is Faith okay? She cancelled our earlier appointment. I thought maybe she was sick or something."

How the hell was he supposed to address these concerns? "I don't think she's sick. Something just came up." *Like Rowen's cock.*

"Good. I mean, I hope everything's okay." She moved slowly into the club and then stopped, still speaking to the floor. "She encouraged me to come in when the club was open. I thought tonight was as good a night as any." Suddenly, she jerked her gaze upward and to the left.

She didn't look at him directly, but it was the first time he got to see her eyes, which were indeed a deep green like a natural spring. He swallowed his reaction. Damn, those eyes would bring a man to his knees. Perhaps she knew that, and it was why she never met anyone's gaze. Doubtful.

She nibbled on the bottom corner of her lower lip for a second and then opened her mouth to speak. "Don't I need to pay a fee or something?"

Carter searched quickly through his mind for an answer. "No. You're covered. You're practically an employee here. Employees don't have to pay membership dues." *Good one.* He was proud of himself for coming up with that on the fly.

"Okay." Her brow scrunched adorably for a moment before she took her beautiful face away from him again to watch her feet. Tonight was the first time he was seeing her without her uniform T-shirt on. She still wore jeans, but instead of tennis shoes, she had on a pair of black flats. They were slightly scuffed, but they looked comfortable. She also wore a black blouse. It was too big on her and hung off her shoulders, but he got the impression this might be the best outfit she owned, which pissed him off for some reason.

He barely knew this woman, and yet he felt protective of her in a way that defied logic. He hated that she might not have the funds for a carefree shopping trip or possibly even a decent meal, judging from her weight and the way her clothes fit her. His instinct also told him she was humble and would be horrified if anyone tried to help, especially since she had asked about the membership fees.

He needed to speak to fill the silence. "So, you know every inch of this place better than most members, of course, but being here in the off hours when the lights are on is totally different from the ambiance of the club in action."

"I see that." She faced the main room, folding her arms under her chest. He knew she wasn't cold. The night was warm and the inside of the club was kept at a comfortable temperature to accommodate the fact that many members often wore little to no clothing when they played.

Which meant her stance was closed off. Not shocking.

She flinched when a whip whooshed through the air to their right and then seemed to stop breathing for a moment as she turned to watch a Dom warming up. His submissive was naked and facing the St. Andrew's cross. Her wrists were secured to the X above her head, and her feet were spread wide with her ankles also strapped to the lower corners of the X.

Carter knew the Dom. He was one of the employees. Tyler. He was doing a demonstration tonight. At least Carter knew his scene would be safe and a good one for Brooke to watch, but that didn't mean she wouldn't have a trigger reaction to watching someone get whipped.

If his instincts were correct, Carter felt more confident than ever that Brooke had been abused. Abused women often didn't handle some scenes well. He knew BDSM could be therapeutic for some abuse survivors, but he was not the least bit qualified to make this judgment for Brooke, especially since he knew very little about her actual circumstances.

Brooke inched toward the scene as if drawn by a magnet. Carter wasn't sure she even realized she was moving. Panic gripped him. Brooke was hard to read, but he felt an incredible concern over her reaction. If there was any possibility she had been abused, he wasn't sure she could remain quiet and not interrupt the scene.

But she surprised him. She stopped along the outer wall, leaving plenty of space between herself and the scene, and then she watched, riveted by Tyler's movements.

No. That wasn't it at all. She never even glanced at Tyler. She kept her gaze pinned on the sub. The woman swayed back and forth with every crack of the whip even though Tyler had not touched her once.

He was performing a bit of a mindfuck. The submissive was blindfolded.

Brooke flinched every time the whip whistled through the air, but she kept her arms crossed and leaned against the wall. Carter wasn't sure she was fully aware he stood next to her. She was transfixed by every movement of the sub.

Carter kept his gaze on Brooke, fear creeping up his spine. Fear mixed with a certain level of sadness. He was no longer afraid that Brooke would inadvertently interrupt the scene, but now he was nervous about what watching a woman being whipped would do to her emotionally.

He'd give anything to have a window to her past, to know what she'd been through in her short life. He knew from her paperwork that she was twenty-two years old, ten years younger than him. Under normal circumstances he would be certain he had lived through more, endured more, and suffered more than someone a decade younger than him.

But not Brooke. In some ways, perhaps he was right, but he

had a feeling she had experienced far more than him and lived through a level of suffering no one would be envious of.

Carter had fought in several tours overseas in his eight years of military service. He'd seen a great deal of death and destruction. Images of humans being blown to pieces would haunt him for the rest of his life. Visions of women and children dead in the streets of the towns they had once loved were burned into his mind.

What about Brooke? What had she seen? What had she endured?

Brooke was transfixed by the scene in front of her. She'd watched Faith practice with her whip on several occasions, but this was the first time she would witness someone swinging it at a living human.

She found herself intrigued in a nearly perverted way. She wrapped her fingers around the material of her blouse at her throat and held it tight while the man with the whip scared the living daylights out of the blindfolded woman secured to the cross.

She knew the man's name was Tyler. She'd heard several people mumbling his name around her before she'd completely blocked everyone out to concentrate.

It seemed like she was on the set of a horror film where the stupid girl opens the door to see what's on the other side, only to get killed. Brooke had a similar sensation. She should turn away, rush down the stairs and out the front door. She should never have come here on a night when the club was open. Worst idea ever.

A part of her knew her entire world was about to change. She would not be the same person after she watched this scene. For good or bad, she would be altered. And there was no telling which direction things would go.

As if she were watching a train barreling into the depot too fast to avoid the unexpected cars already on the track, she couldn't look away. She was aware that Carter stood close to her, but she ignored him, focusing on the woman on the St. Andrew's cross, still wondering how on earth anyone would subject themselves to an intentional beating, while at the same time wishing *she* was that woman.

She knew she wasn't normal, that her way of looking at things was warped. But there was no way to change her past, a past that shaped her future and landed her right where she stood now.

When Tyler lowered his whip and approached the woman, Brooke was fascinated to find him soothing her with a hand on her back. He whispered something in the submissive's ear that made the woman nod several times.

He was completely in control when he stepped back and lifted the handle of the whip. This time when it whizzed through the air, the tip of it hit the submissive's butt, raising a red welt.

The woman arched her belly forward as if she could somehow avoid the contact, but she only had a few inches of wiggle room. And besides, something else was off.

Brooke didn't blink while she watched Tyler strike the woman again about two inches lower than the first welt. It was at that moment Brooke realized what was odd. The woman didn't scream. She didn't even struggle. In fact, she moaned. As if the entire scene was enjoyable.

Brooke grasped her blouse tighter. A lifeline of sorts. She held her breath, totally mesmerized by the performance. It was a choreographed dance, Tyler moving back and forth behind the woman like a stealthy panther stalking its prey. His legs crossed over each other perfectly, his knees bending each time he lifted his arm.

The only reason Brooke took her gaze off the submissive for

even a moment was to absorb the intensity that was Tyler. Before she could be lured into his web, she jerked her gaze back to the woman. Her butt cheeks were now covered in thin lines. Red welts that would hurt and make it difficult for her to sit down for a few days. There was no blood, however.

For some reason Brooke found that fact disappointing.

You are really and truly a freak.

Who in their right mind would stand in the middle of a BDSM club and watch a woman being whipped while feeling an overwhelming sense of jealousy? Envy crept up Brooke's cheeks, leaving them flushed and warm.

She might not know many things about life. She wasn't worldly. She didn't have possessions. She lacked education. Her job was a dead end. And worst of all, she'd come home from work that afternoon to find an eviction notice on her apartment door. She had four days to get out.

She had no idea why she had come to Zodiac tonight. Perhaps it had been a combination of things: Faith canceling on her, her impending eviction, and her life spiraling out of control. Instead of sitting in her dismal apartment staring at the blank walls that would not be hers anymore on Saturday, she'd chosen to escape her life for a few hours, and here she was.

She knew one thing for certain—she would give anything to trade places with the woman currently attached to that cross.

Well, perhaps not anything, because she did have a pile of hesitation. The list of reasons holding her back was peculiar. For one, she would never be able to take her clothes off in public like this woman. She didn't have it in her. Maybe she could do it in a private locked room under Faith's control, but not in public with people staring at her.

Two, she would never let a man yield this kind of power over her. A woman maybe, but never a man. Men were not to be trusted. Ever. That fact, if nothing else, was cemented in her brain.

Three, she didn't have the guts to voice her desires to anyone, so the point was nearly moot. The closest she'd come to asking for what she desired had been with Faith, who had given her many new experiences over the past several weeks in a private room of the club. Faith had consistently held back on the idea of using her whip, however, insisting Brooke needed to work up to such an experience. They had played with a variety of floggers and even a paddle, but not a whip. Yet.

Four, she was scared to death to find out what might happen to her psychologically if she allowed herself to be intentionally whipped hard enough to draw blood or at least welts. She feared she might completely fall apart. Or perhaps the experience would somehow provide the absolution she craved and had for months.

Oh yeah, she was warped. She knew it. But she didn't have to tell anyone else.

"Brooke?" Someone was whispering her name. She ignored it, too lost in the scene to care who was speaking to her.

Tyler had moved on to covering the back of the woman's thighs. Pink lines crisscrossed her legs from her butt to her knees. Brooke could feel the stinging burn of every strike as if she were the one receiving the whipping instead of the woman strapped to the cross.

"Brooke?" Her name filtered in louder this time, above a whisper, and it was accompanied by a hand on her shoulder.

She nearly jumped out of her skin at the unexpected contact, slamming into the wall behind her roughly as she jerked her gaze to the left to see who had touched her.

Carter.

Shoot.

His eyes were wide, palms in the air. He didn't approach her. "Sorry. I shouldn't have touched you."

How did he know that? Her mouth was dry. She stared at him dead in the eye, not blinking. Seeing him truly for the first time. His expression was filled with concern. Her heart raced, but she managed to release the grip she had on her blouse and lower her hand to join the other crossed under her chest.

She was breathing heavily.

"Brooke?" he repeated, his voice gentle.

She licked her lips, still holding his gaze. His eyes were a gorgeous dark blue that held her hostage. His blond hair had grown since she first met him. It was no longer cut so close to his scalp that he looked like he was in the military. She suspected he had been at some point, judging by the fallen soldier tattoo on his biceps. It stuck out of his sleeve far enough for her to recognize the symbol. Besides, most of the time whatever shirt he wore fit him too snuggly.

Yeah, even though she'd never intentionally made eye contact with him, she wasn't dead. She was a living, breathing human who knew a hot male body when she saw it. It wasn't necessary to meet a man's gaze to know what he looked like from the neck down. She could accomplish an amazingly specific description from her peripheral vision alone.

Carter scared her to death, however. Not because she was afraid he would hurt her, but rather the opposite. Every encounter with him had indicated he was a genuinely nice guy. He was polite and courteous. He spoke to her calmly every time. And he never got too close, as if he sensed she had issues with being touched.

He probably thought she had some level of agoraphobia the way she kept her distance from other people, especially him. Including right now.

He was still holding her gaze, waiting. "You okay? Will you follow me? I'd like to get you some water."

She nodded.

For several more seconds he continued to stare at her as though weighing the possibility that she might not look at him again as soon as he broke the spell.

He was right. She needed this magnetic pull to be severed, and she needed to guard herself against ever putting herself in a situation like this again. She'd let her guard down. She'd looked into his eyes, and a part of her fortress crumbled. It would need to be rebuilt. Fast.

Forcing herself to look away, she jerked her gaze to the floor.

Carter sighed. Disappointed? "Come on." He swung a hand out to indicate she should follow him at his side. When she lifted her eyes to see where he intended to put that hand, he lowered it slowly. "Please, Brooke. Follow me."

She did as he asked for some unknown reason. Rationally, she knew it was the right choice. She had no business continuing to observe that scene. It was luring her into a state of hypnosis. It unnerved her to so readily obey the demands of such a large man —or any man for that matter. But Carter was different somehow. She trusted him more and more as the minutes ticked by. She knew better, but she couldn't stop herself.

The devil must have grabbed ahold of her sanity and was now laughing at how easily she had succumbed to a man's suggestion. Never mind that he had only indicated a desire to get her a drink of water, in her head he might as well have asked her to strip naked and spread her legs. She squeezed her thighs together at the thought.

And why did she find herself reacting to him unlike any other man she'd ever met? She needed to get out of this club, go back to her apartment, and get a decent night's sleep. She only had three of those left before she moved into her car. Coming in tonight had been a mistake on several levels.

There was no way she could run without drawing attention to herself, however, so she followed Carter. He rounded a corner, leading her away from the main room and into a kitchen area.

The room was brighter and a few other people were milling around, talking in hushed voices. Carter grabbed a water bottle from a row of them on the counter, twisted the lid off, and handed it to her.

She took it, unable to avoid touching his fingers. She nearly dropped the bottle when she made contact with his skin, making him grip the bottle tighter instead of releasing it while he reached out with the other hand to steady her forearm.

She stiffened, forcing herself not to freak out. People touched. It happened. Sometimes people touched *her* even. She didn't usually react so violently, but bumping into strangers or her boss or other women was not the same thing as making contact with Carter Ellis.

He did something to her, awakened something inside her that was better left dormant.

When her gaze went to his fingers wrapped around her wrist, he suddenly released her as if she'd burned him. "Sorry, Brooke. Instinct." He pointed toward a pair of chairs along the wall. "Come. Sit."

"I should go."

"Not yet." His voice was firm. "Please. You need to clear your head first. That scene affected you."

He was right. She followed him to the set of chairs and lowered her unsteady body onto one of them, gripping her thighs together and glancing down to make sure her blouse was still fully buttoned and hanging loose enough not to reveal any curves.

Luckily she was fully covered. The last thing she needed was for Carter to ogle her body. Out of the question. She'd give him this play because he was right about her being unsteady, but as soon as her brain cells started firing properly again, she was out of there.

"Take a few deep breaths." He was sitting on the chair next to her, elbows on his knees. Several inches separated them, and he made no move to close the distance, though he was rubbing his palms together nervously. "I would swear you fell into a sort of subspace from watching."

"Probably," she admitted before she could stop herself. "Faith says I'm easily swayed toward subspace."

"Well, Faith knows what she's talking about. She's an excellent Domme."

Brooke glanced up and asked him the question on the tip of her tongue before she lost her nerve. "Will she be here Saturday? She mentioned people sometimes make appointments or whatever. Could I get one with Faith?"

Saturday... The day she would move out. The first night she would spend on the streets. Perhaps it was insane and unreasonable, but it suddenly appealed to her to come to the club first. One last appointment with Faith before she faced her new reality. Once she was living in her car, it would be nearly impossible to consider coming to Zodiac for anything other than her job cleaning the place. She hadn't figured out the logistics of where she might shower or even use the bathroom.

Carter broke into her musings. "I don't know. I'll find out for you. Do you still have my card? You could call me Saturday to confirm."

Did she still have his card? She nearly laughed. Not only did she have it, but she could recite it to him from memory. And then she realized she also had Faith's information.

She'd never spoken to Faith on the phone. In the past several weeks, Faith had always been at the club on Wednesdays. Until today. Faith had sent her a text to cancel their usual appointment that afternoon, but that had been the first time they'd communicated by cell phone.

Brooke hadn't responded to the incoming text. She had only the most basic plan, prepaying for limited service in case of emergencies or for work to contact her. A response to Faith hadn't been necessary.

It wouldn't be necessary to confirm for Saturday either. Brooke would simply show up and hope for the best.

With a deep breath, she decided she was stable enough to flee. "I should go." She pushed to standing and spun around to face Carter, trapping him in his seat with the knowledge he would not rush to stand and risk touching her after the way she'd reacted to him already.

He lifted his gaze to her, but she stared at her shoes.

She hurried to say several more things in a string of speech that probably made little sense. "Thank you for the tour and for the water and everything. I'll just go now and come back Saturday." She turned around fast and nearly ran from the club, taking the stairs two at a time when she hit them and then jogging across the parking lot to her car.

Her fingers were shaking as she fumbled with the lock, and she didn't breathe easily until she had the car started and was pulling out of the lot.

Carter hadn't followed her. She was both grateful and disappointed at the same time.

Carter was still worried about Brooke hours later while he worked as the head bouncer. Maybe he should have followed her. It had taken Herculean strength to force himself to let her go. She was so easily skittish, and the last thing he wanted to do was ruin any chance he might have at worming his way into her life.

There was no doubt she reacted strongly to watching someone else's scene. She had been in subspace from nothing more than observing. How far into her head did she wiggle when *she* was the one submitting?

He had considered taking a risk and asking her to submit to him, but it had seemed too soon. She'd hardly made eye contact with him yet. He did think he affected her, but he needed to tread lightly.

The urge to command her to her knees in front of him had been powerful. He would bet anything she would relax and easily submit if someone took charge. Preferably him. No. Definitely him. The thought of some other man doing it made him grit his teeth.

In between members coming and going from the club, he sat on a stool near the entrance and pictured her on her knees between his thighs, head bowed, hands clasped behind her, shoulders back. His cock grew stiff at the imagery. He was in a near-constant state of arousal lately as Brooke occupied his mind often enough that he occasionally forgot what he was doing.

"Hey."

Carter jerked his attention to the left to find Lincoln standing a foot away, a smirk on his face. "Where were you? I've been speaking to you for a while. I just realized you weren't hearing me."

"Shit. Sorry."

Lincoln eyed him suspiciously. "I saw you with Brooke earlier. Did she leave?"

"Yes." Carter sighed. "She was a little freaked out after watching Tyler perform. This was her first night coming in while we're open."

Lincoln frowned. "Do you think it was a good idea to let her leave?"

"I ran out of options. Short of chaining her to the wall, which I'm pretty sure wouldn't have gone over well. She doesn't even like people to make eye contact with her, let alone touch her." He fought the urge to cringe at the admission. Chaining her to the wall might have been a great option. Or it could have completely backfired on him. Either way, he needed to adjust his cock.

"Do you think she'll come back?"

"She asked if she could make an appointment with Faith for Saturday."

Lincoln nodded. "Guess we need to check with Rowen on that issue."

"It would seem that way." Carter glanced toward the stairs that led to the third-floor offices. Something was going on between

Rowen and Faith. She'd arrived about an hour ago unexpectedly and Lincoln had escorted her upstairs to Rowen's office. Neither Rowen nor Faith had come back down.

"Where's Sasha?" Carter asked Lincoln. Ever since Lincoln had finally hooked up with Rowen's sister, the tension between everyone had been sliced in half, but their juggling act to avoid each other in the club was hilarious.

"Upstairs. We're going to play in a bit after Rowen leaves."

Carter chuckled. "You and Rowen planning to arrange your calendars for the rest of your lives just so Rowen doesn't have to see his sister performing with you?"

Lincoln shuddered. "Yes. It makes both of them uncomfortable, and I don't blame them."

Carter shook his head. "You don't let the woman show an inch of skin in the club. How uncomfortable could Rowen be?"

Lincoln smiled. "What's with the twenty questions? Get your own woman, and then talk to me about how much you like to share her with other people in any way, shape, or form." His eyes shot open wider in a mock gesture, and he snapped his fingers as if he'd just come up with a brilliant idea. "I know a certain redhead you could dominate. As soon as you grow a pair of balls," he teased.

Carter rolled his eyes and changed the subject. "I'll be at the Wilson Street house tomorrow, by the way. Meeting the plumber there to figure out what's happening in the kitchen before we drywall." Carter had become the head of Lincoln's construction team, flipping houses, three years earlier when he and Rowen had also become part owners of Zodiac.

"Okay. I might stop by."

"If not, don't worry. I'll get it figured out and organize the crew to start on the back porch."

"Sounds good."

Footsteps coming down the stairs caused Carter and Lincoln to both turn that direction.

Rowen appeared. "Hey." He glanced around. "Taking Faith home." He turned toward Lincoln. "Sasha's gonna walk her down in a minute. I'm pulling the car up."

Lincoln nodded. "Got it."

Carter watched as Rowen rushed down the second set of stairs. Yeah, something was going on between him and Faith. Carter hoped it didn't affect Brooke since she had a rapport with Faith that didn't extend to many other people.

Hopefully Rowen wouldn't prevent Faith from topping Brooke Saturday night. He needed to broach the subject with his friend. But obviously not now. Rowen had fled down the stairs as if his heels were on fire.

CHAPTER 6

Friday morning started like any other day. Brooke climbed out of bed, joined a coworker at an attorney's office they cleaned every other Friday, and finished right on time. At two o'clock, as she was climbing back in her car, she got a text from her boss asking her to come into the office.

Ordinarily she wasn't required to check in with the office often. Her schedule was set. If she didn't show up for work, the various companies she cleaned for would call her boss. Unless she was sick—which had never happened in the four years she'd been working for CCS—she had no reason to touch base daily with the office.

Something felt off. She gripped the steering wheel with both hands as she drove under the speed limit to reach the head office. When she arrived, the secretary greeted her without making eye contact and told her Mr. Zellerman was waiting. She could go right in.

Great. The last thing she needed was to be reprimanded for something, but she'd spent the last twenty minutes wracking her mind to come up with a reason she might be in trouble and nothing jumped out at her.

"Mr. Zellerman?" She eased the door shut behind her and inched forward slowly.

His brow was furrowed, and he didn't stand as he pointed at the chair on the other side of his desk. "Brooke. Take a seat."

She hadn't finished lowering into the chair before he continued, leaning back in his chair. "I'm afraid I have some bad news."

She was afraid she might stop breathing.

"Our client enrollment is way down this year in the Miami area. Headquarters is cutting every corner down to the bare bones."

Brooke said nothing. This could not be happening. Surely she wasn't about to get fired.

He sighed. "I'm afraid we're going to have to let you go." As he spoke, he pushed an envelope across the table toward her. "Today was your last day. The best I could do for you was a two-week severance pay to tide you over until you can get another job. I'm so sorry."

She stared at the envelope, not blinking. Not moving an inch.

"Brooke?"

She jerked her gaze up to his chest and swallowed. "You're firing me?"

"I don't have a choice." He squirmed in his seat.

"But I've been working here for four years."

"I know, but we have others who have been here longer and several people with families. I need to hang on to those who are most desperate for as long as possible."

I'm most desperate.

Her breaths came faster. She was going to hyperventilate. In fact, she leaned forward and rubbed her temples with both hands. "Mr. Zellerman, I need this job."

"I know, Brooke. I know. I wish there was some other way."

Silence filled the space between them. There was nothing else to say. Finally, she reached for the envelope, clasped it close to her chest, and stood. She walked out of his office and then the building without looking at a soul or speaking to anyone else.

When she was back in her car, she started the engine while the tears began to fall. Tonight would be the last night she slept in her apartment, but it had never occurred to her that she might also lose her job. Her entire world was collapsing around her.

On autopilot she drove home, parked, and climbed the stairs to the third floor. The tears she'd shed on the way to the apartment hadn't even dried up yet when she flopped down on her mattress.

After twenty-two bleak years of existence, tomorrow afternoon she would be homeless. Jobless and homeless.

Without removing her stupid uniform or even her dirty shoes, she rolled to her side, pulled the covers up over her body, and closed her eyes. It was three in the afternoon. But she had no idea when she would get to sleep on a mattress again.

She hadn't thought far enough to even devise a plan. All she could do was pack up her meager possessions in her car and make the few dollars she had stretch as far as possible until she could find another job.

Exhausted beyond reason, she finally fell asleep, not waking for twelve hours when her stomach started protesting. It was the middle of the night. She rolled onto her back, took a deep breath, and then pushed off the mattress to start packing.

By five, she had everything she cared about loaded in the trunk and back seat of her car. At least none of her neighbors would witness her shame when she casually left at noon. She returned to her apartment, opened the fridge, and sighed. She had a few slices of American cheese and some bread. She didn't have butter, but toasted cheese was almost as good as grilled cheese.

The important thing was it was hot. She had two cans of off-brand chicken noodle soup too. She made one of them, adding extra water to make it stretch further, and slowly sipped the warm broth.

In the silence of her apartment, she glanced around as the sun came up. She'd lived in this cheap, tiny, one-bedroom dump for as long as she could remember.

And now this part of her life was over, as well as her job.

Maybe she could get work cleaning homes. She could apply with local area companies like the one she'd been with or even go on her own. She had no idea how would she would find clients though.

All the money she had in the world was in an envelope handed to her by her stupid boss yesterday afternoon. She considered using it to get a hotel room, but even a cheap one would eat away at the cash in a few days, leaving her once again homeless with no money. She needed the few dollars in that envelope for gas and food.

She sat on the ratty, worn kitchen chair for several hours. Thinking. Finally, she headed for the bathroom and took a long, semi-hot shower. She had no idea when she might get another chance. When she was finished, she packed up the few dishes and pans she thought might come in handy when she landed on her feet and left the apartment for the last time. She slid her key under the door and walked out of the building.

Brooke had no idea why she came to Club Zodiac that night. She wasn't even positive Faith would be there. She hadn't called or texted Carter or Faith to confirm. She had never intended to.

The truth was she had nothing else to do with her time on a Saturday evening, and chances were after tonight she would never return to the club again. She wouldn't be cleaning it. She wasn't paying for the membership. And she couldn't afford the luxury of pretending she was a regular human being after today.

It was as if she decided to put aside her immense life problems for one more day and focus on the only thing that had brought her any pleasure for the last several weeks. Pain.

She nearly laughed at the irony.

Wearing one of her three pairs of jeans, a long-sleeved, black tee, and her black flats, she climbed the stairs to the second floor —the club's main level. She wasn't sure if she was disappointed or relieved when Carter wasn't the one who greeted her at the entrance. Another employee was working the door. He nodded at her as she passed, but said nothing. Thankfully.

It was after ten o'clock. Several members were already milling around, talking, and preparing to play. She glanced around, feeling out of place. She didn't know these people. None of them. The only person she had a relationship with was Faith, and she had no way of knowing if Faith would be there that night.

And Carter, of course. Where was he?

Why did she care? It wasn't as though she intended to speak to him or would even approach him. He was simply a man who was part owner of a club she used to clean. A large man. Broad. Built. With unbelievable muscles. And messy blond hair that women would kill to run their fingers through.

Good grief.

She shook the absurd thought from her head and took a breath. This was stupid. She should leave. Carter and his partners had probably already been informed of her firing. They would wonder why she came.

She spun around to rush back out the door just as Faith stepped into the main room from the stairs that led up to the third floor. She was with a man. Another owner. Rowen. They weren't touching each other, but Rowen was standing close to her, and he spotted Brooke before Faith did.

He whispered something in Faith's ear, and Faith lifted her gaze to smile at Brooke before heading her direction. "You *came*." There was a surprised lilt in her voice.

"Yeah, uh, but maybe it wasn't such a good idea," Brooke

stammered. "I mean, you're probably busy, and I should go." She started to pass, but Rowen stepped in her path.

His voice was deep, commanding. "Why don't you two talk in my office? I've got a few things to take care of down here."

His office? Why would they do that?

Faith smiled up at Rowen. "Great. Thanks. We'll be back down in a bit." She nodded toward the stairs that continued to the third floor and backed up in that direction.

Brooke followed, feeling foolish.

Faith was so glamourous. She wore an amazing white fitted dress that looked like it was designed just for her. It was short, but tasteful. Her breasts were far larger than Brooke's and showed an impressive cleavage. Again, tasteful. Not that Brooke would ever own anything like that in her life, nor would she have the confidence to wear it. But it looked fantastic on Faith.

The silver strappy heels on Faith's dainty feet rounded out the outfit. Even her nails looked like they'd been done that afternoon. The woman had money. Why had Brooke never noticed before?

Rowen never took his gaze off Faith as Brooke took a step to follow her. He too looked like a million bucks in black slacks and a classy black dress shirt. Even his tie was black. They looked like a couple. Were they?

Brooke followed Faith up the stairs, wondering why they were heading to Rowen's office. Maybe Carter had told Faith about Brooke coming to the club on Wednesday and how weird she acted before running out.

Her hands were sweating, and she wiped them on her jeans as she entered the office behind Faith.

Faith flipped on the lights. "Take a seat. I'll grab us some water." She glided across the room to the mini-fridge and pulled out two bottles. After crossing back to the sofa, she handed one to Brooke. "I'm so glad you came."

Brooke felt ridiculous. What was she doing here? "I wasn't going to come. I'm not even sure why I did." She took a breath.

Faith leaned back, crossing her elegant legs. "Why not? I wasn't sure you would show up, but Carter told me you asked for a time slot with me."

Brooke lifted her gaze. "He did?" What else did Carter tell her?

Faith's brow furrowed. "Of course."

Snap out of it, Brooke. This is your only chance to fully experience BDSM. Make it good. She took a deep breath and lifted her gaze to meet Faith's, forcing herself to pull out all the stops and go for it. "Do you? I mean, do you have time to do a scene with me?"

"Yes." She beamed. "That's why we're up here. I thought we could negotiate what you want from the experience before we go downstairs. We can take our time. I'm only performing with you tonight. In fact, I have a confession to make..." Her voice trailed off, and she glanced down at her water bottle, running a perfectly groomed nail over the top absentmindedly.

For the first time since Brooke had met her, Faith seemed out of sorts.

Finally, Faith smiled and lifted her gaze. "You're the first person I'm telling this to."

Oh God.

"I'm not really a Domme."

Brooke winced. She had no idea what that meant.

Faith shook her head. "That didn't come out right. I am a Domme. I mean, I have practiced as a Domme for a long time, but I'm giving it up. You'll be my last bottom."

"Why?" Brooke squeezed the bottle tighter, confused.

Faith giggled. "I've been pretending it was right for me. Don't get me wrong. I'm good at it. I know that. I've topped a lot of people. But my true self is submissive."

Reality dawned. "You're with Rowen."

Faith beamed again. "Yes. I mean, it's recent, but it's right."

"That's why you didn't come in Wednesday night."

She nodded. "Exactly. I've been submitting to Rowen for the past week. Few people know. It's going to be weird switching and explaining myself to everyone, but I know in my heart it's the right thing to do."

"Wow." Brooke's shoulders relaxed. "Why did you come in tonight? Just for me?"

"Yes."

"You didn't have to do that." No one had ever gone out of their way to do something for Brooke. It warmed her to think Faith cared enough to do this for her.

"I did. For several reasons. I need to top someone one last time for myself, for one thing. And you need me too." She reached out with one hand and clasped Brooke's.

Brooke swallowed hard, afraid she might cry. Her bottom lip trembled.

"You have secrets, Brooke. Deep pain that needs to be let out. I'm not expecting you to share everything with me tonight by any stretch of the imagination, but I'm hoping I can at least break through and help you open up. And then I'd like you to work with someone else."

Brooke jerked her gaze up, shaking her head. "I couldn't do that."

"You can. You're ready. I'm not the only person capable of dominating you."

Brooke continued to shake her head slowly. "No. You don't understand. I'm... I'm..." A tear fell, and then another. She tugged her fingers free and wiped the line of moisture from her cheeks onto the back of her hand, fighting for composure.

Faith leaned closer. "Don't worry about the future right now. Let's just concentrate on the scene we're going to do."

Brooke stared at her. She could do that. No sense worrying about later. It didn't matter anyway. She would be gone. She would never see these people again. There was no reason to stress about Faith's imaginary future plans for Brooke's life.

Faith sat up straighter and pointed toward the floor in front of her. "Kneel in front of me, facing out. I want to braid your hair."

Brooke searched Faith's face. "Why?"

Faith smiled. "It's common. I've always had you pull it up when we played in the past. I'm going to do it for you this time. It will calm you. Put you in the right frame of mind."

Brooke finally broke the stare and lowered to her knees in front of Faith. It felt awkward. Different. They weren't in the club. They were upstairs in an office.

The moment Faith gathered Brooke's hair and ran her fingers through it, Brooke relaxed. It felt so good. No one had ever played with her hair before. "Tip your head down," Faith whispered.

More tension left her body as she stared at her knees.

"Put your hands on your thighs, palms open and facing up."

She followed Faith's instructions, releasing even more pent-up stress. Incredible.

"That's good." While she worked her fingers through Brooke's curls over and over, she continued speaking in a soothing, calm voice. "I'm going to tell you a lot of things in the next hour or so. I know you won't remember all of them, but hopefully the most important things will stick."

Brooke said nothing.

"You're very submissive. It makes you vulnerable. Even the slightest suggestion puts you in a subspace most people aren't capable of. I know you probably think it has something to do with me, but it doesn't. I just happened to be in the right place at the moment you were ready." She chuckled. "Worked out well that we met inside a fetish club."

Brooke managed to smile.

"Promise me you'll be careful. Not every Dom or Domme is as tuned in as I am. I don't want anyone to take advantage of you."

"I promise." It seemed important to Faith to hear the unnecessary confirmation, so Brooke gave her that.

"After our scene, I'm going to ask someone else to take over your aftercare. A transition of sorts."

Brooke flinched.

Faith released her curls to set a hand on her shoulder. "You'll be fine. I promise. I have just the right person in mind."

Who? Brooke wanted to ask, but she decided not to. It didn't matter. When Faith was done with her, she would flee the club and never come back.

"Pull your shoulders back. Straighten your spine."

It took Brooke a moment to comply. Again, it felt awkward. She spent most of her time hiding from the world, her shoulders hunched forward so no one would notice her. Pulling them back made her feel exposed.

She glanced at her chest and rolled her eyes. No part of her was exposed. She wore a baggy, black shirt that revealed nothing. And there wasn't much to reveal anyway. Her chest had always been small. Of course that was partially because she never ate enough to gain weight.

"I'm going to ask you to do things we haven't discussed before tonight. I want you to get a more complete experience. I want you to feel more fully what it means to submit and let yourself relax into someone else's care."

Brooke nodded.

Faith finally finished playing with Brooke's hair and divided it into three sections to braid it. The thick weight of the heavy braid on her back felt comforting in a way. It kept her from being able to hide her face, but she found she liked the fact that it pleased Faith.

"I'd like to secure your wrists tonight. Do you think you can handle the restraint?"

"Yes."

Faith stood and circled around to stand in front of Brooke. She reached under Brooke's chin and lifted her face, forcing her gaze up. "For the next hour, you'll address me as *Ma'am*."

Brooke swallowed, nodding.

Faith lifted a brow.

"Yes, Ma'am."

"Good girl. It humbles you. Puts you in the right frame of mind. Everything a dominant does guides you to the right frame of mind."

Brooke nodded.

"Are you ready then?"

"Yes, Ma'am."

Faith smiled. "Then let's go downstairs."

CHAPTER 7

Brooke was surprisingly calm as she followed Faith down the stairs. She kept her hands clasped behind her back as Faith instructed, her shoulders back, and her head down.

Every instruction was both awkward and soothing. It felt natural. Perhaps Faith was right and Brooke was a natural submissive.

It didn't matter. This was her last night to experience submission, and she intended to be the perfect bottom and fully live in the moment.

She was surprised when Faith led her toward a new piece of equipment Brooke had not paid much attention to yet. A strange circle of chains that looked exactly like a spider web.

Without a word, Faith lifted Brooke's hands above her head and circled her wrists with Velcro cuffs. It was the first time Brooke had been secured by Faith. It felt odd, but comforting. The inability to escape relaxed her.

"How do the cuffs feel?" Faith whispered in her ear.

"Good, Ma'am."

Faith smiled. "I thought you would like them. Another level of submission."

Brooke nodded.

Faith disappeared for a moment and then returned holding three items in her hands—a paddle, a flogger, and a whip. "Look at me, Brooke."

Brooke tentatively lifted her gaze. "Ma'am?"

"You said you didn't want me to hold back tonight."

"Yes, Ma'am."

"I'm going to let you choose which item you'd like me to strike you with, but there's a catch."

Brooke's eyes widened. "A catch?"

"Yes. I'm going to expect you to open up to me. Talk to me. Answer my questions while I top you."

Brooke swallowed, a flush covering her face. "Why...Ma'am?" How was it necessary for her to tell Faith anything about her past?

"Because you're using me to escape and hide from even yourself. If you don't let some of that out, you're never going to make any headway."

Brooke hesitated for a long time, uncertainty creeping up her spine. Finally, she nodded. "The whip, please, Ma'am." It would cause the most pain. She didn't need anyone to tell her that. She knew from experience. The sting would be sharp. She wondered if Faith would break her skin. So far she never had in their previous sessions together.

Stepping out of Brooke's line of sight, Faith took a position behind Brooke, set a hand on her shoulder, and spoke into her ear. "Are you sure you're ready for this?"

"Yes, Ma'am. I want to push myself tonight."

"Safeword?"

"Red, Ma'am."

"I'm going to start now. Easy at first and then harder."

"Yes, Ma'am." Brooke clenched her butt cheeks together when Faith stepped back.

The first strike centered her in a way she couldn't remember ever feeling. The thin leather tip was all that made contact, and it wasn't hard at all, but the tiny sting felt amazing.

The second whoosh of the whip caused Brooke to close her eyes, wondering where it would land. Again on her butt cheek. Lower. Only slightly harder than the first.

Brooke let her mind sink into the scene, her breath leaving her on a sigh. She'd had a horrible day. The worst day of her life.

No, that was certainly not true, unfortunately. But it had ranked up with the worst. She needed this. The escape. The... absolution. The penance.

Rationally she knew she had done nothing wrong to deserve the life she lived, but that had never mattered in the past. Even the slightest mistake on her part—intentional or otherwise—would earn her a beating.

Maybe she deserved it. Maybe she was a bad person. Maybe there was a God in the world and He put her in this club to clean it so she would meet this woman who could give her what she deserved. People said God was not a vengeful being, but if He existed, Brooke saw no other explanation. Why else would she lose her job and her apartment in the same day for no reason?

She gripped the chains with her fists and held on as if releasing them would somehow end the scene. Even though she was secured to the web, she still liked the feel of the cold metal against her palms.

She slid deeper into herself as the whip rained rhythmically down over her thighs and then up toward her shoulders. Every swish of leather through the air was followed by the stinging burn of contact.

Amazing.

Every once in a while, Faith came in close and checked to make sure Brooke was okay, whispering in her ear and expecting a response.

"It feels perfect, Ma'am." It did. It really did. Every strike brought her deeper into her mind, calming her. Soothing.

Magically taking away the pain. Replacing the emotional pain with physical pain.

Physical pain she could handle. Emotional pain was so much worse.

Thoughts of Carter filtered into her mind. Was he in the room? Was he watching? Part of her hoped he was. She wondered if he realized she deserved this punishment and that he was the subject of her most recent series of offenses. Too many to count. Every day he still managed to get under her skin in one way or another. He didn't belong there, and Faith was reminding Brooke of that fact with every strike of her whip.

Faith stopped again, rubbing her hand along the heated welts across Brooke's shoulder blades. She asked the strangest question. "Do you get aroused when I whip you, Brooke?"

Aroused? "No, Ma'am."

"That's a girl." She continued to sooth Brooke's back with her palm. "There's no right or wrong answer, you know."

"Okay, Ma'am." The question was baffling. Who would get sexually aroused from a beating?

"Did someone in your past hurt you, Brooke?"

Brooke's breath hitched, and she responded before she could stop herself. "Yes, Ma'am."

"A man?"

Brooke's heart stopped beating.

CHAPTER 8

Carter had never been more stressed in his life. As the scene unfolded, he didn't move an inch. He had to force himself to stand next to Rowen and watch.

He trusted Faith. Everyone trusted Faith. And he knew this was the last time she would top another person. She belonged to Rowen. Rowen was permitting her to play this out, and Carter should be grateful to his best friend.

He'd never seen a more skittish person in his life than Brooke. When she wasn't playing, she was completely closed off from the world.

But now...

Damn.

There was no way to describe what he was witnessing. It wasn't as if she was less closed off. She was definitely in a zone someplace where no one could reach her. Except perhaps Faith.

Carter would give his right arm to know what Faith was whispering to her and what Brooke was responding. He might never know. The scene was private. None of his business.

But something in his world had shifted in the last half hour. Before, he'd been attracted to Brooke. Something about her had called to him from the moment they first met. That something had grown over the past several weeks. And now...

Damn, she was gorgeous. She was too skinny. She needed to eat more. He hoped she didn't have an eating disorder. That would be a bitch to deal with. He knew she had issues. Lots of them. But suddenly nothing else mattered. She called to him like a magnet. Drawing him closer until Rowen had to grab his arm to keep him from approaching.

"Let them finish," Rowen murmured.

Carter nodded. Of course.

"She's gonna need a soft touch."

Carter nodded again. That was an understatement.

"You've got a soft touch." Carter glanced at his friend. Rowen was smiling, not condescendingly, but with understanding. "You can do this."

"I know I can."

"Be careful." Rowen's words were loaded. Carter knew he was speaking from the heart, worried Carter would get hurt. It was a possibility, but it was a risk he was willing to take.

Carter watched as Faith finally removed the cuffs from Brooke's small wrists and rubbed her arms as she lowered them. She led her to a sofa and sat next to her, handing her a bottle of water.

Damn, he wished he could hear their conversation.

Every once in a while, Brooke nodded. She kept her gaze down, but she wasn't able to hide her face completely because her hair was pulled back in a braid. He liked the braid. Hopefully the next time she wore one, it would be Carter who arranged the curls into submission.

Finally, *finally*, Faith lifted her gaze. She glanced at Rowen and smiled, and then she shifted her attention to Carter and nodded.

Show time.

Carter forced himself to step forward slowly with Rowen at his side. While Rowen set his hands on Faith's shoulders and led her away from Brooke, Carter lowered himself onto the sofa next to her.

He didn't touch her with his hands, but he did let his thigh slide against hers, and he leaned in close to her face. "I watched your scene. It was spectacular."

"Thank you," she whispered. She notably did not call him *Sir*, and for that he was glad. It was too soon. They didn't know each other. He didn't want her to feel compelled to so formally submit to him. Yet.

She lifted the water bottle to her lips, but her hands were trembling, and it slid from her grip.

He reached out reflexively and caught it before it hit the floor. "You're in subspace."

She moaned softly, swaying a bit his direction. He hadn't realized she was in so deep.

He reached out an arm and wrapped it around her, careful not to put pressure on her back. He had no way to avoid the welts since she was so totally covered by the long-sleeved shirt.

She leaned into him anyway, but he didn't think she was fully aware of it. She didn't flinch at his touch, which rang a warning bell in his head. For one thing, no matter how gentle Faith had been, Brooke would still have welts down her back that wouldn't disappear for a while.

For another thing, he knew for a fact she was normally adversely affected by contact with other people, especially him. Especially men, most likely. The fact that she was leaning against his chest spoke volumes about her state of mind.

He wrapped his hand around her biceps and held her closer. Damn, she was tiny. Not just small, but underweight. He tucked her bottle of water between his thighs and lifted his free hand to cup her face for the first time. He stroked her skin. Soft. Smooth. Perfect.

When he tipped her head back, forcing her to meet his gaze,

she blinked, her eyes widening in horror. Her full, pink lips parted.

The temptation to taste those lips was great. He ignored it. "Brooke? You okay?"

She stared at him. "Yes. Of course."

She was not. It was like her mouth was going through the motions but her mind was in another place. The craziest subspace he'd ever seen. Like she was two people.

He needed her to snap out of it. "Take a sip of water." He released her chin to grab the water, glad that her head didn't loll forward.

At least she managed to sip the water when he set it to her lips. If she hadn't done that, he would have panicked. He needed to be careful with her. She was so vulnerable.

When she squirmed against him and winced, he knew she was coming back. He winced with her.

Carter was not a fan of whips. Everyone knew it. Inflicting pain on a submissive was not his gig. He was a firm Dom, but his tastes ran toward pleasure, not pain. He didn't play as often as the other owners or employees at the club, mostly because he preferred a more committed relationship with a woman who enjoyed the more carnal sides of submission.

A woman on her knees in front of him was his dream. A woman trembling with lust, her pussy wet for him, her obedience given freely in exchange for raw sensual pleasure—that was Carter's style.

Watching Faith wield a whip against Brooke had made him grit his teeth. He didn't normally react so violently toward masochism. It didn't bother him a bit that others enjoyed that side of BDSM. To each his own.

But Brooke... She was like a butterfly. Soft. Delicate. Watching her take the strikes and even moan with each one had been his undoing. If she needed that from him, he was in serious trouble.

He could only hope he could introduce her to the softer side of BDSM and convince her to submit for pleasure instead of pain.

Wishful thinking?

Undoubtedly.

But a man could dream.

She swallowed the water over and over until it was gone. Good. She needed it. She also sat up straighter, seemingly returning to Earth from whatever spaceship she'd been traveling on.

When her back stiffened, and she leaned away from his chest, he released her shoulder. "Better?"

"Yes. Thank you." She looked down. "I think I zoned out for a minute."

He chuckled. "That's an understatement. You're very susceptible to subspace."

"Faith said that too."

"Well, she was not kidding. You have to be careful."

Brooke nodded. "Don't worry. I'll never be in a position to submit like that again anyway."

Carter's breath caught. What did she mean?

She flinched, jerking her gaze to his as if just realizing what she'd said.

"Brooke?" He furrowed his brow. "Any time you submit to anyone for any reason, even subtly, you'll need to be aware of your propensity." He knew the entire time he was speaking that she had meant her words literally. She never intended to submit to anyone again. For any reason.

She nodded. "I'm not coming back." Again, she winced, lowering her gaze. "I should go." She pushed off the couch on wobbly legs. "I need to go."

He stood next to her, grabbing her arm so she wouldn't fall over. "You need to sit for a while longer. You're not yourself yet." His heart raced.

She shook her head. "I'm fine. I feel much better. I really need to go. *Now.*" She jumped out of his grip and turned toward the entrance.

He followed her, heart pounding. No way would he let her leave. His gut told him he would never see her again. His gut was rarely wrong. "Brooke…"

Pulling together amazing strength that shocked him, she shook out of her stupor and nearly ran for the stairs. Seconds after that, she took them two at a time.

He was on her heels. He didn't touch her, but he also kept pace. As she pushed through the door and stepped into the parking lot, he kept up.

She spun around, making him stop short to avoid knocking her down. "Let me go, Carter."

"No." He shook his head. "Not gonna happen."

She humphed, turned, and continued rushing across the parking lot. When she got to an older model, beige Pontiac Grand Prix, she fumbled to get her keys out of her pocket and opened the car with shaky fingers. She ignored him, until he slammed his hand on the door, keeping her from opening it.

"Brooke, listen to me." He didn't touch her, but it was hard.

She was shaking as though she were cold. She was flushed too. And when she came completely down from her high, her back was going to hurt. And her thighs, and her ass. She needed aftercare whether she understood that or not.

She was his responsibility now. He'd agreed to see to her, and he fully intended to. No way in hell was he about to let her drive off.

"Carter…" He liked the sound of his name coming from her lips.

"Come back inside."

"No." She shook her head. "You can't force me to stay."

He sighed, his hand still pressing into her car door. He rubbed his forehead, his eye catching the inside of her vehicle. The back seat was filled with boxes. What the hell? He turned back to face her. "Where are you going?"

"Home?" She put her hands on her hips.

"Where is that?"

"None of your business."

"I can easily go inside and look at your paperwork."

She flinched, rubbing her arms. After a deep breath as if trying to calm herself, she lifted her gaze. So rarely had she met him eye-to-eye. If he ever had the pleasure of dominating this woman, he would insist she look him in the eye often. In the most even voice she'd used since he approached her, she said, "I'm leaving now."

He pursed his lips, holding her gaze. Her pupils were no longer dilated. She was not in subspace anymore. As if she'd been doused with cold water, she had snapped out of it. That didn't mean he wanted her to leave, but what could he do? She was a grown woman. Stopping her would not earn him any brownie points. In fact, it seemed in order to keep her from leaving, he would have to physically prevent her. Assault was not on his bucket list.

Fuck.

He pushed off the car and nodded. "Be careful driving."

Her shoulders visibly lowered, and the breath whooshed from her lungs. "Thank you."

She climbed into the car and buckled her seat belt while he held the door. As he shut it, he spotted a pillow and blanket next to her in the passenger seat. Every cell in his body went on alert. His spine stiffened.

She yanked the door shut, leaving him standing next to her Pontiac in shock. When she started the engine, he snapped out of it.

Fuck. Fuck fuck fuck.

She pulled forward, heading for the exit to the road, and he turned around and nearly ran toward his own car. No way in hell was she leaving without him.

His silver F150 might not have been the coolest car on the

planet, but it hauled a lot of shit when he was working construction. He wished he'd chosen his sleek, black Mustang instead tonight because it would keep up easier, but he hadn't.

It didn't matter because it turned out Brooke did not peel out of the parking lot like a bat out of hell. Apparently she didn't realize he was on her tail. She took a right turn as he caught up with her, and since she didn't have a clue what he drove, he followed closely.

Brooke was a cautious driver. She turned her signal on at every intersection and kept to the speed limit. However, he had no idea where she was going.

After a few minutes, he wondered if she was onto him because she turned so many times it defied logic. Soon, she headed into the city and then rounded several more corners.

He dropped back a few car lengths. He even allowed other cars to get between them. Finally, she pulled into a commuter lot next to a highway entrance. What the hell?

He decided then that she must have known he was following her and didn't want him to know where she lived. He kept up the charade anyway. She was not going to get away.

She parked next to the only car in the lot and turned off her engine. It was after midnight on a Saturday. Not much call for ride-sharing. Instead of entering the lot behind her, he decided to drive on by and circle back.

Five minutes later, he was on the other side of the street, lights off, engine idling, watching her car. She had turned the engine off. There was no sign of life. Darkness. Silence.

"What is she doing?" he asked himself out loud. "This is insane. And dangerous." He wasn't the sort of Dom who used whips or canes or crops, but he wasn't opposed to spanking a pig-headed submissive who put her life in danger in defiance.

He waited. Nothing happened.

He waited longer. Damn, she was obstinate.

She had to know he was watching, right?

Five minutes ticked by. And then ten.

Carter grew impatient. Brooke was crazy if she thought he would leave. Maybe she was watching him, waiting for him to give up. What difference did it make? Like he said, he could just look at her paperwork to get her address. She wasn't hiding anything.

At fifteen minutes, he gave up. Impatience ate a hole in him. He put the truck in drive and turned into the lot. He approached slowly, turning his lights off as he got closer, hoping to see in her windshield.

For a moment, his heart stopped. She wasn't in the car. He couldn't see any evidence of her at all. He panicked. Was she so desperate to rid herself of him that she'd taken off on foot?

He parked several yards from her Pontiac, turned off his engine, and jumped from his truck. He jogged the distance from his vehicle to hers and came to a sudden stop when he saw inside.

For a moment, he couldn't breathe, and then he let out a long, slow exhale. She was inside, curled on her side in the fully reclined driver's seat, a pillow stuffed beneath her head, a blanket covering her body.

She didn't move. She didn't appear to know anyone had approached.

Another glance at her back seat filled in the blanks. She wasn't waiting on him to leave so he wouldn't follow her home. She didn't have a home. This car was her home.

He staggered back a few steps, trying to control his emotions. Fuck. Why was she homeless? She had a job. He doubted it paid well, but it was a job. Why was she living in her car?

He ran a hand through his hair, pacing back and forth, trying to pull his emotions together so that when he approached, he wouldn't scare the fuck out of her.

Finally, several deep breaths later, he closed the distance and leaned against her car. Before he could figure out what to do next, she bolted upright. His shadow must have alerted her. At least she wasn't fully asleep. He feared he'd scare the piss out of her if he rapped on the window.

"Jesus," she shouted, setting a hand over her heart. "Are you kidding me?"

He waited.

She turned her head away from him and stared out the passenger window, her chest rising and falling with every breath.

"Brooke," he said loud enough to reach her, "open the door."

"No."

It occurred to him that he'd never heard her cuss. The harshest word she'd said since he met her was *Jesus*, spoken a few seconds ago. "Open the door," he repeated. "I'm not leaving."

She flopped back down on her side and curled into a ball, drawing her knees up to her chest. She looked so small and vulnerable. Was she crying?

Her body shook. Yeah. She was crying.

Dammit.

He lowered his voice. "Brooke... Baby, please open the door."

She didn't obey his command, but she did curl in deeper, turn farther away, and sob harder. He could hear her now.

"Baby, please..." His chest literally hurt for her. What happened in her life to bring her to this moment? He had no idea, but he fully intended to fix whatever it was.

He knew very little about this woman, but it didn't matter. It was enough. She was alone. She was homeless. She was hurting. She needed help. Even if she never gave in to his advances, he would not leave her like this.

She cried for a while.

He waited, both hands on her car door, leaning in, watching, hurting for her, praying she would open the door.

Finally, she glanced at him and blinked. She rolled partially onto her back and stared at him forever. She swallowed— weighing her options?

The standoff continued. He waited some more, not moving. Not giving in. He would never give in.

She clenched the blanket with her fists and pursed her lips.

He waited.

She took several deep breaths, her body relaxing marginally. Streaks of tears dried on her face.

He wanted to wipe them away. He wanted to hold her. He wanted to chase away whatever happened in her life to put her in this position. And he vowed to himself that he would fix this if it was the last thing he did. Even if she never let him touch her. Even if she entered the lifestyle right under his nose and found a Dom who was willing to beat her.

No matter what, he was going to be her friend. Starting now. "I'm not going to leave without you, Brooke. Please, baby, open the door."

More time passed. More waiting.

Finally, after an eternity, she reached for the lock and lifted it.

CHAPTER 9

Brooke was out of ideas.

It didn't seem Carter would ever leave.

She had no idea he'd followed her. What an idiot. There was no way to hide her current problem. She could bluff, but he was too smart. Her car was filled with her belongings, and she was trying to sleep in a commuter lot. That spoke volumes.

She'd never held a man's gaze so long in her life. Not by half. Even through the window, he'd been there, waiting patiently, calmly. So kind. So thoughtful. So giving.

When she gave in and popped the lock, he eased the door open slowly. Still, he didn't touch her. He bent his knees, lowered to her level, and—holding on to the frame—met her eye-to-eye. "Come home with me."

She sucked in a breath. That was the last thing she expected. "I can't do that."

"Why not?"

"You're... You're..."

He smiled. "I'm what?"

"A man, for one."

He frowned. "So? I'm not an asshole. I'm just male."

She was unable to keep from widening her eyes. *There's a difference?*

He winced. "I have no idea what has happened to you to put this fear in you and make you so skittish, but I swear I'm a good guy. I just want to help."

"Help? Me?" She rolled her eyes. "What? By taking me home and turning me into some sort of sex slave or something? I'll pass." She turned to her side again, facing away from him. She tucked her hands between her thighs and wished she could take the last several words back.

Carter gasped and then silence took over for several moments. Eventually, he spoke again. "Obviously some asshole has made you think *all* men are complete pieces of shit. Or perhaps a series of assholes have done that job. However, I need you to understand that we're not all like that. *I'm* not like that. I won't deny I'm attracted to you. It's the reason I'm standing here in the middle of the night after following your sweet ass around the city in circles forever.

"I've been attracted to you from the first moment I set eyes on you. Those damn red curls make my entire body take notice. And your porcelain skin is every man's dream."

She didn't move a muscle.

He kept going. Rambling. "Maybe it's the way you so demurely put me off. Maybe it's the submissive nature I see in you. Maybe it's the way you exude an innocence that tugs at my heart strings. Maybe it's the way you tuck those unruly curls behind your ear when no one is watching. Maybe it's the way you hide. And run. And need. And want. And cry. And hurt. And…" He stopped.

She couldn't catch her breath. What was happening here?

He breathed heavily for a while. "Brooke, I don't have the answers. I don't even have the questions. I don't know what I'm saying or suggesting or what I want. But I'm not leaving you here. So, you either have to move over and let me in or you have to come home with me."

Her face flushed so hot she thought it might catch fire. Go home with him?

He waited. Again. Never moving. Was it a trick?

"I'm not sleeping with you," she blurted.

He sighed. "I hope not. It would totally blow my image of you."

A smile crept across her lips, unbidden. She also couldn't keep from glancing at him before she realized what a bad idea that was.

He returned her smile. "Please. I won't touch you unless you ask me to. Come home with me."

"Unless I ask you to?" she joked. *Joked?* What was happening to her? "You'll be old and gray and lonely if you wait for that sort of invitation."

He laughed, his face lighting up. "If that's the effect I have on women, then I have no business keeping my man card anyway."

"I'm a mess."

"Challenge accepted."

"I have no money. I lost my job. I lost my apartment. And whatever was left of my self-respect."

He flinched. "You lost your job?"

She adjusted her seat and held his gaze, righting herself. "You didn't know?"

"No. What happened?"

She shrugged. "When I got off work yesterday, the company fired me. Something about gradually cutting back."

His brows rose. "They did that to you? How long have you been with them?"

"Four years." She pursed her lips. Why was she sharing so much with him? He was so big. He filled the entire doorway with his frame. He could break her in two with one hand. And yet, for the first time in her life, she found herself trusting a man. A *man*.

Perhaps she was misinformed. Maybe not *all* men were as vile as she'd been led to believe.

Nothing in his stance or his words indicated he intended to mess with her. He went to a great deal of trouble to follow her and wait for her to come around. Who would do that if they had only bad intentions?

"Four years? And they fired you? On the spot?"

"Yes."

"How did you end up sleeping in your car tonight if you just got fired yesterday?"

She lowered her gaze, fiddling with her fingers in her lap. "I was already behind on my rent. It was a bum day. I also got evicted."

"A bum day?" His voice rose. "A bum day?" he repeated.

She flinched, lifting her gaze.

His eyebrows were high on his head. "Baby, a bum day is when the internet won't start up fast enough. A bum day is when the mail is late. A bum day is when my phone has no service in the car and won't send my text fast enough. Losing your job and your apartment in the same day is...well, it fucking sucks. That ranks far higher than a bum day."

She swallowed, opened her mouth, and let words tumble out that should have been kept sacred. "You haven't walked in my shoes. Losing my job and my apartment in the same day doesn't even make the top ten worst." Immediately she regretted her admission. She jerked away from him and faced the passenger window again. "I'd love it if you walked away and let me be."

"Well, that's not going to happen. Yesterday might have been a bum day, and it makes my blood boil that it wasn't the worst day of your life, but your bad luck is over. Can I trust you to follow me to my house? Or do I need to drag you out of this car and set your sweet ass in my truck?"

Renewed tears fell. She tucked her lips in and kept her head down low, hating the braid that prevented her hair from hiding her face. She didn't even lift a hand to wipe the tears this time. Let them fall.

Again, this god of a man waited patiently. He didn't touch her. Nor did he retreat. He stood stock still while she considered her options. When she thought she could speak again, she whispered, "If I leave my car, someone might break in and steal my things."

"Then you'll follow me," he decreed.

She nodded. "Yeah."

"Don't even think of trying to lose me, Brooke. I'd much rather go to bed eventually tonight than spend the entire night driving around Miami looking for you, but I won't stop."

She lifted her gaze. "I'll follow you."

He smiled. "Good girl." Righting himself, he tapped her roof and then turned away.

She watched his enormous frame as he sauntered toward a silver truck. His butt was fantastic. His shoulders were wide. Even his gait was sexy. Sexy?

She jerked her gaze away from him. *He's a man. Stop staring. They're all scum.*

It wasn't hard to follow him. He drove cautiously and gave her plenty of time to keep up. He didn't even take the highway. It took twenty minutes, but eventually he pulled into a nice neighborhood and turned several corners before he slowed. A garage door opened at the house on the left. There was a black sports car in the garage. He pulled behind it, rolled down his window, and pointed into the garage.

He wanted her to park in his garage?

She came to a stop next to his truck while he got out, rounded her hood, and leaned against her window. "Park in my garage. It's a nice neighborhood, but it's late. You don't want to unload all this stuff tonight. And there's no reason to take any chances. Your car will be safe inside my garage."

She swallowed the lump in her throat as she did his bidding. And then she opened the car door and stepped out. She hadn't been this nervous in a long time.

"Come on." He angled his head toward the door as he shut the garage.

She followed him, hands shaking.

85

He was attracted to her. He'd said so. But he'd also given her no reason to think he intended to sleep with her in exchange for this kindness.

When she entered his kitchen, she shut the door behind her with a soft snick while he reached for a panel to the side, disengaged the alarm, and then reset it. Finally, he faced her. "Relax. You're safe here."

She leaned against the door. Safe? He had no idea what safe even meant.

She realized she'd left everything in the car. She needed some of her things. "I need to get some stuff. Can I sleep on your couch or something? I'll just stay this one night. Tomorrow I'll figure something out."

He stalked toward her, making her heart race as he got closer. When he was a foot away, he set one hand on either side of her head and leaned in closer. He didn't touch any part of her. "Brooke, I'm sure I have everything you'll need tonight. And I have a guest room. You'll sleep there. You're not leaving here in the morning either. Where would you go?"

She said nothing, trying not to breathe. He smelled so good. Whatever soap he used and…man.

He held out a hand. "Give me your keys."

She glanced at his palm and shook her head. "No way." She gripped them in her palm.

"Brooke, give me your keys."

"I'm not a hostage."

He sighed, his head hanging low in front of her, the top of his messy blond hair catching the soft light coming from the lights above the stove. The only lights on in the house. He spoke to her feet next. "You're not a hostage. You're a flight risk. I don't trust you. I want to help you. I'm *going* to help you. The only way I can ensure that is if you give me your keys."

She stuffed them in her pocket, defiant. She had no idea why she kept challenging him like this, but she couldn't stop. Perhaps she was testing him, wondering where his breaking point was. How long would he go before he snapped and took a swing at her?

Instead, he chuckled and stepped back, running a hand through his hair. A grin spread across his face when he faced her next. "Fine. I'll give you two choices. Either you give me your keys and I let you sleep in my guest room, or you sleep in my bed with me so I can ensure you don't try to run in the night."

She gasped. For a moment, she lost her certainty about him, and then she saw the twinkle in his eyes. He was not going to hurt her.

He was also not going to sleep with her. She dug in her pocket, pulled out the keys, and handed them to him, dropping them in his palm without touching his skin. Self-preservation.

He grinned again. "See? That wasn't so bad. Come on. I'll show you around." He sauntered through the kitchen, not looking back.

She took in her surroundings. The kitchen was pristine. White. White tile. White granite. White cabinets. Not the sort of kitchen a murderer would try to hide a crime.

Shuddering at the thought, she followed him. Her choices were limited after all. The attached dining room was less colorless. He had a mahogany table and chairs that rested on a thick, dark-brown carpet. There was even a floral center piece in the middle.

He continued through the family room, also inviting. A soft, brown leather sectional angled toward an entertainment center. The carpet was the same as the attached dining room. Thick. Inviting. Homey.

She closed her eyes and forced herself not to look any longer at his environment. He might have her keys, but she was not staying here more than one night.

A hallway opened up on the other side of the family room. Carter kept walking. He flipped on a light, illuminating their path, pointing right and then left. "Office. Guest bath." Right again.

"Guest room." Left again. "Master bedroom." When he reached the end, he stopped and turned around.

She paused, unsure what to do next.

"Everything you need is in the guest bath. My sister lives in Minneapolis, but she visits me at least twice a year, and she thinks my bachelor pad is uninviting, so she makes it…girlier when she comes." He smiled.

That explains the silk flowers on the dining room table.

"She says every home should have guest provisions, just in case. Open every cabinet and drawer. You'll find what you need."

Brooke nodded. "Thank you." She stared at the floor.

Carter snapped his fingers as if just remembering something important, turned to the right, and headed into his room. The lights went on and he returned a few seconds later holding a T-shirt. "Here. Something to sleep in."

She took it from him, murmuring, "Thank you."

He cocked his head to one side. "Is your back okay? From the whip, I mean?"

Mortification flooded her. If he thought she was going to show him her back or her thighs, he was crazy. "It's fine." It felt warm, but it didn't sting at all anymore.

He nodded. "Good. I know Faith is an expert. She knows exactly how hard to strike for the results she intends, but it's harder to be sure when the submissive is clothed."

"It's fine," she repeated.

"Okay." He hesitated. "You won't take off in the night on foot, will you?"

She shook her head, staring at the white T-shirt instead of him. "No."

"Then, I'll let you sleep. If you need anything, yell or just come get me."

She nodded.

"Brooke…" He sighed. "I have no idea what you've been through, but I sense it hasn't been pretty. I'm not your enemy. I'm not an asshole. I'm a nice guy. Give me a chance. I won't let you down. It would seem too many people have let you down in your short life. I will not be one of them."

She nodded. Tears started to fall again as she considered the fact that it was possible he was not lying. She turned abruptly before he had to watch her cry again and entered the guest bath, shutting the door behind her. She pursed her lips to keep from sobbing out loud and turned on the faucet.

She'd never been in a bathroom this nice. Not one equipped with a spare toothbrush and toothpaste. Not a bathroom she had not cleaned herself. Not a bathroom with brown swirled granite counters. Not a bathroom that undoubtedly had unlimited hot water, a toilet that flushed without jiggling the handle, and a faucet that shut off completely.

She opened the drawers to find that indeed there were several unopened toothbrushes and a tube of name-brand toothpaste. She could have insisted he let her grab her belongings from the car. She didn't need to open a new toothbrush when she had her own right outside in the garage, but he had ignored her suggestion. So, she used the borrowed items and then the toilet. Even his toilet paper was soft and gentle.

Like his speech and his demeanor and everything else about him.

Carter Ellis was going to bring her to her knees.

CHAPTER 10

It took Carter an hour to stop pacing and sit on the edge of the bed. He hadn't shut his bedroom door, just in case. He wanted to hear her if she left her room or, God forbid, the house. Though it was unlikely she would leave her car and belongings. And besides, if she opened a door or window, the alarm would go off.

Nevertheless, he struggled to relax. When he finally pulled the comforter off the bed and slid under the sheet, he closed his eyes and tried to slow his mind. He was crazy to chase this woman. She made it painfully obvious it would take a lot of hard work to break through her hard, outer shell.

She was also broken in a way he didn't think he had the skills to fix. Someone had abused her. Perhaps an ex-boyfriend or her father. Whoever it was, they had done a fantastic job of fucking with her mind. If he met the guy, he would probably kill him with his bare hands.

No matter how irrational it was to pursue her or even befriend her, he couldn't stop himself. He was drawn to her in a way he could not describe. And she needed help. Desperately. A place to live, for starters.

Monday morning, he could fire their cleaning company—the

one that let her go—but doing so would not put her back on her feet. It was only one job. If he paid her outright to do the work, she would still need several other clients.

He cringed at the idea. Helping her get a dead-end job was not the way to go. He needed to ask her what other skills she had. How much education did she have? Maybe she could go to a temp agency and get placed somewhere in an office instead of cleaning.

Maybe she likes cleaning, asshole.

It wasn't as if he could single-handedly hire her to work at Zodiac without checking with Rowen and Lincoln first. Plus, it was a bad precedent. Maybe there was something she could do for him at his day job. He nearly laughed trying to picture her with a hammer and nails.

Carter's day job was in construction. There wasn't a lot Brooke could do in the area of renovating houses. Maybe Lincoln or Rowen would have some ideas. Or even Sasha or Faith. Someone.

He had no idea why he was spending so much time trying to solve her employment problem. She could get a job on her own. She didn't need him to interfere. In fact, she would probably resent it. But something in him squeezed off his airway when he pictured her taking crap from anyone anywhere at a job that was going nowhere.

Was she sleeping? He glanced at his open doorway. She hadn't made a single noise since she'd finished in the bathroom and shut the door to his guest room with a soft snick.

Picturing her wearing nothing but his T-shirt made him fight a groan. It was his own fault for handing her the soft cotton shirt in the first place. If he'd let her grab some belongings from her car, he wouldn't be reaching down to adjust his cock right now. But some part of him hadn't wanted to return to the garage and fully face what comprised her entire worldly possessions, so he'd insisted she borrow his things tonight. Besides, he liked the idea of knowing she spent the night wearing one of his T-shirts.

It was horrifyingly wrong of him to sport a hard-on for the broken woman across the hall who had given him no indication she was interested in him, and in fact had deflected every small advance he'd ever made.

He couldn't help being attracted to her, though. It was out of his control. Those damn curls... Had she taken the braid out before she went to bed? He visualized her tossing and turning, her slender body rubbing against his shirt and the sheets.

None of those visions helped a bit, and before he knew it, he had his hand inside his boxers, jerking his cock up and down. He gritted his teeth to keep from moaning while he pictured his muse across the hall. It wasn't a hardship. Her full pink lips... Her green eyes... Her dainty hands... He imagined her palm and thin fingers wrapped around his cock and bucked up into his grip.

In fewer strokes than reasonable, he came, every wave of his orgasm making his body jerk until he was gasping for breath and staring at the ceiling. Damn, he was fucked. There was no way he could avoid pursuing this woman, and she was probably going to disregard the chemistry between them.

After he caught his breath, he headed to the bathroom, cleaned up, and then flopped back down on his bed. It was going to be a long night.

Brooke woke up slowly, her first thought was that she had slept hard. Her second thought was that the room was too bright. She bolted to sitting, chest pounding, afraid she had overslept and was late to work.

It took her several seconds to realize where she was, and then she panicked.

There were noises somewhere in the house, which meant Carter was also up. She had no idea what time it was. As she slid from the bed—the best bed she'd ever slept on in her life—she glanced down at her rumpled clothes. Her shoes were on the floor next to the bed, but she was still wearing yesterday's clothes.

Carter had lost his mind if he thought she would put on nothing but one of his T-shirts and sleep nearly naked in his house. God, no. It would never happen. She had no idea why he'd insisted she use his things instead of her own, but in retrospect it was for the best. It would make things easier this morning when she only needed to retrieve her keys from him before she fled.

After slipping her black flats on her feet, she ran her fingers through her messy hair and headed for the door. She needed to get out of this house fast. Staying with Carter even one night had been a horrible idea. She didn't want to be beholden to him or anyone. It was a slippery slope.

When she opened the bedroom door and stepped into the hallway, she nearly slammed into a pile of boxes. Heart pounding, she spun around to find several boxes on both sides of the doorway. Her boxes. Her stuff. The rest of her belongings were also gathered in piles on top of the boxes.

Oh, God. Oh, no. No no no no no. She rushed down the hallway toward the family room and then moved through it to get to the kitchen.

Carter was sitting on a stool at the kitchen island, sipping from a mug, and staring at a laptop. He lifted his face and smiled. "Hey, sleepy."

She ignored his good mood and pointed behind her. "Why is my stuff in the hallway?"

"I didn't want to disturb you by bringing it into your room. I'm surprised you slept through me getting it that far. I tried to be as quiet as possible. There are bags under your eyes. When was the last time you had a good night's sleep?"

She stared past him, catching his movements in her peripheral vision. *I've never had a good night's sleep.* Shaking that thought from her head, she continued. "Carter, I can't stay here. You shouldn't have done that. You didn't have permission to touch my things."

He sobered and took a deep breath. "Yeah, I knew you would say that. That's why I didn't ask permission." He slid off the stool and turned his back to her, heading across the kitchen toward the counter. "Coffee?"

She didn't respond. Fisting her hands at her sides, she tried not to scream. Rarely in her life had she let her voice rise above a whisper. Mostly because she wouldn't risk making someone mad. That never boded well.

She kept her feelings contained, as usual. But inside, she was boiling over. How dare he?

He glanced over his shoulder. "You didn't answer me. Coffee?"

"No, Carter, I don't want coffee. I'd like my keys, please. I need to leave."

He didn't respond. Instead, he preceded to fill his mug and then returned to set it on the island. After settling back on the stool, he set his chin on his palm and stared at her.

She didn't move. She had no idea what to say or do next.

"You're not leaving, so stop asking. You're staying here while you get back on your feet. We can discuss your options later, but first you need to eat. When was the last time you had a full meal?"

She glanced at the floor, still fuming, trying to contain herself. How defiant could she be with him while he ordered her around before she made him mad enough to hit her? Maybe it would be best to completely push him to that point now and get it over with. Then she could prove her point, pat herself on the back, and get out of his house.

"Do you like eggs? Scrambled? Fried? Boiled?"

She still didn't move. Her stomach grumbled loud enough for him to hear it, though.

"Bacon or sausage? Pancakes or toast? Give me something to work with here, Brooke."

She swallowed, a tear sliding down her face unbidden. Why did he have to be so nice? Why did he have to be so attractive? His blond hair was slicked back from a shower, the top already slightly mussed. His jeans fit him perfectly, giving her a splendid view of his butt when he'd stood at the counter before. He also had on a worn green shirt with ARMY written on the front. She had no idea if he was in the military, but she suspected he had been at some point.

She didn't want to reach up and wipe the tear from her cheek, hoping not to draw attention to it. She didn't even know where it came from. No man had ever been this nice to her. Not without expecting something in return. Heck, no human had ever been this nice to her. Except Faith.

The stool scraped the tile floor, indicating he was on his feet again. Seconds later, he was right in front of her. He slowly cupped her face with his palm as if he thought she might break—or lash out at him. And frankly, she had no idea why she didn't. On both counts.

When the pad of his thumb brushed away her tear, another fell in its place. His voice was whisper soft. "You're a conundrum. So fragile and so strong at the same time. I actually believe you could walk out my door, sleep in your car for a few nights while hitting the pavement hard, and find a job.

"I believe you could do it. You've got a deep inner strength even you aren't aware of." He held her face with his entire palm but didn't force her to lift her gaze from his enormous, rock-hard chest. "But here's the thing: You don't have to. You got lucky. You found a safe place to fall. Maybe fate put you in my path last night. Think of it that way. It's not safe to sleep in your car. It's safe here in my house."

She licked her suddenly dry lips and spoke to his chest. "I can't repay you."

"I'm not asking you to."

"I like to do things on my own."

"I know you do, baby."

It tugged at her heart when he called her *baby*. Infuriating her. She jerked free, backing up a few steps. "Stop. Stop being nice to me. Stop trying to fix things. I don't need your help." She needed to push him. It was the right thing to do.

She needed to prove to herself that he was just like any other man. Not to be trusted. Violent. Angry. She kept going. "I'm not your slave. You can't make me stay here." She forced her gaze to a random spot across the room instead of continuing to look at his chest, the T-shirt pulled so tight across his pecs the entire definition was evident.

He remained several feet in front of her, his stance loose.

She let her voice rise to an uncharacteristic decibel. "I want my keys. I want to leave. You can keep my stuff. It's all junk anyway. I just want to leave."

He slowly crossed his arms, but she didn't dare look at his face to catch his expression.

She kept going. "I'm not going to sleep with you. So if that's what you had in mind, forget it. You'll have to rape me if that's your intention. But if you don't give me my keys, I'm going to walk out the door on foot."

Still no reaction.

Tears fell down her face in earnest now. She was rambling stupid stuff that made no sense. "I'll call the police. Tell them you're holding me hostage. Tell them you hit me. I'll tell them you assaulted me." There. That would piss any man off. The threat of accusing him of something he didn't do.

He stepped forward.

Then she made the mistake of lifting her gaze to meet his, needing to see his expression. Needing to see his furious face and watch as he lost his temper. But that wasn't what met her gaze.

Shocking her entirely, she saw nothing but concern and sorrow. Not pity. Just sadness. He inched closer, closing the gap until he stood in her space and lifted both hands to cup her cheeks. He wiped her tears with the pads of his thumbs, so many tears she hadn't even realized she'd shed.

He said nothing, just held her gaze until her body shook with uncontrolled emotions and she nearly collapsed. When her knees buckled, he wrapped her in his arms and pulled her into his chest.

She buried her face against his shirt, the soft cotton the only barrier between her cheek and his heat. And then she cried. Not soft sobbing. Loud, obnoxious, ugly weeping. Years of pent-up frustration rushing out of her.

She couldn't stop it. It kept coming. Her body shook violently.

He scooped her up, turned them around, and stepped into the living room to sit on the sofa, nestling her in his lap.

She cried into his shoulder and neck, soaking his shirt while she lifted her arm to fist the front of it against his chest.

He held her tighter, drawing circles on her arm with his fingers. His lips landed on her ear and he whispered close, "I've got you. Let it out. You're going to be okay."

Carter was wrong. She was never going to be okay. She was born broken. She would never be fixed. There was nothing in the world that could fix someone like her. It was too late. She was not good. She didn't deserve comfort.

And yet, if anyone could fix her, it would be Carter. There was no doubt the man had willpower. Eventually, he leaned to one side and reached out with his hand to grab something. A moment later, he held a pile of tissues in front of her.

She took them, more tears falling at his kindness. She pushed away from him a few inches to wipe her face and blow her nose. "Stop being nice to me."

He sighed.

Lifting her gaze to meet his eyes again, she became aware of his hard body. He was hard everywhere. Even his thighs were hard. And she wasn't about to ponder the hard length of him pressing into her leg. To shake that image from her mind, she blurted out the most absurd thought. "Do you work out ten hours a day?"

He smiled. "No. But I work out a lot. I enjoy it. The adrenaline rush invigorates me. A long hard run or an hour of tough weight training rejuvenates me."

She shuddered. "Freak." She'd rather be beaten bloody than forced to run or lift weights. She shivered again. That thought was far too close to the truth than she wanted to admit.

He laughed. "I've been called worse."

"You aren't going to let me leave."

"No. But," his face sobered, his eyes drawing closer together, "let me set you straight on a few things."

She tucked her lips in between her teeth.

"I can't imagine what the ever-loving fuck has happened to you to make you so distrustful, and I'll let you tell me on your own time when you're ready, but I'm not your enemy. I didn't do any of those things. And I never will. I realize you were spewing all the venom to get a rise out of me. Testing me. But it won't work."

She flushed. How had he figured that out? "What are you? A psychiatrist?"

He smiled. "No, but you're transparent sometimes. You're hurting. You think you want to be left alone. You don't know how to accept help. Get over it. I'm not holding you hostage. You're not my slave. Even though I'm part owner of Zodiac, I'm not a sadist, so I won't be hitting you either. But most importantly, I'm not going to sleep with you without your permission.

"So, I'd appreciate it if you didn't accuse me of any of the above again. Eventually it will tarnish our relationship."

"We have a relationship?" she asked before she could stop herself.

He smiled wider. "Of course. It's a weird wobbly one, but I think we made headway this morning. Now, what do you like to eat for breakfast?"

"Honestly, I have no idea."

Instead of flinching in shock or questioning her weird answer, he took it in stride. "Then I'll pick something today and something else tomorrow, and you'll have every breakfast food known to man over the next few weeks until you know what your favorite is."

"You're going to cook for me?" *For weeks?*

"Yep." He surprised her when he wrapped his arms around her and pushed to standing as if it required no effort at all. He lowered her to her feet and steadied her with his hands on her shoulders. His expression grew serious again. "You need to eat. You're so frail."

He was right. She knew she was too skinny. But it was intentional. It kept men from finding her attractive and giving her a second glance.

On the flip side, it had not worked on Carter.

Her cheeks burned at the thought. She was still standing so close that he was touching her in about eleven different places. She couldn't remember the last time someone had so caringly held her.

CHAPTER 11

"Carter..." Her voice caught in her throat. Something was happening to her. It scared her to death. Parts of her body that had never been alive came to life. She wanted to lean into him and ride the foreign feeling. She didn't dare, but she wanted to.

He leaned down, kissed her forehead, and then brushed his nose across hers. "Food. Then we'll talk."

He slid one hand into hers, threaded their fingers, and led her to the kitchen.

Staring at the place where they were connected, she felt fear creep up her spine. She shouldn't be doing this, feeling this, letting down her armor. It was dangerous. She would get burned.

When they reached the kitchen, he lined her up with a stool, lifted her by the waist, and settled her on her butt. "Now, let's start over," he said as he held her shoulders again. "Coffee?"

"I don't like coffee."

He grinned. "Headway. Excellent."

"Or maybe that's not true. It's been a long time since I tried it. I used to like the smell of it. But..." she needed to shut up. She was revealing too much.

"But what?"

She shrugged. *But then I spilled it once...*

Instead of pressuring her further about her past, he shocked her again with the oddest question. "Does it bother you if I drink it? Would you rather not have to smell it?"

She stared at him, her lips parting. Her heart raced. Carter was a nice guy. He was not an asshole. Either that or he was an amazing liar. She didn't believe that, though. He had no idea how sharply she had rounded an insurmountable corner with his offhand question. So caring. He would stop drinking coffee because the smell bothered her?

Who would do that? Her voice was soft, ragged. "No. Of course not. I'm fine."

"How about tea? Do you want a cup of tea? I think my sister stocked me with some when she was here last."

"Sure." The truth was she hadn't had tea in a long time either. Her beverage of choice—the one she could afford—had been tap water.

When he released her to spin around and start filling mugs and grabbing tea bags and sugar and cream and a spoon and even a saucer, she let her shoulders relax for the first time in twenty-two years. "You're not going to hurt me," she mumbled, not intending to speak out loud.

He spun back around fast. "Never." He grabbed the edges of the counter at his back so hard his knuckles turned white. His head was shaking. "Brooke, never."

"What if I want you to?"

He turned a little white.

She kept speaking. Now that the floodgates were open, she couldn't stop. "I liked what Faith did to me. I mean, I *really* liked it. You can do that, right?"

He hesitated, his lips parting. "I don't think so."

She flinched. "Why? What do you mean? Don't you do that sort of thing too?"

"Not usually. No. I have on occasion. I'm trained. I've worked with most instruments enough to know about safety and to ensure no one who comes to the club does anything dangerous. I can spot an imposter. I can guide a new Dom. But I've never been a sadist. It doesn't work for me. I prefer a more...sensual BDSM experience."

"What does that mean?" She curled up her nose.

He released the counter finally and turned around to fill her mug with hot water. She thought he was going to ignore her question, but as he set everything she might want behind her on the island, he gently spun her around to face the counter and finally spoke again. "For some people BDSM is about the release they get from a spanking or even something harsher like a whip. But not everyone comes to the club looking for that kind of release."

He rounded the island to lean on the other side, facing her before continuing. "I know you learned a lot from Faith, and I'm so glad she was there for you. You were learning. She's a fantastic teacher. She earned your trust. Hell, she made me so jealous a few times I thought I would lose my marbles." He grinned at the admission.

Brooke sucked in a sharp breath. "She made you jealous? Of what?"

"Of her time with you. Of getting you to look at her. In the eye. Of getting you to open up and speak and smile and blush and even letting her touch you. I've never been so envious of another person."

Brooke gasped. God, he really did like her. He had for a while. She felt like she owned him an explanation. "She's... She's..."

"A woman."

She exhaled. "Well, it's not that exactly. I just, I don't know, I trust her to give me what I need."

He nodded slowly. "Would you be able to trust a man to give you what you need?" He leaned closer. "Would you trust *me*?"

She swallowed hard. Would she?

He sighed. "I get it. I understood it all along. It's written on your face. You don't trust men. You've been hurt. Anyone can see that if they look hard enough. That's why I didn't pressure you. I wanted to get to know you slowly."

She smirked. "Like you're not pressuring me now?"

"Okay, until last night. Until I thought you would drive away in your car and I would never see you again. That lit a fire under me."

Her skin flushed further. "I can't promise you anything," she whispered as she glanced down at her tea, knowing he'd stirred something foreign inside her and it would only be a matter of time before she let him in. The inside of her mind was a jumbled mess. So complicated. He made it seem so black and white, and it was far from it. There was no way for him to understand her. There was no way for her to explain herself. And she didn't want to. She wasn't ready. She couldn't even form sentences from the clutter in her head.

"I'm not asking for promises, baby. I'm only asking for a shot. I won't pressure you. I won't do anything to make you uncomfortable. I just want to get to know you. I can and will earn your trust. All I ask for in return is that you not run. Please."

She watched his earnest face again.

There was desperation in his voice. "Please promise me you won't run. Stay here. Please. Figure stuff out. Find a new job if you want. Or take a break from life and stare out the window. Watch TV. Read a pile of books. Eat ice cream from the carton. Take long baths. Sleep late. Find yourself."

She had no idea how to respond. It was overwhelming.

"Let me be a soft place to fall for now. We'll worry about the rest later."

"What if it doesn't happen for me?" She squirmed on the stool, knowing whatever "it" was, it was already happening. He probably knew it too.

He shrugged. "Then we go our separate ways. No harm done."

"I can't ask you to cover me financially."

He leaned closer. "You didn't ask."

She nodded slowly. This was insane. She should not agree to this weird proposition.

"Faith isn't going to work with me again," she pointed out to change the subject to something safer. As if her need for submission was safer.

"I know." She didn't doubt he knew all about Faith and Rowen.

"What if I need to explore that side of me further? I think I liked her using that whip on me last night." She swallowed her fear and continued. "I wanted her to hit me harder."

"I know," he said gently. "But I'm not sure you were ready for the whip, and I'm certain you aren't ready for something harder. You're very susceptible to subspace, baby. It would not be safe for you to submit randomly to people. Not everyone is equipped to handle a submissive that far in her head."

"You can," she pointed out, shocked by how bold she could be.

He nodded. "Yes. I can. But I won't. Not with you."

"Even if it's something I want?"

He inhaled slowly. "At the risk of sounding condescending, you need a therapist. You need to see someone. Work out whatever happened to you in your past. I'm not saying BDSM and even masochism can't play a role in your life in the future, but it wouldn't be healthy to use it as an escape so you don't have to face your past."

His words were harsh. They stung. He was right. But he had no clue what he was talking about at the same time.

She couldn't believe how long she had held his gaze. "You're right. I've never had a therapist. I've never had the money for anything that frivolous." She held out a hand. "And don't even try to offer to pay for something like that. We aren't there yet."

He nodded.

"Thank you. Someday, yes, I'll get help. But for now, what's the harm in letting out my stress through masochism?" Whoever had taken over her body and given her the strength to voice her wants concerning this subject was as alien as a green Martian. The truth was, she'd felt freer last night while Faith was whipping her than she had in years.

"No real harm, but there are other forms of submission that aren't nearly as...painful."

"I enjoy the pain."

He nodded slowly again. "I know you do. But if you truly want to explore BDSM further, let me show you some other aspects of the lifestyle. You might like them." He winked.

What did that imply? "You said you prefer the sensual side of BDSM. Explain what that means."

He glanced away, seeming to choose his words carefully. "Some people are in the lifestyle because they get a different kind of rush. A sexual rush. A lot of people, actually."

She blinked. "Right. Of course." She looked away from him too. "I don't think I'm like that." She couldn't imagine getting something sexual from a whip. She'd had an adrenaline rush. She'd slipped into her mind and let her troubles slide away, but sex? No.

He was smiling when she looked at him again. "Maybe." He shrugged noncommittally. "But you won't know until you try."

"So, you like to dominate women to have sex?" She had obviously not paid much attention to what anyone else was doing inside the club.

"Well, that's oversimplifying, but yes. It's considerably more complicated than that. I'll show you someday."

"Not today?" She sat up straight. It would be best to prove him wrong sooner rather than later. If he got it in his head that she might get something sexual out of BDSM, he would be sorely disappointed.

He laughed. "Not today. Definitely not today." He reached across the table, picked up her mug, and turned toward the microwave. After a silent ninety seconds, he set it in front of her again. "Drink it this time. Or we'll be reheating coffee and tea all day." He picked up his mug next to repeat his actions.

She lifted the cup, blew on the edge in that irrational fashion everyone did, and then took a sip. Deciding it needed sugar, she added a spoonful. After another sip, she set the mug down. "I think I like it."

He was grinning from several feet away, his foot kicking the fridge shut, his arms full of a precarious balance of items. "Excellent. You won't go thirsty this morning. Now let's see what kind of eggs you like." He turned away, and she spent several minutes silently watching his back as he worked.

She had never so blatantly stared at a man before. She hadn't blatantly stared at anyone before. It still scared the hell out of her. She'd been taught to lower her gaze and keep to herself. This was foreign, but a dam had broken, and she liked it.

Maybe she'd been misinformed. Maybe not all men were out to hurt her.

Carter's jeans hung from his hips perfectly. His T-shirt rose above the waistline when he reached for things. Not shocking since they probably didn't make T-shirts to fit a man like him. A buff man with muscles that had muscles.

He should frighten her. And he did. But she was getting over it.

She stared at the tattoos extending from the sleeves of his T-shirt. The fallen soldier on one side. Another intricate design on the other side.

She was watching him so intently that she forgot he could see her when he turned around. He'd been facing her for several seconds while she ogled his chest, his waist, his thighs, and even the bulge in the front of his jeans before she nearly jumped out of her seat. "Oh, God. Sorry." She turned away.

He came forward. "For what?"

"I was staring at you," she pointed out.

"What if I liked it?" He set a hand on the counter at her side, the other on the back of the stool. His breath hit her cheek when he spoke again. "Do you like cheese?"

She couldn't help giggling. Just like that, he erased her embarrassment. "Yes."

He shoved off without touching her, leaving her with the sensation that instead, he had touched every inch of her.

She went back to watching him, losing her embarrassment. "Are you in the military?"

"I was." He glanced over his shoulder. "Army. Served eight years."

"How old are you?" she boldly asked.

"Thirty-two." He set the spatula down and turned around, leaning against the counter. "I met Rowen when I enlisted at eighteen. I'm from Minneapolis. He only served four years. When I got out, he offered me a job at Zodiac. I took it. A few years later, both Rowen and I bought into the club, joining Lincoln as part owners."

She watched him closely, trying to keep her gaze on his face while he spilled his life story.

"When I bought into the club, I also started managing Lincoln's construction endeavors. He flips houses. Buys them. Fixes them up. Sells them. I do a lot of the work myself and contract out what I can't do or don't have time for. That's my day job. Three nights a week I work at Zodiac. That's me in a nutshell."

She couldn't stop herself from asking a question. "You mentioned a sister. Are your parents still alive too?"

"Yes." He nodded. "They also live in Minnesota. I visit occasionally, but I fell in love with the weather in Miami. I'm not excited about returning to the north." He held her gaze, a smile on his face for another moment, and then he turned around to stir whatever he was cooking.

She enjoyed staring at his back again as his muscles flexed, swallowing the emotions that came to the surface as she considered how openly he had shared his entire life without flinching. She couldn't share even a moment of hers. Not with someone like him. Someone wholesome and pure and good and kind and perfect. He didn't need her messy, stupid, ugly life tainting his goodness.

The next time he turned around, he had two plates of food in his hands. The entire kitchen had filled with the fantastic scent of bacon above all else. She couldn't remember the last time she'd had bacon.

"Lord, Carter," she murmured as he slid a plate in front of her. "How am I supposed to eat all this?"

He eased onto the chair across from her and handed her a fork. "With a fork." He winked. "But I won't say anything if you'd rather use your fingers. Whatever works," he teased.

Her plate held more food than she'd eaten in one sitting in her life. In addition, it was a comical assortment.

"You don't have to eat it all. Just the parts you like."

"You made three kinds of eggs," she pointed out. One was scrambled. One was hard cooked. And one was over easy.

"You weren't sure how you liked them, so now you'll know." He took a bite from his own plate that had even more food on it than hers, and pointed at her food with his fork. "Eat."

She was battling a ball of emotion in her throat again. She had to swallow it down before she could eat a bite. Finally, after counting to ten while avoiding his gaze, she managed to lift her fork. She went straight for the scrambled eggs covered in cheese and moaned around the bite.

"Folks, we have winner."

She rolled her eyes and picked up a piece of bacon next. And moaned again.

"Seriously, when was the last time you ate?" he asked.

"Hot food? That didn't come from a can?"

He blew out a breath.

She answered her own question, looking at her plate. "It's

been a while." She stabbed into the hard-boiled egg next. It was equally delicious, but then again, nearly any food would taste great to her.

A bite of one of the two slices of toast on her plate was next. She was in heaven.

For a while, they ate in silence. When she was stuffed and feared she might make herself sick, she stopped. There was still food on her plate, including the runny egg.

Carter's plate was empty. "Note to self, she doesn't like her eggs half cooked."

"I'm so full," she explained.

"Okaaay," he drawled out. "I was just making a joke. I never expected you to eat three eggs. I was only trying to figure out what you liked."

Brooke had never been permitted to leave food on her plate. Besides, she hadn't been in a position most of the time to do so anyway. She was always hungry. "I should finish it."

Carter jumped down from his stool, rounded the island, and snatched the plate. It still contained a slice a bacon and half a piece of toast, in addition to the egg. He opened the cabinet door under the sink, shook the remainder of food in the garbage, and rinsed off the plate.

Seconds later, he was back. He looked serious again as he took her chin with two fingers. "You're way too skinny. And I'm not saying that to hurt your feelings. It doesn't matter to me how much you weigh. I'm attracted to you for about a dozen reasons that have nothing to do with your weight. But you need to eat to get healthy. You'll have more energy and feel better after a week of my cooking. I promise.

"However, I have no doubt you cringed when I tossed the rest in the trash. It will be hard to get over that. It's ingrained in you, I'm sure. So, I'm just going to come right out and tell you I'm going to overfill your plate every time we eat because I never want you to be hungry when you're finished. You eat what you want until you're full, and you look away when I toss the rest. Got it?"

She nodded. "I'll try." It didn't seem like it was up for debate. She had far more important things to argue with him about. Eating wasn't on the list. She met his gaze again. "I'm sure I'm keeping you from whatever you normally do on Sundays. Let me clean up. You can go do whatever you need."

"I don't do much on Sundays. We're going to spend today together, and I'm going to help you make some decisions."

"Right. Of course. I need to get a job, for starters. I can't mooch off you forever."

He rolled his eyes. "Nope. You need to relax, for starters. Take a breath. Find yourself. I meant, I was going to help you pick a movie." He chuckled. "Or a flavor of ice cream. Stuff like that. Ordinary everyday things. Forget about finding a job for today."

She groaned. "You're so bossy."

A slow wicked smile spread across his face. "Oh, baby, you are not wrong."

What did that mean?

She was afraid to ask.

CHAPTER 12

Two hours later, Carter sat in the corner of his sectional with his computer on his lap, pretending to be interested in the screen. The truth was, he hadn't logged in to the damn thing yet.

Instead, he had listened intently while Brooke moved around in his home, taking a shower and puttering around in his guest room. She had pulled a few things out of some boxes, but left the rest.

She reappeared at the entrance to the family room with her beautiful hair hanging in long, damp curls and clean clothes on. He knew for a fact she didn't have much to wear because he'd personally unloaded her car. She would lose her shit if he suggested taking her shopping, so he kept his mouth closed on that subject for now.

Her jeans were worn, but they looked comfortable. They were also too big on her frame. As usual. What he really wanted to know was if she had lost weight or if she intentionally hid behind baggy clothes. She wore a T-shirt today. Navy. Plain. Also too big. And tennis shoes. Old but cleaner than the ones he'd seen her working in.

"You find everything you need?" he asked, sitting up straighter.

She had reverted to not meeting his gaze again. One step forward, two steps back. Probably given the time to think, she'd talked herself into retreating. She fiddled with the hem of her shirt as she came farther into the room. "Yes, thank you."

He needed to find a way to reach her, get her to open up and toss him a bone. "Come here," he requested, half commanded. He watched her closely as she approached. Her hands were shaking, and she tucked her fingers under the edge of her shirt and gripped the hem.

It was too soon to attempt this, but he'd been dying to know how she might react to other types of submission since their earlier conversation. She thought she needed to be struck with an object. It was possible she was wrong.

He had no doubt she was submissive. That had been apparent from the moment he met her. But could he channel that into something that felt good instead of whatever horror existed in her past?

When she was about two feet from him, she stopped. He rounded his body to sit facing her and shut his laptop, setting it aside. He reached out a hand. "Give me your hand." He put an intentional commanding lift in his voice. Just enough to test the waters.

She willingly obeyed, reaching out with one hand. "What are you doing?"

"Trying something." He was sitting. She was standing. He considered this for a moment and decided to let this awkward Dom/sub position remain for now. "Look at me." It wasn't a stretch since she liked to keep her head bowed and he was beneath her. It might play in his favor.

She met his gaze, her lips curling into her mouth.

"I told you earlier about other types of D/s. I'm going to give you a taste."

Her brow furrowed. "Now?"

He smiled. "We already started about two minutes ago."

She flinched, glancing away from him.

"Eyes on mine."

She jerked her gaze back.

He slid his hand to more fully encompass hers until his thumb lay on her pulse point. "Strapping a submissive to a cross or a spider web or a spanking bench in order to inflict some level of pain isn't the only way to practice D/s."

"I know." She tugged on her hand.

He held it tighter and reached to grab her other hand, pulling her a few inches closer until she stood between his legs. "Intellectually perhaps, but I want you to experience it."

"I'm not having sex with you, Carter."

He smiled. "You've made that perfectly clear a few times. I'm not suggesting we have sex. As I've said before, you're gonna have to ask me to have sex with you," he teased, hoping to lighten the mood around the subject. He shook her hands at her sides.

Her cheeks turned red. She looked away again and took a step backward.

He held her steady, not releasing her hands. "Don't back up. Eyes on mine."

She hesitated.

"Brooke, look at me," he repeated with more force.

She swallowed but did as he demanded. "Will you let go of me? I feel…weird when you're touching me. I can't…think right."

Thank you, God. He shook his head. "Nope. I like you a little off-balance."

She licked her lips. Full. Pink. Sexy. Her heartrate sped up under his thumb.

"Are there any marks on you from last night?"

"No."

He lifted a brow. "You're sure?"

"Yes."

"If there were, would you tell me?"

She gave a slight smile. "No."

He smiled back. "Figured." He continued to hold her gaze for a moment and then tugged on her wrists. "Lower to your knees."

She flinched, hesitating. She would do that a lot. He needed to take things slow and give her that play. It was to be expected. Finally, she slid to the floor in front of him.

His cock jumped to attention at the simple move. This was going to be hard. For him. His instinct was to push her because he knew she had a deeply submissive side that could easily be tapped into. But *she* didn't know that. And she had secrets. He would be an ass to push her beyond a small taste right now. Just enough to plant the seed. Make her think.

She shivered.

He released her hands. "Clasp your hands behind your back, baby." His words were gentle. Controlled. Soft.

She complied, but her form was too slouched.

"I like your head tipped toward the floor, but straighten your spine and pull your shoulders back."

She took shallow breaths as she followed his directions.

He set a hand on her head and stroked her hair. "This is the basic pose of a submissive. I'm sure you've seen it at the club."

"Yes."

"It puts you in a frame of mind. Centers you in a way."

She dipped her head farther, her hair completely blocking his view of her face.

"The next time we do this, I'm going to pin your hair back. It's allowing you to hide."

She might have flinched slightly but otherwise said nothing.

He smoothed his hand down to her shoulder and set his other one on the opposite shoulder. When she didn't try to shake free, he let his thumbs lightly stroke the soft skin at her neck. "Relax."

She released a slow breath. *Good.*

"Submission can be as simple as this right here. It's liberating in a way to assume a position under someone else's control. To do as they say. It doesn't have to be more. For many people, all it takes is to consciously turn their care over to another for a while. Can you feel it?"

"I think so," she whispered.

He kept stroking her skin as she relaxed further under his care. The shift in the air was palpable.

"Spread your knees a few inches."

She stiffened a bit, but then inched them out.

"Is the carpet enough under them? Or are you uncomfortable?"

"It's enough."

"If I expected to keep you in this position for long, I would put a pillow under your knees." He smoothed his hands down her arms and gently rubbed the skin of her biceps. Besides her face and her neck, no other part of her was exposed for him to touch. He'd give anything to have her naked before him like this. Not today. But one day. *Please, God.*

"Keep your shoulders back," he commanded when she leaned forward.

She pulled them back on a sharp inhale.

He pushed again, testing her. "With your arms behind you, your spine straight, and your shoulders back, your chest is forced higher. Can you feel that?"

"Yes," she murmured. She shuddered again.

"Spread your knees a little more."

Her movement was negligible, but she did it.

"Feel the vulnerability?"

"Yes."

He rubbed her arms with his thumbs. "There's nothing sexier than a submissive on her knees."

She chuckled and not in a good way. "Whatever."

He released her arm with one hand and lifted her chin. "You doubt me?"

She shrugged. "No one has ever accused me of being sexy, so yes."

"Then they're all blind. It's my lucky day."

She winced. "It's intentional. I don't like attention."

He slid his hand around to the back of her neck under her hair. "I don't doubt that. You do hide behind baggy clothes. But you can't hide your gorgeous hair or your porcelain skin or your full lips. Nor can you hide your demeanor. Your essence. I see you."

She flinched.

"I see you, Brooke."

Now she looked away.

He leaned closer. "I see you."

She held her breath. Her pulse picked up, her chest rising and falling.

"I have a question. One I've been curious about for a while." He squeezed her neck, massaging it gently until she rolled her head into his touch subconsciously. One more point for team Carter. He cleared his throat. "Do you buy your clothes too big on purpose, or did you lose weight recently?"

She hesitated, biting her lip before responding. "I've actually gained weight recently."

His eyes shot wider. "Well, let's improve on that."

"I'd rather not. It's intentional too."

"Being underweight?"

"Yes."

"Do you have an eating disorder?"

"No."

He closed his eyes as he figured out one more piece of her. And then he couldn't stop from leaning his forehead closer until it touched hers. "You think men won't look at you if you're too skinny." It wasn't a question. And she didn't answer.

He read her so well. It was unnerving. Like he was clairvoyant. It was also a relief in a way, as twisted as that was. She didn't have to tell him things. He guessed them. With incredible accuracy. Was she such an open book that others had always seen through her façade too?

His lips were inches from hers. She'd never been this close to being kissed. Half of her wanted him to kiss her. More than half actually. She wanted to throw caution to the wind and feel the softness of his lips against hers.

His fingers were massaging her neck with the perfect amount of pressure. No one had ever touched her so tenderly either.

Nineteen things were happening to her body all at once, assaulting her with an abundance of sensation. Her breasts felt heavy, which was saying something since they were not large in the first place. She was also aware of her nipples. They were hard points against her bra.

But the most disturbing thing of all was the space between her legs. A warm tingling had started when he told her to spread her knees, and in the last few moments wetness had leaked into her panties. It scared her. It was foreign. She wasn't sure she liked it. And she was way too embarrassed to say anything.

She really should have educated herself better on this subject. The truth was, she never intended to be in a position like this in her lifetime, so it hadn't mattered. She'd overheard other women talk about arousal and how their men made them feel—most often in public restrooms of all places—but she had simply walked away and blocked out the possibility for herself.

Until now. Until Carter. Oh, yeah. She was scared to death of these feelings.

"I can feel your pulse picking up," he whispered. His eyes closed, and he ran his nose up the side of her face and across her forehead.

She gasped.

He smiled, his eyes still closed. "Yeah, that's what I want to hear."

A flush crept high on her face.

He tipped her head back toward the floor with his hand on her neck. And then he surprised her by leaning back, no part of him touching her. "Concentrate on what you're feeling. Focus on your position. Your breasts are high and tight even though they're hidden from sight. It doesn't matter because you know it. I don't need to see it. You can feel your nipples stiffening as I speak."

Oh God.

"You're in this position because I told you. That's submission. It's powerful. It's relaxing while at the same time invigorating. You probably can't decide if you'd rather take a nap or go for a run."

He was so right.

"Your hands clasped behind your back open you up to me even though you have on baggy clothes. Your knees are wide enough for me to slide a hand over your pussy if I wanted." Every word struck a chord.

Silence. She took deep breaths in the silence. Her panties were definitely wet now. She was close to squirming. She should not have let this happen. It snuck up on her.

"It's normal, you know. Perfectly normal. Many people experience submission this way. Following my directions and listening to my voice is enough command to put you in a subspace without the pain.

"Not that I'm implying there's anything wrong with enjoying a whip or a paddle or even a hand on your bottom. I'm just pointing out there are other ways to submit that might give you the same results without the physical release of being struck by a whip."

She held still, absorbing his words. Even though she wasn't sure she fully understood, she was lured by the tone of his voice.

He leaned forward again, not touching her but closing the distance. "That release you got from Faith's whip, was it not similar to the release you feel right now?"

She pondered that concept. He was right and he was also wrong. Every time Faith's whip landed on Brooke's back or thighs or butt, another piece of her stress flew away from her body.

But what she felt at the moment was different. The buildup

was the same. She felt similar to how she had felt before Faith started swinging the whip. She thought about how Faith had taken control, secured her to the chains, and whispered in her ear.

Carter had instead commanded her to her knees and secured her hands at her back with an imaginary bond. But then he'd spoken to her in the same fashion. Reassuring her. Complimenting her. Praising her. The problem was she wanted the whip now. The part that would let her fly away, taking her pain with it.

"Talk to me. Tell me what you're thinking."

She opened up to him. "I feel the spell of submission, but now I want the release from the contact."

"Exactly."

She lifted her gaze to question him with her eyes.

He smiled. "Close your eyes."

She did as he asked.

"What if the release was sexual in nature instead of physical? What if I pinched your nipples right now instead of striking your bottom?"

She gasped. She could actually feel him doing just that.

"What if I cupped your pussy and pressed my hand against your wet heat?" His voice was deeper now. Gravelly. Aroused?

She wasn't sure how she felt about that, but at the same time she could almost feel his palm pressing against her sex, and it made her jump.

"I think you're getting it." He leaned closer. "What if instead of spanking your bottom hard enough for you to let go of your pain, I thrust my cock into you until you came so hard you got a better high than from any paddle?"

Her sex spasmed, freaking her out so badly she jerked her eyes open. Her gut told her to run.

"Don't move." He must have read her mind. "Don't move a muscle." He held his hands out, palms up. "I'm not touching you. Don't worry."

She remained in her spot, but her heart beat so fast she pictured it thumping out of her chest. His words had sent her someplace foreign and scary.

She could feel panic slipping in as memories flooded her mind, taking control of her. She swayed forward, assaulted by the past.

Never let a man get to you. Never let one of those bastards touch you. They are all liars. Every one of them. Every single one of them is a lying, cheating, conniving piece of slime. You hear me, girl? You keep your head down and your pants on. You hear me? Don't let them in. You will get hurt.

Someone was calling her name from far away. "Brooke. *Brooke.*" Hands landed on her shoulders and shook her slightly.

She screamed, her eyes shooting open as she tried to remember where she was.

Someone was in her face. Too close.

Carter.

"Baby, look at me."

She tried to focus. Yes, Carter. He wasn't a bad person. He wasn't. She knew he wasn't.

He tugged her arms until she released them from behind her back, and then he lifted her onto his lap, nestling her against his chest. "Jesus, Brooke. You scared the shit out of me." He rocked her, holding her close.

It felt good. *He's not a bad man.*

"Your eyes rolled back and you left me," he continued to explain. He kissed the top of her head.

For a long time he held her while her breathing returned to normal and her heart rate slowed down. He stroked her back with his fingers.

It felt right. The demons fled. Her reality was shifting. The world as she knew it was a lie. Everything she'd been told was a lie.

She lifted her face and looked at him. "I'm sorry."

He frowned. "Don't be. I shouldn't have pushed you so hard. It's my fault. I feel awful."

She shook her head. "No. It's not you. It's me. I'm a mess. Forgive me."

"No, baby. God, no. You have things to work out is all. I knew that. I just don't know what they are. I can help you, but you have to tell me what I'm facing." He cupped her cheek.

She leaned into his touch and nuzzled his hand. It felt right. It felt nice.

He sighed. "When you're ready, I'm here."

"I know." Was he, though? How long could he wait? She was not at all in a place where she could share yet. She had never visualized telling anyone a word about her past. She'd intended to take it to her grave. Until one minute ago. She needed to process this and consider the implications of letting someone in, especially a man.

His hand eased into her hair and he threaded his fingers in it before dragging them through the locks and doing it again.

"I like that." She closed her eyes.

"Then I'll do it."

No pressure. No stress. Just comfort and acceptance.

CHAPTER 13

Three days later...

"Fuck," Carter muttered at the piece of tile in his hand. He tossed it aside, leaned back on his ass, and wiped his palm over his face.

"You okay?" Lincoln asked.

Carter sighed as he stared at his boss and one of his best friends.

Lincoln stood several yards away, leaning over a stack of paperwork at the kitchen island. The top was nothing more than a piece of plywood at the moment because the granite hadn't come in yet, but it was currently serving as a desk.

"I might be in over my head."

"You think?" Lincoln chuckled, turning to face Carter, his hip against the edge of the island. "You've been fucking with that piece of tile for half an hour. You've cut three pieces so far," he teased. "I'm going to have to go buy more if you keep measuring it wrong."

Carter rolled his eyes.

"She's way under your skin, isn't she?" Lincoln knew the gist of what was going on. It wasn't a secret. They all knew Carter had run out of the club Saturday night to chase her down and hadn't returned. Several people had covered for him for the rest of the night.

In addition, Carter had spoken to Rowen twice and Lincoln once since then. "Yes," he admitted. "I'm twisted so tight around her finger that I can't concentrate. Was it four inches I needed or four inches I was supposed to cut off?" He kicked the stupid piece of tile, sending it careening away from him.

Lincoln was grinning. "I knew you'd fall one day, but I hadn't expected it to be so hard and so fast that you lost your marbles."

"I have all my marbles, asshole. I'm just...adjusting."

"Uh-huh. Where is she now?"

"Looking for a job."

"And how do you feel about that?"

"I think it's too soon. I think she needs to take some time off and figure things out. Face her demons. Fuck, I need her to talk to me. Let me in."

"You can't force her."

Carter flinched. "You think I don't know that? Hell, I'm betting someone has forced her to do all sorts of things. That's the problem. I'm walking on egg shells."

"Maybe she needs a job so she doesn't feel like she owes you or something."

"I'm sure, but I still don't like it. Yesterday when I got home, she was on her knees in the bathroom scrubbing the tile with a small brush. It took me half an hour to get her to stop. She feels like she has to earn her keep or something. I don't like her thinking she's my domestic slave. It makes my skin crawl."

"Did you tell her that?"

He smiled, finally relaxing. "I told her if I caught her cleaning my house again, I would borrow Faith's whip and use it on her."

Lincoln laughed.

"I'm pretty sure it didn't give me the desired result. She might have had an orgasm."

Lincoln laughed harder.

Carter was exaggerating. But her eyes had gotten huge, and she'd actually made a joke for the first time since he'd met her. *"Promises. Promises."*

He was so screwed.

"Does she realize you aren't sadistic enough to use a whip on her?"

"Yes. I'm trying to convince her she can channel that energy sexually instead, but she's not buying it."

"Well, you've said yourself she was probably abused, so that's an enormous hurdle. If some man, or even a string of men, abused her physically or emotionally, it's gonna take time for her to trust again."

Carter pushed off the floor. He needed to stretch. "Yeah, I'm not sure it was a boyfriend." He winced, partly at the thoughts running through his mind and partly at the strain in his back muscles.

"What makes you say that? Seems like a classic case to me, from what little I know from Faith and you and Rowen."

"Maybe, but what if it wasn't a boyfriend? What if it was her dad or something?"

Lincoln nodded slowly. "Could be."

"She's so...innocent. I don't get the feeling she's even had sex." Which scared the hell out of him. As soon as the idea had popped into his mind after her weird reactions to him the other day, he had changed his direction mentally, considering other options. An abusive father would explain things.

The idea that she might be a virgin slowed him way down. He'd put some distance between them immediately and kicked himself for speaking so crudely to her about her nipples and her pussy.

It took Carter two days to relax enough not to worry she

would pack her car and run if he left her alone. But she hadn't fled, thank God.

"Go home," Lincoln said, interrupting his thoughts. "It's late anyway. If you cut any more tiles wrong, we're going to run out," he joked again. "I've already got you covered at the club tonight. Spend some time with Brooke."

"Thanks." Carter slid back into his own mind as Lincoln stuffed papers in his computer bag and left. Carter followed him.

When he pulled up at his house, he exhaled in relief. Her car was still there. When would he stop worrying about her being a flight risk?

The house smelled fantastic when he opened the door from the garage to the kitchen. The room was a mess, but it made him smile. "You're cooking," he told her back.

She spun around from the stove, flustered, her hair tucked behind her ears. "Yeah, okay, maybe. I mean, I'm trying." She pointed at a magazine on the island. "Found a recipe. Might have been optimistic."

He bent down to remove his work boots and left them by the door before he approached. When he leaned over the pot, he moaned. "That smells great. It looks good too. Why are you worried?" It was some kind of soup. He hoped.

She shrugged, tensing because he'd leaned into her space, but she didn't move away. Progress. "Don't you work at Zodiac tonight?"

"Nope. Aaron or Dayton will fill in. Maybe Tyler. They're all usually there. I'm all yours."

She forced a smile. He didn't buy it.

"I'm going to take a quick shower, okay?"

"Of course. It will take a while for this to cook. I should have started earlier."

He leaned over the recipe to make sure he wasn't crazy. *Beef vegetable soup.* As he thought. No way to mess it up. She would be fine. "No worries. We can eat later." He reached for her hand and brought it to his lips to kiss her knuckles. Every day he tried to close the gap between them a little more. Baby steps.

She didn't pull away. In fact, she leaned closer, her breath catching.

Again, progress.

Twenty minutes later, he was back. The kitchen had undergone a transformation in his absence. The mess was gone. The counters sparkled. "Wow, did an army of elves come and help you clean, or was I gone longer than I thought?" He brushed her hair from her shoulder where she stood stirring.

She put the lid on the pot, turned it down to simmer, and faced him. "Ha ha. I'll have you know I'm an expert at cleaning. I have few skills, but that's one of them."

He took her hand and lured her into the family room, plopping down on the couch and tugging her down next to him. "Don't sell yourself short. I'm sure you have other skills."

She shook her head. "No. I'm quite serious. And I seem to have a new problem. Did you know you need a social security number to get a job?"

He nodded. "Of course." He narrowed his gaze and cocked his head to one side. "Don't you have it memorized?" Who didn't know their social security number?

"No. I don't even know if I have one."

"Everyone has a social security number. How did you get your last job?"

"I don't know. I didn't do it myself. I wasn't even there."

Hairs stood up on the back of his neck. "Who got you the job?"

"My mother."

A slight breeze would have knocked him off the couch. *Progress* suddenly had new meaning tonight. "Your mom? Where is she now?"

Brooke took a deep breath, blinking. "She died about six months ago."

Some of the pieces fell into place. "She lived with you?"

"Yes."

"So, she was helping pay the rent."

"Yes."

Houston, we have a foundation. "I'm so sorry for your loss."

Her gaze fell to his lap and she murmured a quiet *thank you.*

He wanted to ask about her father, but decided it wasn't prudent. One thing at a time. He needed to thank his lucky stars she'd given him this one piece, not push his luck. But maybe he could at least push this same issue. "Was she sick?"

"No."

Okay, that was *not* informative. It was downright bone-chilling. "Do you want to talk about it?"

"No. Could we not?"

"Of course." *I mean, I won't be able to sleep worrying about it, but sure, let's table it. Good plan.* He needed to get back on track. "Okay, so she must have had your social security card. Have you looked through the boxes?" They had stacked her meager possessions in the corner of the guest room. He wasn't sure she had opened them, with the exception of the ones that held her few clothes.

"Yes. I searched everything. She only had one file of papers. It wasn't in there."

He tipped his head back to think and then had an idea. "Your previous employer would have it. Let's go there in the morning and see if they'll give it to us."

Her eyes lit up. "Good idea." And then she scrunched her nose. "Although the last person I feel like speaking to is the man who just fired me."

"Yeah, that's why I'm going with you."

She pursed her lips, and just when he thought she might argue, she surprised him. "Thank you."

More progress.

"What was your mother's name?"

"Ann."

How generic, he thought, a chill racing down his spine.

It was after midnight before Carter was able to slow his mind down enough to relax. As far as he knew, Brooke had been asleep for a while. He still left his door open every night. She made no comment, but she still closed hers.

Suddenly a scream filled the darkness, and he bolted upright. It took a moment to untangle himself from the sheets, but he was on his feet and running across the hall before the piercing sound stopped.

He didn't hesitate to open her door and rush into the room. She was under the covers, tossing around. She was no longer screaming, but she was mumbling. "No. Please stop. No. It won't happen again. Please." She yanked her arms over her head in a protective stance and curled onto her side.

Fuck. She was having a nightmare, one he hated more than anything. He set a hand on her shoulder, afraid to scare her and make things worse. "Brooke," he whispered, shaking her slightly.

She continued to struggle. "I didn't mean to do it. Please..."

He swallowed the tight ball in his throat and grabbed her flailing hands, afraid now that she might hurt herself or take a swing at him. "Brooke, baby, wake up."

She tugged on her wrists, but he held tight, pressing them into the pillow.

"Brooke." That time he nearly shouted.

She stopped, her eyes flying open, her body stiff. Her expression was wild and confused. "Carter?"

He released her and sat on the edge of the bed. "You had a nightmare."

She groaned and turned her face toward the pillow. "I'm sorry."

He set a hand on her shoulder. "Baby, you don't have to apologize for everything. It's okay. People have bad dreams."

"Did I say anything?" she asked the pillow.

"You were mumbling." He hated to lie, but telling her the truth would hurt also.

Her breathing gradually slowed, and he climbed over her small body and spooned his front against her back. Risky.

She didn't pull away. Instead, she settled into his embrace.

He was on top of the sheet, but it had worked its way down to her waist. That was when he realized what she was wearing. His T-shirt. The one he'd given her Saturday night. The one he was certain she had not worn that first night. He felt sure she had slept in her clothes.

Relief flooded him. She had her own clothes now. It spoke volumes that she'd chosen to wear his shirt. He set his head on the pillow behind her and breathed in the scent of her soft curls. Clean. Not something fruity or floral. Just clean.

When he assumed she'd gone back to sleep, she finally spoke. "I'm a disaster."

He stroked her arm, running his hand down until he threaded his fingers with hers under her breasts. It was the closest he'd ever gotten to her. "Everyone has a closet, baby. Yours is just kinda jammed. But it's not your fault."

She giggled. "How do you always say the right things?"

He smiled against her hair. "I have many talents."

"I bet you do." She sucked in a sharp breath as if wishing she could take the slightly suggestive sentence back.

He pulled her tighter against him. Now was a good time to take some risks. "You're wearing my shirt." He punctuated his statement with a kiss to her shoulder.

"It's soft. It...smells like you. It comforts me."

"I like that. Maybe I should wear one of yours."

Another giggle. "Lordy. I know my shirts are too big for me, but your chest is huge. I don't think you'd even get your head through the neck hole."

"Good point. I suppose I could set it over my pillow so I could breathe in your scent when I sleep. It's only fair."

"Doesn't seem like you need it right now. You're lying on my pillow." Damn, she was getting bold.

He was too choked up to respond. Besides, she had blindsided him.

"Will you stay?" she asked tentatively.

"As long as you'd like." His heart skipped a beat.

She snuggled closer. "I feel safer and calmer when you're near me. When you touch me. I never thought I'd say that to anyone."

He closed his eyes, nuzzled her neck, and kissed her sensitive skin again. "I'm here. You're safe."

"Thank you." Her voice cracked.

He continued to hold her as her body eventually relaxed and she fell back asleep.

He continued to hold her while he watched her face in the dim light of the room as the worry left and the lines loosened.

He continued to hold her until the sun came up.

CHAPTER 14

At nine in the morning, Carter set his hand on Brooke's lower back and guided her into the head office building for CCS. He'd gotten up early and ensured that his guys were on the job site working on the house they were currently renovating. They could survive without him today.

His first thought as they entered her former place of employment was how pumped he felt that she let him touch her without flinching. His second thought was that the place was bustling. Phones were ringing. The receptionist looked frazzled. And two men in company polos were struggling over a printer behind the front desk.

He didn't see any signs of the doom and gloom the owner had painted for Brooke on Friday afternoon.

"Hey, Brooke," the receptionist greeted. She tipped her head to the side. "What are you doing here? I thought you quit?"

Brooke's brow furrowed. She didn't answer. Instead, she asked, "Is Mr. Zellerman in?"

"Yep. He just got here. Let me see if he's in his office."

Carter watched her reach for the phone and decided she was oblivious to whatever happened between Brooke and the owner.

She mumbled into the receiver and then set it back down. "You can go on back."

Brooke didn't respond. She turned to the right and led Carter down a short hallway to the owner's office.

The man he assumed was Mr. Zellerman stood as they entered. "Brooke. Nice to see you. Did you forget something?" He glanced hesitantly at Carter and then back at Brooke.

Carter rounded Brooke and reached out a hand. "Carter Ellis. We need your help actually."

"Oh?" His brows went up.

"Yes. It would seem Brooke doesn't remember her social security number, which is making it difficult for her to get a new job. She can't find the card anywhere, and we're hoping you have it on file and can jot it down for her."

Sounded simple enough. A reasonable request. What excuse would anyone have for not giving someone their own social security number? If the guy balked, Carter would head down another path and push the issue about why Brooke was fired in the first place.

Something was fishy.

Mr. Zellerman lowered himself slowly onto his office chair. His face was pale.

Carter didn't want this to become a problem. A preemptive strike was in order. "Brooke told me about the cutbacks you're having to make. I'm sorry to hear about it. The economy is tough these days." He decided not to point out that he owned one of the places Brooke used to clean.

Mr. Zellerman ignored Carter's taunt and leaned forward on his elbows. He was growing paler, and his hands weren't quite steady.

Carter lifted a brow, hoping his expression alone proved he was not about to get dicked around. He also hadn't taken a seat. Nor had Brooke at his side.

Finally, the man glanced down. "I don't have it."

"Her social?"

Zellerman swallowed as he lifted his gaze. "Right. I never had it. Ann never gave it to me."

"How is that possible?"

Brooke interrupted. "That's why you paid me in cash…"

He nodded.

"Why would you do that?" This story was getting thicker and more confusing.

"Her mother asked me to. I, uh, I felt sorry for her."

"Do you have her mother's social?"

Zellerman shook his head, leaning back again, looking defeated. And guilty. Of what? "Never had hers either."

"How long did she work here?"

"Fifteen years."

"Fifteen years?" Carter's voice rose, and Brooke wrapped her fingers around his forearm. He didn't know if she was trying to hold him back or draw strength from him. "Why the hell did she not use a social security number? It must be a mess in your accounting. Why would you agree to that?"

Zellerman looked like he might pass out. He licked his lips, glancing around. "She…uh…" His eyes grew wide. His hands were shaking. "Look, man, it wasn't my idea."

Carter's blood boiled. "Never mind. Don't you dare answer that question." He narrowed his gaze, pinning Zellerman to the chair, knowing his assumption was correct. This asshole had let Brooke's mother work for him in exchange for sex. Now that Ann was no longer living, Zellerman had no use for Brooke.

"Look," Zellerman continued, "I felt sorry for them, okay? The woman came in here fifteen years ago desperate. She told me her husband was abusive and she was on the run and she didn't want him to be able to track her. So, I gave her a job. She was a good employee. She worked hard. When Brooke turned eighteen, she begged me to let her work for me too. I did it. But you're right. It's a mess. I can't take the risk anymore."

"I'll bet," Carter spit out sarcastically. "I mean, why keep Brooke? She isn't half as valuable as her mother." He slid his hand into Brooke's and turned around. They weren't going to get anything from Zellerman.

Carter honestly believed the man didn't have either Brooke's or her mother's social. He was leaving out the juicier part of the story, but he wasn't lying. "Let's go," he said to her in a far calmer voice.

She followed him without a word, not speaking until they were back in his truck. And then she turned to him. "I feel like the two of you were having a silent side conversation in a language I don't speak."

Carter was furious. And a little sick. He didn't meet her gaze as he started the truck and pulled out of the lot. The only thing keeping him from vomiting was the realization that it seemed incredibly unlikely that Zellerman had made a similar arrangement with Brooke.

"Carter?" she prompted.

He reached over and took her hand when he came to a light. He needed to be sure. "Did Zellerman ever make a pass at you?"

She flinched. "No."

Carter narrowed his gaze at her, trying to figure out if she was telling the truth. "He never propositioned you?"

Her eyes went wider. "For sex?"

He nodded.

She flushed, her free hand going to her throat. "No. Never. I hardly ever saw him."

The car behind them honked. The light had turned green. Carter pulled forward.

Brooke tugged her hand back, crossed her arms under her chest, and turned to stare out the window. She didn't say another word.

He waited until they were back at the house, the engine off, before he turned to face her again. "Brooke…"

"She was sleeping with him, wasn't she?" she asked the window.

"I'm guessing." Damn, he hated this development.

She shuddered. "That bitch," she shouted before she grabbed the door handle and yanked it open. Two seconds later, she stomped around the hood and entered the house.

He was so stunned at her outburst, he struggled to move. When he finally caught up with her, she was in the kitchen, slamming around and pulling stuff from the fridge. "You want a sandwich?" she asked.

He glanced at the clock. It was ten in the morning. Granted, she needed to eat more, and he was glad she was doing so, but he wasn't hungry yet. "No. You go ahead."

She got so frustrated with the twist tie on the bread bag that she ended up tearing the plastic, ripping an enormous hole down the side, and sending several slices flying into the air.

For a moment, time stopped. She stared at the mess. And then her entire demeanor changed and she jerked her gaze to his. She was white as a sheet. "I'm so sorry. I'll clean it up. I'll put the bread in a Ziploc baggie."

"Jesus, Brooke. It's just bread. You look like you killed my cat."

"You have a cat?" Her eyes widened.

He couldn't help it. He laughed. "No. But we can get one if you want." *I don't want a cat. What the hell am I talking about?*

She blinked and then glanced down at the mess and rushed toward the pantry. She returned with a large Ziploc, not making eye contact.

He rounded the island, took the bag from her hand, and tossed it on the counter. Next, he grabbed her shoulders and turned her to face him. "What's going on? Talk to me."

She shrugged. "Nothing. I need to clean up the mess. I shouldn't have blown up like that. Sorry. I didn't mean to do it. It won't happen again."

He froze. He'd heard those words before. Last night while she was having a nightmare. "Brooke..." He pulled her closer. "Look at me."

She glanced at the counter.

"Forget the damn bread. It's just bread. Look at me."

She flinched first, and then lifted her gaze. There was fear in her expression.

"Did you think I was going to be mad?"

"Aren't you?"

Fuck. Fuck fuck fuck. "No. Shit, Brooke. No. Over bread?"

"I broke the bag. I lost my temper. I broke the bag," she repeated, her voice trailing off.

Ignoring the mess, he backed her away from the kitchen and then turned her around and led her to the sofa. They always made more headway when they were sitting on the couch together.

She was wiping a tear from her eye when he sat her next to him. He pulled her into his embrace and cupped her head against his chest. "Baby..."

She started to cry.

He rocked her back and forth, holding her. Had anyone ever held her?

Eventually, she relaxed into him and tucked her sweet hand around his chest.

"You're allowed to lose your temper, Brooke. It's normal. We all do it."

"You don't. You didn't even get very angry when Mr. Zellerman didn't give you my social security number." She tipped her head back and looked at him with red-rimmed eyes.

"I was furious." He wiped several curls from her face. "But it wasn't going to do any good to scream at the man. First of all, he wasn't worth it. He made me sick to my stomach. And second of all, he didn't have what we needed."

She said nothing for a moment, and then, "He was sleeping with my mother."

"Seems like it."

"Gross."

He chuckled. "Agreed, but that's a far different reaction from the one you had before."

She flinched and scrunched up her nose. "Yeah. Well, my mom… She…"

He changed the subject because he wanted more information and intended to take advantage of the moment to get it. "Did she tell Mr. Zellerman the truth?"

"About what?"

"Your dad." He smoothed his hand up and down her hair. "Was he abusive? Is that why your mom left him? Is that who abused you?" His upset stomach turned into something more like a full-on need to vomit. He wanted the information, but he dreaded it at the same time. What sort of man kicks a kid around?

She didn't respond. Instead, she did that evasive thing, looking away.

"Brooke?"

"I don't know. I don't remember him."

What the hell? Could she have all this pent-up anxiety like an abuse victim without remembering the incident? "I'm confused."

She shrugged. "I don't remember him," she repeated. "I used to ask her when I was little, but it always made her mad. She never told me anything."

"What about the rest of your family? Uncles? Aunts? Cousins? Grandparents?"

"I don't have any, I guess."

Now he was really freaking out. The implications were too many to count.

She pulled away from him, shivering, closing off.

He didn't want to break this connection. He needed her to talk to him so he could help her. It seemed pivotal. He knew only one way he might be able to get her to soften to him. He grabbed her waist and spun her around, setting her on the floor in front of him. "Knees, baby," he prompted.

She instantly righted herself between his legs, her knees hitting the carpet.

"Good girl. Hands clasped. Shoulders back."

She did as instructed without hesitation.

He was seriously concerned about how easily she could submit and the fact that he was about to take advantage of her vulnerability, but enough was enough. He needed answers. To help her ease into the role, he stroked her hair. She tipped her face into his palm and mewled softly.

Damn.

He gripped her shoulders next and nudged them back, encouraging her to straighten a bit and fix her form, knowing the effort to please him would help ground her. "Knees wider, baby."

She complied again.

"Good girl. Now, talk to me."

"I told you what I know," she whispered.

"There are a few dozen holes."

"I can't fill them."

"I bet you can fill some of them."

She let her head dip farther, her hair curtaining her face.

"You have all the classic signs of an abuse victim, baby." He stroked the top of her head as he spoke, hoping to soften his words. "It's obvious to me. It was obvious to Faith. Even Rowen and Lincoln speculated. I assumed you had an ex-boyfriend who beat you, but then all signs indicate you haven't ever had a boyfriend at all."

She shivered. "No. I haven't."

He pinched his face for a second, a silent ridiculous fist pump going into the air to verify she hadn't been with anyone. And then he stopped himself. That was not necessarily true. If her father abused her, he also could have raped her. If he did, and if he was still living, Carter would hunt his ass down and kill him. He was trained in plenty of useful combat skills. Eight years in the army ensured it.

"So, if you didn't have an abusive boyfriend, then it must have been your father," he pointed out, hoping she would open up or remember.

She shook her head too quickly and then lifted her gaze. "Carter. I don't remember him. I'm not lying. If I ever knew him, I don't recall. Maybe he was abusive to my mother like she told Mr. Zellerman? She never said anything about it to me, but it would make sense. She hated men."

"She hated men?" *Ahhhh*. He sighed. "Did she tell you that?"

"Every day of my life."

He winced. "She told you men were bad all the time."

"Yes. That's why I'm so hesitant. I've never given anyone a chance to prove otherwise. I couldn't have even glanced at a man while she was alive, and it took me until now to have the guts to speak to you. I'm still leery." She flushed. "Sorry."

"Don't be. You should be leery. You're brainwashed." But Lord, there were still holes in this story. He worked through his thoughts out loud. "Maybe your father was abusive to both you and your mother, and she took off with you to protect you, and she was so freaked out about the way he treated you both that she went overboard and pushed you to hate men to keep you irrationally safe."

"Maybe..."

"It happens all the time. That would explain why she didn't want to give out your social security numbers. She didn't want him to be able to track you down. Did you live in hiding?"

"Yes. Always."

"Did she take you to school and then pick you up right after?"

"I never went to school."

His entire body jerked. "You never went to school?"

"No. She made me study, though. At home."

"Jesus. She was totally hiding you so he wouldn't find you. She must have been so scared. I feel kinda bad now for judging her for sleeping with her boss. She did everything she could to keep you safe."

Brooke's face scrunched up and then she laughed. Not like a normal laugh. Out of control.

"What's so funny?"

"My mother?" She continued laughing, gasping for air, trying to pull herself back together. Somehow she managed to do all this without releasing her hands from behind her. She even kept her shoulders pulled back while they rose and fell with her odd cackling. "I can't begin to tell you why she was hiding me or from whom or what, but she didn't keep me safe."

"What do you mean? I'm not following."

She sobered and stared at him. "For someone who has spent as much time as you have trying to figure me out, you're sort of dense."

He felt pretty stupid now, but he was still in the dark. Suddenly, it hit him. He closed his eyes, tipped his head back, and groaned. "Your *mother* abused you."

She said nothing.

He needed to wrap his mind around that before he looked at her. When he lowered his gaze, he found he was far more horrified by her revelation than she was. Of course, it wasn't news to her. She'd known it her whole life.

"I'm seriously stupid."

She smiled and shrugged. "I mean, it's a common mistake, I'm sure. Most abusers are men."

"Why didn't you tell me?"

"It's embarrassing. And I didn't trust you. I don't trust anyone. The first person I really let myself go with was Faith. Until my mother died, I didn't have friends. I had acquaintances at work and stuff, but nothing substantial."

"And you ran out of money."

"Yes."

"How long did you live in that apartment?"

"I don't know. I don't remember another home."

"What did your mother do with you when you were young?"

"One of the neighbors kept me when I was very small. A really old lady. Mrs. Thurston. She was nice. As soon as I could take care of myself, my mother left me home alone. She made me lock the door, answer to no one, and left me with chores."

"How old were you then?"

She shrugged. "Too young. Probably four."

His eyes shot open wider. "Baby, jeez."

"I could open a can by then. I didn't use the stove. I wasn't allowed to, but I could eat a can of cold soup." She shuddered. "To this day, I don't like canned soup. I didn't even add water to it."

His mind was reeling. Jesus.

CHAPTER 15

She was on a roll, so she kept talking, letting it all spill out. "Carter, I have no life experiences. I don't even have a high school diploma. My mother did the bare minimum to prove to the state she was homeschooling me each year, but I never took a graduation exam. Half of what I know about the world I learned from watching TV. After my mother died, I started going to the library and a nice librarian helped me learn to use a computer. I've been going there in the afternoons several days a week for months."

His eyes were drawn together when she glanced at his face, and his hands were on his knees, gripping them tightly. His voice was low, caring. "Tell me about the abuse."

She knew she was shocking him, but it was too late to stop the flood, so she closed her eyes, lowered her head, and kept going. "It was sporadic. I could never see it coming. She would be supernice and fun for weeks at a time and then snap. I had to be so careful because I was always waiting. Anything could set her off. Like she was a different person." It still boggled her mind, and she shuddered remembering how she walked on eggshells all her life.

Carter lifted a hand and cupped her head again. "Those are the cycles of abuse."

"Well, whatever it was, she got worse over the years. I could predict the days I would be beaten the moment she got out of bed. On her bad days, she was out of control from the get-go. She would rant and throw things. Nothing I did would stop her. There was never any way to keep from receiving her wrath.

"It was like she waited, watching all day for me to mess something up so she could take her anger out on me. Anything would do it. If I didn't shut a door or shut it too loudly or didn't wash my hands long enough or use enough soap or scraped a plate with my fork or my shoestrings weren't straight. Anything."

Carter leaned forward and set his forehead on the top of her head, hauling her closer with his hand at the back of her neck. "I'm so sorry, baby."

She didn't even shed tears. It felt weird, but purging this pent-up secret was a relief. "Afterward, she would leave me alone for the rest of the day. I usually didn't move a muscle or make a single sound. The next day she would get up and be back to her happy self. She wouldn't mention the beating, but she would take me to the park or fix my favorite foods or let me watch a movie, her ways of apologizing I guess."

When Carter pulled her forward closer, she lost her balance and released her hand to steady herself against his shins. She turned her face to one side and set her cheek on his thigh. He didn't respond to the break in form. Instead, he tucked her hair behind her ear and stroked her face.

He spoke in a soft voice. "None of your neighbors ever called the police? Child Protective Services never showed up?"

She shook her head. "My mother was very careful to ensure no one heard us. I can't imagine what she would have done if I'd ever screamed or cried loud enough for the neighbors to hear. I never tried." She shuddered.

"Jesus."

"I know it's kinda deep and maybe makes no sense, but I always felt relieved after she beat me because I knew life would be fantastic for several days." She sucked in a breath, trying not to let her voice crack. "I knew I was a good girl again…until I was not, and the process started over."

"It makes perfect sense, baby. You were a child. You internalized what happened to you the only way you could. Let me ask you something else."

She nodded against his thigh. Whatever he wanted to know, she would tell him. "Okay."

"Do you see the correlation between your mother beating you and this new desire to submit to various types of masochism?"

She had thought about that. "Yes."

"When Faith did a scene with you, did you feel relieved afterward?"

"Yes. It was amazing." She lifted her face to look up at him. "I can't explain it, but after she did that last scene with me, I was flying. Like I was…" She wasn't sure how to finish that thought.

"A good girl," he suggested.

She smiled. "Yes."

"You're not alone. Lots of people turn to BDSM after abuse of some sort. It can be cathartic. Relaxing. Somehow imitating the abuser's method of absolving you of your perceived crimes."

She nodded. He made so much sense. "That's exactly it." Her heart raced. She was mentally exhausted from purging herself of her entire life, but physically she was shaking with the need to experience what he suggested. "Would you do it for me?"

He held her gaze. "Now, you mean?"

"Yes. Please, Carter. It's like an itch. My skin is crawling with the need to feel that pain. Now that I've experienced it, I want to do it again. I've never felt so relieved and alive as I did every time Faith worked with me. From the moment she first struck me with her flogger, I knew."

She couldn't read his expression, but he was clearly

considering her request. "I'm not sure it's the right thing to do. You're so fragile. There are a lot of things I'd like to do with you, but it's hard for me to reconcile causing you pain."

She lowered her gaze, setting her forehead on his knee. "Please. You're the only person who can do it. You're the only person I would ask."

His hand was on the back of her head, fingers working absentmindedly through her hair. It felt so good. So right. Relaxing. "I'll make you a deal."

She blew out a breath. She'd make nearly any deal.

"Try submitting to me my way first. If you don't feel the same euphoric release from my type of dominance, then I'll give you what you need."

Slowly, she lifted her face. "I'm not sure I fully understand what 'your way' entails."

A wry grin spread across his face. "I'm asking you to submit to me sexually. Let me make your body hum until you come so hard your vision blurs."

She sucked in a sharp breath and leaned back a few inches, her hands on his knees, her face flushing hot. "You want to have sex?"

He shook his head. "Nope. I won't even take my clothes off. I want *you* to have sex."

She cocked her head to one side. "What does that even mean? I'm pretty sure it takes two people to have sex."

He shrugged. "Semantics. Many people would argue that what I'm going to do to you would constitute sex. I won't use my cock to penetrate you—not today anyway—but I will make you wish I had."

If it was possible, the flush grew hotter. It spread down her neck and chest. Her stupid body responded to his words, irrationally coming alive. She'd never craved anything sexual in her life until she met Carter, and lately it had been happening with more and more frequency.

You're twenty-two years old. Your mother was wrong about a lot of things. Maybe she was also wrong about sex. Maybe it wasn't a bad thing to let a man touch her. If any man was ever going to touch her, it would be Carter. She trusted him.

He waited patiently while she thought, his hands covering hers and squeezing. "You don't realize this, but I'm going to tell you over and over until you believe me. You're so damn sexy it takes my breath away. You can't even hide it. Not with the loose jeans and not with the baggy T-shirts."

He was right. She didn't believe him. "I'm too skinny."

"Did your mother tell you that?"

"She's the reason for it. She said men liked women with bigger breasts and a better figure. That's why she monitored how much I ate. She insisted it was safer if I wasn't attractive. Men wouldn't bother me if I didn't give them a reason to."

He cringed. It looked like he wanted to punch something for a moment, and then it passed and he inhaled slowly. "Your mother was wrong. For one thing, looks aren't the only thing that draws two people together. I'm not going to deny that I did a triple-take the first time I saw you because I thought you were stunningly gorgeous, but what really drew me into your web was getting to know you. Your kind spirit. Gentle manner. Loving heart. Hell, you're struggling to feel anger toward that blasted boss of yours, and he fucked your mother for money."

She flinched. Surely it wasn't quite as ugly as Carter suggested. "That's basically what happened."

She nodded. "Okay. Maybe. But if it weren't for him…"

Carter narrowed his eyes. "Enough about Zellerman. Let's close that door and never look back."

"Good plan."

"Back to my point. I'm so attracted to you that you're automatically gorgeous in my eyes. I'm gonna stuff you full of food because I want you to be healthy and I never want you to go to bed hungry again, but I don't care a bit what your dress size is."

"I told you I've put on weight in the last few months."

He sighed.

She smiled. "I don't know how much, but my pants are tighter."

"How did you keep them on before?" he half joked.

She lifted her shoulders. "I managed."

He shook his head, his expression going serious. "Submit to me."

She considered his request again. She had concerns. "What if I can't, you know, uh…"

He grinned, cupping her face. "You can."

She closed her eyes. "You don't know that. I'm broken."

"You're not broken. Every time I mention anything sexual, your body jumps to attention."

At that sentence, her body did exactly what he suggested.

He leaned closer, tipping her head toward the floor. His lips landed on her ear, tickling her with his breath. "Submit to me."

"You promise if I don't like it or it doesn't work, you'll punish me instead?"

He kissed her neck. "I'm not going to use a whip on you if that's what you mean. But I will spank you if you still think you need it after I make you come."

She flinched, a gasp escaping her lips. Her traitorous body came to attention too. She started to believe he could do it, but would it be enough? "What if I need both?" she boldly asked.

"Then I'll give you both."

"Okay," she whispered as consent.

"Trust me?"

"Yes." She didn't know why. It wasn't even rational. She had only known him a few days, but she also realized she knew him better than anyone else alive.

"Good girl. Now, I want you to do as I say. Submit to me fully. I'll make the decisions. Your only job is to obey them."

She shuddered.

"You're doing fantastic already. I love how responsive you are to my voice."

He couldn't see her face with it tipped so far to the floor, but she bit her lower lip to keep from making a sound.

"What safeword did you use with Faith?"

"Red."

"You want to keep it?"

"It's fine."

"Red if you need me to stop. Yellow if you want me to slow down."

"Okay."

He stood and circled behind her. When his hands landed on her shoulders and pulled them back a bit, she slid under his control. It was that easy. Did he realize it?

His fingers trailed down her arms, and he gently pulled them behind her, tapping one to get her to clasp her wrist.

She did as he wanted.

As his palms slid back up her arms to her shoulders, she shivered. He wasn't kidding about her breasts. They always got heavier and lifted on her chest when he put her in this position. She found she wanted him to touch them. She craved it. How had she come so far in such a short time? She'd done a one-eighty.

Next, his hands were in her hair again. "Lift your head a minute so I can pull your hair back."

She followed his orders, staring at the couch while he ran his fingers through her curls. Her eyes slid shut. Her lips parted, and before she could stop herself, she let out a soft moan.

"Oh, baby, I like that."

She pursed her lips together, slightly embarrassed. "I like it when you play with my hair."

"I know you do. And I'm going to do so often." He kneeled behind her, continued to divide her hair into sections, and then braided it down her back. Where he got the hairband, she had no idea, but he produced one.

As if he read her mind, he answered her unspoken question. "A good Dom always has hairbands in his pocket. If I have nothing else with me, I at least have rubber bands." He held her shoulders again and leaned closer, speaking against her ear. "I love how your porcelain skin flushes when you're aroused."

Was she? Aroused? Oh yeah.

He nibbled a path down her neck, tugging the collar of her T-shirt to continue a few more inches to her shoulder.

She leaned her head to the side to give him better access. His lips felt amazing on her skin. Surprising her again, he massaged her shoulders, his firm hands loosening the tight muscles.

"That feels so good."

"Wait until I get my hands on the rest of your body. You're in for a treat."

Somehow her body must have been taken over by an alien being, because the thought of him massaging her entire body made her sex quiver.

He laughed.

It was really annoying that he could read her so well.

Rising onto his feet again, he reached for her biceps and gave a slight lift. "Let's move to the bedroom. I want you to be comfortable. This floor is hard, and the couch will be awkward."

She stood on wobbly legs after kneeling so long, but an edge of fear crept up her spine at the idea of going to his bedroom. It felt safer submitting to him in the family room.

He set his mouth on her ear again. "Don't panic. The location changes nothing. I'm still going to keep my pants on. But you're going to be more comfortable on my bed than the carpeted floor."

"Okay." With her hands still clasped at her back, she followed him. She hadn't been in his room yet, but he never shut the door, so she was aware of what it looked like. It was unavoidable. It loomed in her line of sight every time she exited the guest room across the hall.

When they entered, he stepped away from her to pull the

comforter to the foot of the bed. She was going to have to dig deep to continue down this path. Her complete lack of experience scared her to death. She worried about what he would think. What if she didn't react in the way other women did? She had a legitimate fear about embarrassing herself or disappointing him.

To tamp down her nerves, she focused on his room. The furniture was mahogany—dresser, bedside tables, head- and footboards. Everything matched. The furniture in the guest room was white, but it matched too.

She stared at his bed next, the sheets were dark gray, the comforter navy. The carpet beneath her feet was also gray.

Carter sat on the edge of the bed, facing her. "Come here."

She slowly inched forward. This was it. Sort of. He'd promised not to take his pants off, but he'd made it clear he intended to do everything else to thoroughly claim her body.

She was apprehensive, but also curious. When she got within a foot of him, he reached out for her and pulled her closer. "Relax your hands at your sides. You're gripping them so tight you're going to have sore fingers."

Letting them fall to her sides made her feel more vulnerable for some reason.

At her shiver, he rubbed his hands up and down her arms. "Close your eyes. Concentrate on relaxing into my touch. You don't have to watch." His enormous hands eased to her back, and he rubbed them up and down, drawing her closer.

She enjoyed his touch, and he was taking things slow enough that she wasn't in a panic.

Suddenly, his hands were at her waist, gripping her hips. His thumbs stroked the skin just above her jeans, reaching under her T-shirt. And then he flattened his hands under the edge of her shirt, the warmth from his palms directly on her waist making her crave more of his touch.

He took his time, though, shocking her with his ability to drive her desire higher every step of the way. When he finally eased his hands up her sides and smoothed them around to her back, she was beside herself with the desire for more.

And then her shirt disappeared between one heartbeat and the next, whipped over her head and tossed to the floor before she could process the movement.

She pursed her lips, wondering what he saw and how he reacted.

Again, he knew her mind. "Look at me, Brooke."

She blinked her eyes open to find him staring at her face. His hands were on her again, holding her steady at her ribcage. But his thumbs were moving, stroking the undersides of her breasts.

He lowered his gaze to her chest, his breaths shallow as he licked his lower lip. "Damn, you're beautiful." His voice, so sincere, was undeniably reverent. He meant every word. He was not just saying that to make her feel good.

He truly found her attractive.

"I've wanted to see what you keep hidden under those baggy clothes for weeks. You're even better than my imagination." He slid his hands around to cup her breasts, and she gasped at the initial contact, swaying closer to him. When his thumbs brushed over her nipples, they tightened beneath her bra.

For the first time in her life, she wished she was wearing something sexy. Lace and silk instead of a sensible white cotton bra and panties.

Carter didn't seem to care, though, and it hardly mattered since the next thing he did was unclasp the fastener in the front and draw the straps down her arms until the white, utilitarian bra fell to the floor.

His pupils dilated as he drank her in. She decided it was much less nerve-wracking to watch him undress her and see his expression than to hide behind her eyelids, guessing what he was thinking.

When he cupped her breasts again, his palms on her bare skin, she gasped. This time his thumbs came in direct contact with her nipples. That was the moment she believed him. Her body was on fire. A tight ball was growing in her stomach, coiling tighter by the minute, needing release.

He continued to play with her nipples until she had to glance down to see what they looked like. She was shocked to find the tips firm and darker than usual. The globes were also swollen and didn't look nearly as small in his hands as her imagination conjured.

"Perfection," he whispered. Growing bolder, he molded her breasts in his palms and squeezed gently, and then he pinched both nipples between his thumbs and fingers.

She came up on her toes, straining closer. A soft moan escaped her lips.

"Oh, yeah. So perfect."

When his hands smoothed down her belly, leaving her breasts wanting, she almost begged him not to stop. But there was more to come, and she was curious about the rest too.

He went straight for the button on her jeans, popping it and then lowering the zipper. "Kick your shoes off, baby."

She rushed to use her toes and heels to remove the flats as his hands slid inside her jeans, easing around to cup her butt. She lost her balance and reached out to grab his thighs as she swayed too far forward. Mimicking the way he'd touched her breasts, he molded his palms to her butt.

Before she had fully accepted his touch, he hastened to shove her jeans down her legs and used his foot to finish getting her out of them.

She lost her nerve for a second, crossing her arms over her chest as the cool air of the room reminded her she now wore nothing but a pair of panties in front of a man.

She fought the sound of her mother's voice in her head, shaking it away. It didn't belong here in Carter's bedroom.

He closed his fingers around her wrists and tugged. "Hands at your sides. Do not cover yourself." His tone was commanding. It brought her back to center. As she lowered her arms, he met her gaze. "Good girl." He gripped her chin with two fingers, holding her face in front of his. "Do not hide from me. You're a beautiful woman. I'm going to convince you of that until you know it in your soul. Keep in mind that you're supposed to be submitting to me. You don't do anything unless I tell you to, understood?"

She nodded as much as he would allow her. The reminder calmed her. It was much easier to give herself to him if she did it in submission than if she let herself try to control things.

"Deep breaths."

She inhaled and exhaled several times.

"Eyes on mine."

While she stared into his deep-blue eyes, he released her chin and lowered her panties down her legs without looking. "Step out."

She kicked them off, but she thought she might hyperventilate.

"Breathe, baby. In. Out."

She followed his instructions, calming under his command.

"That's a girl."

Wetness. Heat. A pulsing need between her legs. Totally foreign.

His hands were back on her waist, smoothing up to cup her breasts again. "Hold still for me."

Hold still? She was about to crawl out of her skin and he wanted her to remain still?

Another wry smile. "That's your job right now. Don't move. Just feel. Let me explore."

She wasn't sure her legs would hold her up, but she dug her toes into the soft carpet to steady herself, swaying slightly when his thumbs brushed over her nipples again. Her mouth fell open. "Carter…" She didn't know what she intended to say next. Stop? Please? More?

Overwhelmed with sensation, she concentrated on breathing while he continued to push her to new heights.

When he leaned forward and flicked his tongue over her nipple, she came up on her toes again. "Feet flat on the floor." He lifted his gaze. "Would you rather I restrain you so you don't have to work so hard to remain still?" His eyebrows rose. He was serious.

A flutter took over her belly all around the tightness. She'd been restrained only one time, and that was Saturday night when Faith cuffed her hands to the spider web before she used her whip. It had been oddly freeing to be unable to escape the "punishment."

"Brooke?" He was waiting for an answer. Holy cow.

She licked her lips. "Um…" Her chest pounded. She found she liked the idea, but she also felt strange asking to be restrained while he tormented her sexually.

His hands rubbed up and down her sides from her thighs to her breasts, over and over, warming her, bringing her to new heights. He waited.

She closed her eyes and let her chin dip. "Yes."

"Good girl. I think you'll be able to relax and enjoy yourself more if you don't have to worry about keeping your hands at your sides or behind you."

She nodded, more wetness leaking irrationally between her legs. The sensation was so completely foreign, she didn't know how to process it. There couldn't be many twenty-two-year-old women as inexperienced as her.

Carter stood and then patted the mattress. "Climb up. Lie in the center. Stretch your arms above your head."

Her blood pressure had to be through the roof as she did as he instructed, spreading her body out for him. The fact that he was seeing her naked was weird enough, but now he was going to have complete control to touch her everywhere, and that should freak her out.

Instead, it drove her desire higher. When she reached the center of the bed on her hands and knees, she hesitated, pondering the difference between lying on her back so that Carter could ravage her body sexually in a way she was completely unfamiliar with and stretching out on her stomach instead to receive a flogging or spanking or even a whip.

She knew he wouldn't go for that right now, but half of the reason she was shaking so badly was because she wanted him to strike her. She was torn over the juxtaposition between his gentle touch that would bring her someplace new and the firm smack of leather or a palm that would give her the kind of relief she was familiar with.

He climbed up beside her, setting a hand on her back. "You okay?"

She nodded, yanking herself back to the task. *Give this a try. Do it.* She turned over, settled onto her back, and fought the urge to cover her chest or draw her legs up. So far out of her comfort zone.

Ironic. Her comfort zone was off-kilter—consisting of the desire to be beaten instead of loved. She met his gaze and got bold. "Will you take off your shirt? At least give me something sexy to look at."

He grinned, straddling her as he grabbed her wrists and pulled her arms over her head. "You think my chest is sexy?"

She rolled her eyes. "I'm inexperienced, but not blind or from another planet."

He chuckled, leaning closer. The slight pressure of his butt on her thighs was welcoming. At least he wasn't staring at her sex. Yet. "I'm going to kiss you."

Her lips parted at his words. She wanted that.

He lowered his face and claimed her mouth, gently at first, pressing lightly and nibbling her lower lip before doing the same to the upper one. And then he opened his mouth farther and angled his head to one side. He licked the seam of her lips, sending a current down her spine.

Only Carter could have made her first kiss so beautiful that it brought tears to her eyes. The same man who was about to give her a giant pile of firsts. When his tongue slid into her mouth to tangle with hers, she fell further under his spell, enjoying the minty taste of his toothpaste from that morning mixed with his own flavor. Who knew people had a flavor?

She found herself lost in the kiss, lifting her head toward him to deepen the contact, moaning around his lips as he grew more demanding, devouring her as if he would starve if he didn't destroy her with that kiss.

It worked.

By the time he pulled back enough to nibble across her cheek and over to her ear, she was putty in his hands. He flicked his tongue over her earlobe and then whispered close, "You're mine."

Her heart skipped a beat. What did he mean?

"I'll never get enough of you," he continued. "I'm wrapped so tightly around your finger, I'll never be able to unravel. I'll never want to."

She flushed, biting her bottom lip at his words. He couldn't know that. He hadn't even had sex with her. What if she sucked at it?

"Do you believe me?" he asked.

She shook her head. "No."

"Figures. I'll just have to convince you." He was still smiling as he rose over her again and then tugged her hands farther up toward the headboard. "Grab the rungs, baby."

She wrapped her fingers around the spindles and held on tight.

He leaned across the bed, opened a drawer on the nightstand, and returned holding a length of rope.

Her stomach dipped. He was really going to tie her to the bed. Yes. She wanted this. He watched her face as he worked the rope around her wrists in what she determined was an intricate, specific manner. When he was finished, she gave a slight tug.

He fulfilled her request next by pulling his shirt over his head and tossing it aside. Lord, he was broad. And hard. And muscular. The desire to flatten her palms on his pecs was strong. Her hands were a bit occupied at the moment, however.

He kissed her nose and then her lips as he slid down her body. His palms landed on her breasts so fast she gasped at the renewed contact with her sensitive skin. "So perfect." He squeezed them both, molding them with his fingers. "Your skin is exquisite. Your nipples are the sexiest shade of pink."

She wanted to point out how small her breasts were, but decided against it. Judging by his expression, he was not concerned about size. In fact, he looked like he was about to devour her.

And she wasn't too far off because he pushed even farther down her body, leaned over her chest on his elbows, and sucked a nipple into his mouth.

She arched into him on a moan. So good. Sooo...good. She had really been missing out.

After suckling and tonguing her nipple for so long it stood at attention with a new level of sensitivity she hadn't known existed, he switched to treat the other nipple in the same fashion. "You're delicious," he murmured. "I need to taste the rest of you." He wormed his way farther down her body before she realized what he intended.

She squirmed, mortified that he was going to put his mouth on her. *There.* And stare at her. *There.* This was the first time she'd even been naked with a man, and she was tied to his bed with his mouth all over her. It was overwhelming. "Carter..." His name sounded more like a mewl than anything else.

He lifted one knee and then the other to nudge her legs apart and settled between her knees. The farther he moved down her body, the more nervous she got. When his hands landed on her thighs and pushed them wide, his face inches from her sex, she held her breath.

It was too much. Sensation overload rocked her body. "Carter, please. That's too much. I can't…"

He didn't give her a chance to finish before he set his nose on her sex and inhaled deeply.

She didn't know how red her face was before that moment, but it was on fire now. She couldn't find the words to argue further because he set one hand on her lower belly and held her down while he lifted his face for only a second. In a flash, his tongue flicked over the tiny nub at the top of her sex.

Holy mother… Her vision swam at the contact.

He did it again, and she squirmed hard against his hand. Too much. Way too much. "Shit. Carter."

He flicked his tongue rapidly over the sensitive ball of nerves she had never taken the time to explore. Apparently she should have because it felt amazing and scary at the same time. If she hadn't been such a prude for the last twenty-two years, she wouldn't be in such a state of shock now.

The pressure in her belly grew, sparks zinging from the ball in her stomach and trailing outward to her entire body. She gasped, trying to focus, but unable to think of anything except the extremely unusual sensations bombarding her. Something was happening. Something was going to break free. She thought she might implode into millions of pieces if he didn't stop.

Intellectually she knew women had orgasms. But surely not this fast. Without having sex? It was unexpected. It was taking her by surprise like a freight train running over her body. She didn't even have the brain cells to beg him to stop anymore. She could use her safeword if she remembered what the hell *red* even referred to. But she also didn't want to miss the finale, whatever that entailed.

Suddenly, he lifted his face. She could feel him looking at her. "Did you just say *shit?*" he teased.

She didn't respond. He was worried about her language now?

"I've created a monster," he continued. "One flick of my tongue over her clit and she loses all her inhibitions. What will happen if I thrust my tongue into her pussy?" All this talk in third person was making her head spin.

But that was nothing compared to what happened next. With his hand still holding her belly and his other hand pressing her thigh wider, he sucked that tight bundle of nerves into his mouth.

She screamed, the unnatural sound ringing through the room. Her entire body stiffened as he suckled, drawing the little nub rhythmically into his mouth while his tongue resumed flicking the tip.

Digging her heels into the mattress, she gripped the headboard tighter as if she might float away if she didn't hold on. She crept closer and closer to the edge of an unusual precipice. So much sensation slamming into her. She couldn't breathe right or think.

And then she was right there, gasping as it grabbed her, luring her closer, not willing to let go. She couldn't stop it. A second later, she flew over the side of the mountain, the nub exploding with her release. Pulse after pulse of her orgasm throbbed against Carter's unrelenting lips.

She soared on the high, gasping for air as he slowly eased his attention until he finally released the bundle of nerves with a reverent final kiss. "Fucking amazing." His voice was so deep she didn't recognize it. She was lucky she could even process words.

He kissed her belly and dragged himself slowly up her body a few inches until he could set his gaze on her face.

She blinked, still trying to find words or make sense of the world.

He smiled. "Which is better?"

She frowned. "Which…what?" she managed.

"Sex or a whip?" He grinned wider. "I promised you that you could get the same release from an orgasm as you got from Faith's whip. Was I wrong?"

She closed her eyes, thinking about his words. "I don't know yet."

"Then you'll need more convincing."

She flinched when she realized his intention as he eased back down her body and stared once again at her sex. This time he explored more thoroughly, making her hyperaware of his gaze on her private parts. She squirmed.

"Stay still," he ordered. "Let me look."

It was too much. She had endured his mouth because she hadn't had a chance to fully process his intention before he sucked the brain cells out of her head, but now that she was postorgasmic, she was more aware of his intense examination. "Carter…" She wiggled to get out of his line of sight.

He lifted a hand and gave the inside of her thigh a swat.

She froze, her breath catching.

"Stop squirming around, baby. I'm still dominating you. We aren't done."

The sting on her thigh was shocking but in a good way. It sent her arousal right back where it started before she came so hard she saw stars. What the hell?

"I think my girl likes a combo of punishment with her sex," he pointed out.

"Is that a thing?" she asked before she could stop herself. Weren't they supposed to be comparing the gentle touch of sex with the roughness of physical pain?

He lifted his gaze again. "Of course. In fact, I might have created a monster. Some people get aroused from a spanking or flogger or whatever. So aroused they can come from the contact alone."

Her sex gripped tight at his words.

She swallowed. Yeah, she really wanted him to slap her again. "Do it again," she boldly demanded.

He shook his head. "Maybe, but not because you command it, baby." He flattened his hand on the heated skin of her thigh. "Don't try to dictate what you want when I'm dominating you. That's called topping from the bottom. I'm in charge. Unless you need to use your safeword, you do as you're told when we're playing."

She nodded. It seemed like he needed confirmation. A nod was all she could give him. If that swat to her thigh was any indication of what her future might look like under his domination, she was suddenly certain she would sign up for this life. It scared her.

He resumed his perusal of her private area, spreading her lower lips apart with his fingers to expose her more thoroughly.

She clenched her butt cheeks, hoping he wouldn't notice the movement.

"Baby, you're so wet for me." He probed the opening to her sex, making her insane with need. When he flattened his tongue on her again, she gritted her teeth. "So pink. So pretty." He gave a tug to the curls above her sex. "Sexy as hell."

She turned her head to one side, trying to endure this intense situation while her arousal built rapidly back to the same level it had been at moments ago. If she came like that again, she would be reduced to a blubbering idiot.

He dipped his tongue inside her and moaned as if he were enjoying an ice cream. And then a finger slid through the opening, burrowing deep. His moan turned into something deeper. "Jesus, baby. So tight."

She bucked futilely to escape his touch. Too much sensation again. Way too much. Her mind was turning to mush.

He pumped that finger in and out of her until the arousal reached a new height, her belly fluttering. Her thighs shook. She wouldn't survive this. Did women die from sex?

"Can you take another finger, Brooke? You're so tight. I want it to feel good this time."

She tried to process his words. Had he asked her a question? Please, God, no.

"Brooke, can I add a second finger?" he asked again, continuing to pull the first one slowly in and out of her channel.

She twisted her face toward him. She needed to come. God help her, she needed to come again. "Please."

He smiled. "Good girl." A second finger slid in with the first, stretching her, filling her so full she winced for a moment. Yes, she was not going to live. She would be the first woman in history to die of a heart attack from an orgasm.

"Come for me, baby. I want to watch." He pressed the fingers from his other hand against her swollen nub as he spoke, sending her over the edge again.

She cried out incoherently as this second orgasm consumed her, the pulsing from that bundle of nerves combining with the grip of her channel around his fingers.

She had so been missing out.

CHAPTER 16

Carter was unable to utter a word as he released Brooke's hands and then arranged her sated body so the he was spooning her from behind. He held her close until she shivered, and then he reached down to the foot of the bed and pulled the sheet up to cover her.

His cock was so hard it threatened to explode in his jeans, and it would have to wait. He'd pressured her to submit to him. It might have been too soon to have taken her as far as he had. It was definitely too soon to also claim her with his cock.

Besides, she was in a subspace that made it impossible for her to consent. So far every time he'd watched her submit to Faith or himself, she'd succumbed to some level of subspace. She was sensitive to submission. He needed to remind himself of that often. She needed aftercare right now.

Her breathing didn't even out for several minutes.

He smoothed a hand over her hair, brushing it away from her forehead and tucking it behind her ear for a long time before he spoke. "You okay, baby?"

"Yeah, I think so. That was intense." She shuddered.

"Talk to me. Tell me what you're thinking."

"I'm thinking I just let a man see my naked body and ravage it, and I'll never be the same. I'm freaking out a bit, wrapping my head around it."

He considered her words. "You're so gorgeous when you come. The moment you stopped worrying about your exposure and slid into your head was precious. I wanted you to experience everything sex can be and see another side of submission. It's not all about whips and chains. It can be gentle and sexy and just as fulfilling."

"Mmm." She snuggled into him.

His heart beat faster as hers slowed down. He wanted her. He wanted to own her. He'd known he teetered on a dangerous precipice with her for weeks, but now that he'd tasted her, felt her come apart in his arms, dominated her sexually to the point of total submission, he would not be able to let her go.

She was his. He'd told her so before he made her come, and he knew it with absolute certainty.

Did she agree? He didn't have the balls to push her right now. She needed to rest, wrap her mind around what she'd given him.

It didn't matter. He would convince her again later. And again and again and again, until she believed him.

There were hurdles, and he couldn't ignore them. For one thing, she was like a newborn in some respects. She had no life experiences. She hadn't even gone to school, let alone college. She needed the freedom to expand her wings, experience life, and make her own choices.

If he pushed her to accept him as a permanent fixture in her life, it might backfire on him later. She didn't have enough experience to know what she wanted. It wouldn't be fair to claim her as his own without giving her options.

Would it?

Half of him wanted to ignore those very real facts, wrap her in a tight bubble, and keep her. But that would make him no better than her mother. He couldn't shield her from the world just because he thought she was perfect for him in every way.

Fuck.

He was also ignoring another important fact—she might be inherently masochistic. He had told her he would give her the pain she craved if she didn't believe an orgasm gave her the same relief. Now he didn't have the guts to ask her again if she found the scene in his bedroom to be equivalent. Could he replace gentle hands, his mouth, and eventually his cock with her craving for whips, paddles, and floggers?

He watched her face as she fell asleep, her full lips parting on a sigh, her brow relaxing. So precious.

When she was fully at rest, he slid from behind her, tucked the comforter around her body, and tiptoed from the room. He left the door open in case she needed him or called out, but he padded down the hallway.

The first thing he did was clean up the mess they'd left in the kitchen, reminding himself she needed to eat soon. She had been hungry, or at least pretended to be before he'd dominated her body so thoroughly.

When he had the kitchen put back together, he grabbed his computer and opened it on the table.

He had a mission. Find out who she really was. Perhaps it was a bad idea and he would be opening a can of worms that would explode in their faces, but he knew one thing for sure—if he was alone in the world and there was any possibility he had family out there somewhere, he'd want to know.

Grandparents. Siblings. Her father.

He shuddered when he considered the ramifications of finding her father. What if the man had been abusive? Now that Carter knew her mother abused her, he shifted his thinking a bit, but it wasn't uncommon for someone who was abused to pass on the legacy because it was all they knew.

There were other possibilities. Maybe her mother was the only abuser, and her father had spent the last twenty-two years looking for his lost daughter.

Far more alarming was the idea that the woman who'd raised her wasn't her mother at all. Brooke could have been kidnapped. Considering how hidden her mother had kept her, it was a real possibility.

With nothing to go on but her name, he started searching. An hour later, he had nothing. Not a trace of Brooke Madden anywhere. No trace of Ann Madden either. He needed more information. When she woke up, he would feed her and then encourage her to go through all those boxes to see if there was even a hint about her past in them.

Shoving from the table, he headed for the kitchen to make sandwiches. Before he had them finished, she stepped quietly into the room. "I fell asleep," she whispered.

"Yeah. I might have worn you out." He grinned.

Her face flushed a lovely red as she glanced away. She was fully dressed again, even her shoes.

"I made you a sandwich." He nodded at the stool across the island from him. "Let's eat, and then I have an idea."

She eased into the room, took a seat on the stool, and lifted a bottle of water to her lips, downing most of it in seconds. "I was thirsty."

"I bet. Sorry, I should have made you drink something before you fell asleep."

Her hands were shaking when she picked up the sandwich. "Starving too."

He opened a bag of potato chips next and then cut up an apple, all the while trying to ignore how much he hated thinking about how many years she'd gone without proper food. Most of her life, if he had to guess.

"Mmm," she moaned around the first bite before swallowing. "Turkey and cheddar beats PBJ any day of the week."

He reached for his own sandwich, fighting the knot in his

throat. Before Brooke, he would have thought this lunch to be stupid and boring. Now, he had a new outlook.

He needed to change the subject before he got so sentimental it turned into melancholy. "I think we should go through your things and see if we can find some information about your mom or anyone else in your family."

She hesitated, stopping herself before putting a chip in her mouth. "I don't think I have anything that would help," she said without looking at him.

"Brooke, look at me."

She lifted her gaze reluctantly. It was the only way he could read her better. Her eyes couldn't hide her feelings.

"We need to find out who you are. If we find out you have no living family or even a father, at least you'll have closure. But what if people have been looking for you for twenty-two years? Think of the pain they've endured."

She nodded, sighing. "You're right, but it scares me to death. What if you were also right about my father? What if he abused me and my mother?" She shuddered.

"It's possible. But you're a grown woman now. He can't hurt you. And I'll be with you every step of the way. I'm not sending you out to hunt people down on your own."

"Don't you have to work? You can't continue to spend every hour with me. I'm keeping you from your real life."

He set his sandwich down, slid off the stool, and rounded the island. Slipping his arms around her, he set them on the edges of the counter and put his mouth to her ear. "I have people who work for me. They're fine for a few days without me. And *you* are my real life." It was the only way he could fathom telling her how he felt without scaring the shit out of her.

Screw the fact that he'd known her for only a few weeks. Never mind that she didn't know who she was or where she came from. She was his.

Please, God, make that be true.

Her voice was barely above a whisper when she responded, but his ears were close enough to catch every word. "When you touch me, I lose myself."

He set his nose in the crook of her neck, inhaled her scent, and then kissed the spot. "When I touch you, you realize you're mine." He was taking a risk continuing along this line, but it wasn't as if he intended to give her up easily, so it was better she understood the score.

He tucked one arm under her breasts and held her back against his chest, still nuzzling her neck.

Her breath hitched. "You make my head spin. I just found out this morning that my entire life might be a giant lie, Carter. I need to figure some things out."

"I know, baby, and I'm going to help you."

She leaned closer. "Okay."

Thank God. "Eat your lunch, and then we'll dig around in your boxes."

She nodded.

An hour later they had all the boxes spread on the floor and Carter was riffling through a pile of old papers. So far he had found nothing interesting. Her mother's name was Ann Madden. That was it. Not revolutionary. Also not helpful.

Suddenly, his fingers hit a book on the bottom of the box. He grabbed it and lifted it out, shaking off the dust. It must have sat on a shelf or something for years before she dropped it in the box.

"Bingo," he said as he held it out toward her.

"What is it?"

"A yearbook from twenty-three years ago. It has to be your mother's. From high school." He frowned at the date. Her mother had been very young.

"How old was your mother when she died?"

168

Brooke shrugged. "No idea. She never admitted her age to anyone." She climbed over several piles of stuff and tentatively reached out. Flipping it open, she turned to the M's. "She's not in here." Her shoulders fell.

Carter lifted her chin with his fingers. "Let's take it to the kitchen. I bet she's in there." *Under a different name…* He was certain of it, though he was less certain about how Brooke would react when they found her. He threaded his fingers with hers and led her from the room.

"That book isn't much older than me," she pointed out. "You think my mother had me in high school?"

"Looks like it." He gave her hand a squeeze.

"Do you recognize the name of the school?" she asked as he pulled out a chair for her to sit and then scooted her in.

"Yes. It's on the outskirts of West Palm Beach, only about an hour from here."

She jerked her gaze to him as he sat next to her. "You think my mom went to high school that close to here and never mentioned a word about my family?"

"It could make sense. If she had limited finances and needed to get away and hide somewhere, Miami wasn't a bad choice. I mean, it worked, didn't it?"

She nodded. "Apparently. I feel so stupid. I stopped asking questions years ago. Every time I tried to get information out of her…" Her voice trailed off. "Well, it didn't go well."

Carter seriously wanted to go back in time and kill the woman himself. He set his hand on the yearbook and leaned in closer to Brooke. "You never told me how she died."

"She had a stroke."

"A stroke? So young."

"Apparently."

"Were you with her?"

"No. She was at work. We weren't cleaning at the same location that day. The owner of the business called an ambulance.

She died before I got to the hospital."

"How did you afford the expenses and the funeral costs?" There were so many holes in Brooke's life that he didn't know how to begin to fill them.

"I didn't. We didn't have insurance. The coroner's office cremated her. I never even went to pick up the ashes." She covered her face with her hands and ducked her head. "I was so angry with her."

Carter wrapped an arm around her back and drew her side in closer. He tucked her head against his chest and threaded his other fingers in her hair. "Baby, I'm so sorry. I can't imagine how difficult that would have been." He wondered if Brooke was angry with her mother for leaving her or for years of abuse or both. It didn't matter.

After several minutes, Brooke took a breath and sat up straighter. "I'm okay. Let's find out who my mom is." She opened the yearbook to the first page.

Carter turned her face toward him and gave her a quick kiss. "It's going to be okay. We're going to figure this out." He hated making that promise because he feared things were going to get a lot worse before they got better.

Most importantly, he would bet money Brooke was either taken from her father or stolen from someone else. Both scenarios would be difficult to swallow.

Starting on the first page, they scanned through hundreds of pictures. It took a long time since they paused many times to consider anyone who resembled Brooke's mother. Since there was no one named Ann Madden, Carter felt confident Ann Madden had not been her name in high school. It made sense. If she was in hiding, she could have been using an alias, which would also explain why she never gave her employer her social security number.

After the first few pages of searching, he'd gone back to the boxes and grabbed a few pictures of Ann. It didn't help that he'd never met the woman. It was hard enough for Brooke to identify a postage-stamp-sized picture of her own mother. It was nearly impossible for Carter.

He did his best to help, though, asking lots of questions. "Was her hair always the same length?"

"Yes."

"Was it always brown? As far back as you can remember?"

"Yes."

"What color were her eyes?"

"Brown."

Carter stared at Brooke's profile while she scoured the tiny black-and-white photos. She was a redhead with green eyes. Of course that meant nothing since both characteristics were recessive, but it still gave him pause. It was going to be very disturbing if they found out Brooke had been abducted.

Brooke grew impatient. "Ugh. I can't find her. We're already on the T's and she's not in here yet. What if I missed her? Maybe she was blond or something. Maybe this isn't even her yearbook." She leaned back and rubbed her temples.

Carter rubbed her shoulder. "She's in here. I'm sure of it. There aren't many more to get through. Let's finish the rest of the alphabet and then we'll consider other options."

Brooke sighed and bent back toward the book. He scrolled down every page with her, squinting his eyes and glancing at the photos occasionally.

Suddenly Brooke flinched. "Oh my God," she murmured, her gaze locked on the page. She slowly set her finger on a picture on the bottom row of the W's. "That's her."

Carter swung the book closer to him. He leaned in and compared the small black-and-white picture to the photo in his hand. "I think you're right." He glanced at the name at the end of the column. "Laurie Wilson."

"Laurie Wilson," she repeated. "I've never once heard that name." Her eyes were glazed over when she lifted her face. "It never occurred to me in my entire life that my mother wasn't who she said she was. I assumed she had left my father and I had no other family. What if I have family out there somewhere?"

She jerked the book back in front of her and flipped to the front, tapping the name of the high school. "What if I have family in West Palm Beach?"

"One way to find out." Carter grabbed his computer from across the table and dragged it closer. He'd spent a lot of time looking for Ann and Brooke Madden. He hadn't been searching the correct names.

Perhaps Brooke wasn't even her real name.

His hands were unsteady as he typed in Laurie Wilson and West Palm Beach, Florida. It took just seconds before the screen filled with that name. Every caption was similar: Laurie Ann Wilson...missing child...runaway...seventeen years old...please contact the West Palm Beach police department. The information went on and on, but as soon as they had the gist of it, Brooke stopped talking.

Carter grabbed her hand as he continued to read several articles, but she was stiff and unmoving. Every time he glanced at her, he found her despondent. Frozen. Unblinking.

Finally, he copied several key pieces of information into a blank document and shut the computer, he turned to fully face Brooke and pulled her out of her chair and into his lap. "We have answers. This is a good thing."

She didn't respond.

He lifted her in his arms and carried her to the couch where they could sit more comfortably. "Baby, talk to me."

She fisted his shirt in her hand, but she didn't say a word.

After several minutes, he did the only thing he thought might work—he slid her to the floor in front of him and settled her on her knees.

She immediately pulled her shoulders back and clasped her hands behind her back. It was almost scary how easily she submitted to him. He would never let her go in a million years. No one else would know how to handle her. So much damage could happen to someone like her in the wrong hands.

He stroked her hair back, but let her keep her face cast downward. "Talk to me, Brooke. What are you thinking?"

She hesitated, but finally she spoke. "My entire life is a lie."

He couldn't argue the point, but he would at least try to come up with possible bright scenarios. "She might have had a good reason for running away. We won't know until we do some more research." Given how young Laurie Wilson would have been, he felt confident she had run away pregnant. It was unlikely a teenager would have abducted a baby.

"What if she didn't run away? What if my father kidnapped her?"

The thought had crossed his mind. Damn, she was sharp for someone so distressed. "It's possible, but you don't even remember him."

She lifted her gaze, surprising him with her sudden openness. "Maybe he kidnapped her, got her pregnant, and then she ran away from him. That would explain why she kept me hidden."

He nodded. It was a possibility. "Perhaps, but why didn't she go back home? Her parents were worried sick."

Brooke bit her lip, her brow furrowed in concentration. When her eyes shot wide with excitement, she blurted out another possibility. "Because he could easily find her there again if she went home."

Carter was shocked. Brooke was ahead of him. "That makes sense. I wonder how old you were when she escaped, then. Did you say you thought a woman in the building where you lived watched you as a baby?"

"Yes. Mrs. Thurston."

"Does she still live there?"

"Yes." Brooke smiled. "Two doors down from my apartment."

173

"I think we need to pay Mrs. Thurston a visit." He leaned down to kiss her forehead.

Brooke nodded and then she lowered her face again and leaned against Carter's thigh.

He kept one hand in her hair and one on her shoulder, giving her time to process.

She calmed for a few minutes, and then she squirmed, her agitation growing.

He applied more pressure to her shoulder. "You okay?"

She didn't say anything for a long time, and then she lifted her body, straightened her spine, and pulled her shoulders back again. "I need you to dominate me, Carter."

He stiffened slightly. She wasn't talking about sex.

"It's like there's all this...stuff...inside me. It's frustrating. It's bottled up. Like years of...stuff. It needs release. The only way I know to get that release is from having it beaten out of me."

He closed his eyes, pursing his lips, unsure how to handle this situation. "Baby..."

She flinched. "Please." Her head tipped back and she met his gaze. "Please, Carter. I need the release. If you won't do it, I'll find someone else. But I'd rather it be you."

He searched her eyes. "I'm worried about your ability to know what you need. I don't want to harm you emotionally."

She blew out a breath. "Before Faith, I didn't understand it either. This...this, thing. It's like a burden I carry. When my mother would hit me..." She paused, and then started again. "It was like my mother had to get the punishment out of her and then she could be a good mom again. If she didn't purge the need to hit me, she would get angrier and angrier and more withdrawn every day until she finally snapped."

Brooke looked past Carter, and then said something that chilled his blood. "When she would start to slide into one of her weird, dark moods, I..." Her voice trailed off.

Carter waited a bit and then encouraged her to continue. "You what, baby? What did you do?"

She slid her gaze back to his. "Sometimes I intentionally acted out to get her to punish me so that we could go back to the good times." A tear slid down her face.

Carter fought the emotion building up inside him too.

"I'm a freak."

"You're not."

"Who does something like that? What kind of person misbehaves so that they will get beaten?"

"Baby, you did what you had to do to survive. Everyone copes in their own way."

She blinked through tears that kept falling, and then she spoke again as if she hadn't heard him. "Do you know what kinds of things I had to do to get my mother to punish me?"

"Tell me." She needed to get this out of her system.

She swallowed hard. "It didn't take much. I could spill something, even water. Or I could forget to bring the mail in from the box downstairs. Or I could leave the lid up on the toilet. Or I could set my dishes in the sink without rinsing them. It was so easy."

Jesus. "You were a child, baby. You weren't responsible for your mother's actions." When did Laurie Wilson/Ann Madden stop abusing her daughter, though? Or had she? He was afraid to ask.

"How did she punish you?" he encouraged.

"All different ways. Sometimes she used her hand or a wooden spoon or a belt or a spatula or a hair brush." As she spoke, her words came out in a rush.

There were no visible scars on Brooke's body, so he didn't think any of the punishments had been severe enough for her to need medical care. He prayed anyway. "Did she draw blood?"

"Sometimes. When I was little, it happened a few times, but then she seemed to control herself better. It was as if she figured out exactly how hard she could strike me to make it hurt without ruining my clothes or needing to clean me up afterward."

Carter's heart seized for the little girl who'd been beaten bloody as a small child. "How often did she punish you?"

"Maybe once a month when I was smaller. When I got older, it lessened. Sometimes she would go months without striking me."

"When was the last time?"

Brooke swallowed, more tears falling. Her face was pale. Finally, she whispered, "About a year ago."

He wiped her tears with his fingers. "I'm so sorry, baby." Her mother was truly fucked up.

She winced. "Who does that?"

"I don't know. Some people are disturbed. They can't stop themselves. And if they never get help…"

"No." She shook her head. "I mean, *me*. What kind of person lets their mother continue to abuse them at the age of twenty-one? I'm so weak. So stupid." She looked away again.

Carter cupped her face, his heart breaking. "Brooke, you can't blame yourself. You were caught in a world where you didn't know better. You didn't have the skills to move out and make it on your own. I'd even bet your mother knew that and did it on purpose so you couldn't leave her."

She nodded, but her words didn't agree. "Still, I should have left. I should have stopped her. She was no longer bigger than me. I didn't have to let her hit me. Why did I do that?"

He knew the answer. "For the same reason you're asking me to punish you now. For the release. You're used to it. I assume it purges your stress and leaves you feeling calmer afterward."

She seemed to think about that for a minute and then her brows lifted. "Will you do it?"

"No." He shook his head. "I don't think it's a good idea. I don't like the headspace you're in. I'm not sure it's safe. Maybe someday in the future, but I'd want someone else with me. Rowen or

Lincoln or someone who could help monitor and make sure you were safe."

She surprised him by shoving away from him and stumbling backward. After landing on her butt, she scrambled to get to her feet and rushed from the room.

Scared out of his mind, he pushed off the couch and followed her as she raced down the hall and then entered the guest room where she'd been sleeping until last night.

She shoved the mess of boxes and papers and memorabilia out of the way and found her purse. When she opened it, she stared inside and then threw it against the wall and spun around.

He stood in the doorway, wondering what she was thinking, nervous as hell.

She stomped back toward him. "I need my car keys. Did you take them? I'm not your prisoner. Give me my car keys."

He flinched, taken aback. "Baby, I didn't steal your keys. They're on the kitchen counter. You left them there yesterday. But you can't leave here right now."

She came at him and gave his chest a shove. "Don't tell me what to do. I can leave if I want. I'm not staying here."

He didn't move. It wasn't like she could possibly force him out of her way. He was too big. He outweighed her by over a hundred pounds. She didn't even have the ability to inflict pain on him. "Baby, calm down. Please. You're too angry to drive."

She stomped a foot and spun around. "Now you're going to tell me how I feel? Get out of my way, Carter. I'm leaving."

He blew out a breath. "You're not. Not right now." *Not ever.* No way in hell would he let her drive off in this state of mind.

She shoved at his chest again, not managing to budge him.

He gripped the doorframe, not wanting to touch her with his hands. He could take her wrath. He didn't want to do anything that might accidently injure her if he tried to stop her.

What he wanted to do was wrap her in his arms and hold her

close so she could cry until her frustration passed. But that wasn't in the cards. Not yet.

She picked up a pile of papers and threw them across the room toward the window. They went flying, but they were only paper. They didn't give her any satisfaction. Instead, they fluttered to the floor.

A loud scream filled the air as she rushed toward the window next and then reached for the locks.

"Shit," he muttered under his breath. He went after her, leaping over boxes and piles of clothes until he reached her.

By the time he got behind her, she was pulling on the bottom of the window. He wrapped his arms around her middle, pinning her biceps to her sides.

She struggled, flailing and then kicking at his shins. "Let me go," she shouted. "I'm serious, Carter. *Let me go.*"

"No, baby. I'm not going to let you go." He held her tighter, lifting her off the floor and turning away from the window.

She screamed.

He worried the neighbors would hear her and call the cops. Just what he needed. So he put his hand over her mouth to stop her as he aimed for the bed. After dropping her unceremoniously on the mattress face-first, he climbed over her and held her down. He tried to use enough weight to keep her from getting away, but not so much that he might hurt her.

She continued to struggle, shoving at the bed with both hands and kicking her legs back.

He said nothing more, just held her while she squirmed.

Breathing heavily, she tugged at her arms and then bucked her head back. He leaned to one side to avoid getting a bloody lip. Her steam ran out fast, though, and her fight lost its oomph. After a while, she gave up, her entire body sinking into the bed. She was still gasping for breath, but she stopped flailing.

He waited until he thought she was truly done and then set his head down next to hers, his lips close to her ear. "You're okay," he whispered. "I've got you. You're going to be okay."

She started to cry, just as he knew she would, sobbing, gasping for air, and crying hard.

He eased off her and turned her onto her side so he could pull her against his chest. With one hand, he brushed her hair from her face. With the other, he grabbed a pile of tissues from the nightstand.

After wiping her face gently, he handed her the tissues. And then he waited while she continued to cry, keeping his arms wrapped around her.

For a long time, he said nothing, expecting her to fall asleep when she wore herself out.

CHAPTER 17

Brooke's mind was racing, overloaded with so many thoughts and emotions she couldn't process them all. And she had no idea where to begin. Finally, she gathered enough sense to speak. "You don't understand."

"I'm trying, baby." He stroked the back of her hand where he held it between her breasts.

"After my mother died, I was lost." She had no idea why she felt the need to explain herself further, but it felt good to get it out. "I was a zombie. Even though she'd abused me my entire life, I still missed her. I had no one else. She left me alone in the world."

"I'm so sorry, baby. I can't imagine what that feels like."

How did he know just the right things to say to her? It melted her soul a bit every time he showed her such compassion. "I was just going through the motions day in and day out. Going to work. Making not enough money to live on. Surviving. Running out of time. Scared to death."

He held her closer, comforting her. Helping her relax.

"And then one day I happened to be at Zodiac when Faith was there practicing. I didn't know anything about BDSM, but I knew

I was intrigued. The first time I saw her swing that whip, I knew I wanted her to use it on me. Maybe it makes no sense to you, but—"

He interrupted her, "It makes perfect sense."

She sniffled, drawing his hand up to her cheek and tipping her face into his touch. "I craved that feeling. The release. Maybe I'm crazy and need mental help, but it's who I am. I'm pissed at my mother for making me this way, but I can't change the past."

"I understand," he soothed.

"I'm, like, addicted or something. It's like a drug to me. I used to go for weeks or even months without it, but now that I've had a taste of what it can be like in a controlled environment, I want to experience it again."

"Okay. Let me make some calls. We can go to the club in a few days and I'll have Lincoln spot us."

"Why? Are you afraid you'll hit me too hard? I thought you said you'd at least practiced with other toys before. I mean, I know it's not your usual thing, but you're part owner of the club. You told me yourself you knew how to practice sadism even though it isn't your preference." She didn't want to wait a few days, nor did she want an audience. She wanted Carter to do it. Now.

Except if he wouldn't do it, she would find someone else. She wanted to purge the need now. Today. Not later. Someone else was better than no one at all.

"It's not me I'm worried about. It's you. I can't pay close attention to your emotional state while I'm also striking you from behind. I need to see your face, or at least have someone else watch your expression. Gauge your reaction."

She shook her head, digging her heels in. He needed to understand she wasn't playing here. She meant business. She twisted her body until she landed on her back looking up at him. "Please."

He frowned at her. "Why the urgency? Do you feel like you need to be punished for something right now?"

She glanced away. "I don't know. Maybe. Yes. Probably."

He stroked her arm. "So you feel like you've done something that deserves punishment?"

She closed her eyes, not wanting to see his face. "Yes. Lots of things. Yelling at you. Trying to run away. Freaking out." In a whisper, she added, "Finding you attractive. Wanting to do things with you that are..."

He stiffened. "Are what?"

"Naughty." She could hardly breathe at that admission.

A few seconds ticked by before he spoke again. "Baby..." He took a deep breath. "You're not naughty. You're human. People yell. They get mad. They stomp and fight and argue. It's human nature."

She knew he was right.

He set his forehead against hers, his lips a fraction away from her mouth, though she didn't open her eyes. "And it's perfectly normal for you to be attracted to me. Thank God you are. I'd hate to be the only one aroused in this relationship. That would suck." His last few sentences were lighter.

She still didn't move, trying to process his words.

"There's also nothing wrong with wanting to practice some form of masochism. Thousands of people enjoy it. But I don't want you to associate it with specific incidences as if you need to atone for yelling or getting aroused. At some point you need to learn to separate the craving for release from some misguided belief that you're inherently bad. Because you're not."

She let her eyes slide open. "That makes sense." It did. She understood. It would take time and a lot of frequent reminders for her to change her way of thinking, but she knew intellectually what he said had merit. "It's like something inside me builds up until it needs release. Maybe it has nothing to do with anything I did to deserve being beaten.

"At this point, I think I'm grasping at any reason to justify the punishment. It's what I've always done. It's like a game. Eventually I sort of controlled my environment, gauging my mother's moods and reacting accordingly to keep the balance."

"I get that."

She kept talking, her thoughts stumbling over each other. "I've been afraid for a long time that I would never find that release again. And then I met Faith and now you. It's like a gift. There are people in the world who can strike me in a controlled environment and purge my body of whatever it needs."

He lifted his face several inches, his brow furrowed. "I'm not sure I can be the kind of Dom you need. The thought of laying a hand on you makes me very nervous, and not just because sadism is not my thing, but because I'm not sure you're in the right frame of mind to make decisions right now."

"Either do it yourself or let me go." For some reason it was the most important thing in the world to her. "I just found out I don't know who I am. I don't even know if my mother gave birth to me or kidnapped me. I didn't know her name until an hour ago. I might have family. I might have a father out there. He might be abusive. Or old or dead or any number of things. I need the release, Carter."

His brows were close together. He licked his lips. At least he finally considered her request. "I don't like it."

"Why? Because you're afraid I can't handle it? I've been beaten so many times I can't count them. I learned twenty years ago to shut my mind down and pretend it wasn't happening. I later learned to feel the pain in its entirety. Believe me, I can control my emotional state while I'm being struck with any implement in the room."

He was still frowning. "I'm sure you can, but is it healthy?"

"Both you and Faith have told me there are others like me, people who need the absolution a flogger or a whip can provide.

What makes me different?" She was getting to him. She could read it on his face.

"Because you've been abused for your entire life, Brooke. Not a year or an incident—your entire life. You need counseling, not more abuse."

She cocked her head to one side. "It's not abuse when you do it. I'm educated enough on the subject to know that. It's consensual. I'm asking you to do it."

He almost grinned. "You should become a lawyer."

She rolled her eyes. "I don't even have a high school diploma."

"I'll help you get one."

"Don't change the subject."

He grabbed one of her hands and held it in his, flattening it against the bed next to her head. "It'd rather fuck you than strike you with anything."

Her body jumped to attention when he said *fuck*. So crude. It woke up something inside her, something that was no longer foreign. She flushed. "Use a belt on me first, and then I'll let you have sex with me."

He shook his head. "Not a chance in hell."

"Carter." She moaned. "Stop being unreasonable."

He stared down at her, his expression serious. "I've never been so reasonable in my life. It's killing me. I've wanted to have sex with you from the moment you stepped into my line of sight at the club. It's all I think about, but I won't do it. Not this soon. Not while you're so confused and distraught."

She licked her lips. "You said yourself what we did this morning was essentially sex anyway. What difference does it make if you put your, uh, penis inside me?"

He chuckled. "You can hardly say the word, and you want me to fuck you?"

She had an idea. Her eyes widened as she considered it. "How about we make a game out of it?"

"Out of what?" he asked warily.

"I'll pretend to be naughty and maybe even cuss if you want, and you can punish me." It would work.

He shook his head. "No way."

She let her shoulders sag. "Carter," she whined, knowing that noise always made her mother livid.

"Not going to work, baby. Ever," he emphasized as he leaned in and kissed her nose. "I don't do brats."

"That's exactly my point. If I misbehave, you have to put me in my place." She had no idea why she would suggest such a thing, but it seemed brilliant.

"Never. Not my kind of kink. There are people who role-play that way. I'm not one of them."

Her heart beat faster. "There are others who play that way?"

"Yes." He took a deep breath and blew it out slowly. "And if you decide along the way you really need something like that, you'd have to find some other Dom to do it. It won't be me."

He was so infuriating.

"Baby, I'm far more into the sensual side of kink. I like my women to submit to me in the bedroom, on their knees, keeping good form, obeying my commands until they come so hard they can't think straight. Did I not demonstrate that to you?"

Her cheek grew hotter. "You did. And I loved it. But I want more."

Shocking her, he released her and turned away, sitting on the edge of the bed, facing the window.

She scrambled to her knees and came up behind him, wrapping her arms around his chest and setting her cheek against his back. She didn't say anything at first, waiting for him to work out whatever he had in his mind, praying he would give in so she wouldn't have to leave and go find someone else.

He set his hands over hers after a few moments and lifted her fingers to kiss her knuckles. "Okay. I'll give you what you want, but I have conditions."

She jerked up straighter, yanked her hands out of his grasp, and crawled off the edge of the bed so fast, she nearly tripped as she slid to the floor. Seconds later, she was in front of him on her knees. "Anything."

He shook his head as he smiled down at her. "Woman, if you make me regret this—"

"I won't." She waited for him to continue, knowing she would consent to anything he asked.

"Condition number one, I use my hand, nothing else. Not today."

She nodded eagerly. "Done."

"Two, I decide when you've had enough, and no arguing."

"Fine."

"Third, this is the one and only time I'm going to let you manipulate me into doing what you want. I'll never spank you or in any way punish you physically in the future for bad behavior. Don't even try it. If you whine at me or try to play the brat or deliberately disobey me in order to get disciplined, you'll find yourself very frustrated because I'll stand you in a corner and ignore you instead of giving you what you want."

She squeezed her legs together, her mouth falling open in shock. "Like a time out?" The idea sent a flutter to her sex.

"Exactly like a time out. If being spanked is something you crave, you won't get it from any of those means. It's okay to crave the release, but I don't like you feeling like you deserve punishment for a disagreement with me. And I sure as shit don't want you to think being attracted to me deserves a beating."

She nodded again. "Understood." It would take some time to change how she looked at things, but he made perfect sense. However, if he wasn't going to be willing to strike her in the future for misbehavior, what would be an acceptable reason to give her what she needed? If he meant that he only intended to spank her this one time, she didn't think she could agree to that, but at the moment she needed it so badly she didn't want to risk him changing his mind by arguing the point further.

He stared at her face, probably judging her state of mind. "You won't utter another word except your safeword. If I hear anything besides yellow or red, we end the scene. Understood?"

She opened her mouth to agree and then stopped short and nodded.

He smiled. "Good girl. My way or not at all."

She nodded again, though she was confused by her body's response to the way this was playing out. That knot in her belly was back. Wetness leaked between her legs. She was aroused. Not at all what she'd planned.

He was confusing her, smearing the boundaries between sex play and punishment play. Was it calculated or was she that messed up?

"Take off your clothes."

She gasped, opening her mouth to speak and then stopping herself. *My clothes?* She's been naked with him earlier, but that was different. It was sexual. This was a different kind of need. It didn't require nudity. In fact, it required her not to be naked so she wouldn't get so aroused.

He crossed his arms in front of him and waited.

Darn. He was serious. If she wanted to get what she was asking for, she needed to give him what he demanded in return.

Slowly she stood and pulled her T-shirt over her head. Her fingers struggled to obey directions from her mind, but she somehow managed to pop the button on her jeans and lower them over her hips. Next she unclasped her bra and dropped it to the floor. And finally, she wiggled free of her panties.

By the time she was finished, there were red splotches across her chest from nerves.

"Hands at your sides," he commanded.

She pulled them away from her chest, unaware she'd been covering herself. She had to curl her fingers into her palms and dig her nails into her skin to remind herself to stay still.

"Shoulders back."

She did as he said, but her traitorous nipples jumped to attention even without contact. Her breasts felt heavy under his gaze.

He stared at her forever. "Spread your legs farther. Shoulder width. When you submit to me, always keep your knees or feet spread out. I want you to feel the air on your pussy." He leaned forward and lowered his voice as if his next words were too lude to utter as loudly. "I want your pussy open so I can easily reach out and stroke through your folds whenever I desire."

She shivered, a small noise escaping her lips.

He smiled. "I think that makes my little sub wet."

He was not wrong.

"Turn around."

It was awkward, especially keeping her feet spread apart, but she managed to face the window, wondering where his gaze was now.

"Your bottom is so gorgeous. So white and smooth. It's going to look even prettier all pink from my palm."

A quiver shook her body.

"When I'm done with your bottom, it will be too sore to sit down. And then I'm going to massage your body until you're putty under my hands, rubbing lotion into your sensitive skin. Every stroke of my palm over your bottom will remind you who you belong to."

Belong... She found she liked the sound of that. He'd insinuated before that he owned her. She knew he was only playing, but the idea of belonging to him made her heart soar. She'd give anything to be his.

"I'm going to spank you because you've given me no choice, but you're not going to get the reaction you think from it."

She swayed a bit on her feet, wondering what he meant. He couldn't control her reaction to a spanking. Only she could. She knew the second he struck her skin the first time, she would slide into that happy place where she escaped the world and enjoyed the feeling. Whatever other reaction he thought she might have would never happen.

His hand landed on her bottom unexpectedly, sending goose bumps down her legs and up her back. His touch was light, gentle. "Baby, you're going to come so hard for me you won't know what happened."

Come? What? No. Not from a spanking. Would he be disappointed?

She stiffened, worried she couldn't be the person he needed her to be. Maybe this had been a bad idea all along. He'd told her multiple times he wasn't a sadist and didn't want to play that way with her, and yet she'd pushed and pushed and pushed until she'd gotten what she wanted.

But had she? She wanted the euphoric release only being struck with something could provide. The burning sting of a palm or belt or whip. It chased her sins away and left her rejuvenated. Like a new person.

He cupped her butt cheeks with both hands, molding them, pulling them apart until she gasped at the exposure. His palms slid around to the front of her thighs and farther until they nearly touched her sex. But not quite close enough.

Suddenly his hands were gone and he spoke. "Turn around."

She faced him again, her hair falling loosely around her face.

He tugged a hairband from his pocket and held it out. "Pull your hair back."

She was surprised he was letting her do it, but she took the band with shaky fingers and gathered her hair behind her head, pulling every lock out of her face.

"Good girl." He reached for her nipples next, flicking his thumbs over them and then tweaking them both with a quick grip and twist.

She gasped as she swayed forward. The sting was welcome. It brought her fully alive, but it also sent another wave of arousal to her sex. Pain and arousal?

She remembered how he'd elicited the same thing from her with a swat to her inner thigh earlier. What the heck ride was she on here?

After briefly cupping both breasts a little too firmly, he released them, wrapped a hand around her wrist, and angled her to one side of his thighs.

By the time she realized he intended to take her over his knee, she was already falling forward.

She'd never been in this position before. Faith had spanked her on a bench and then used other toys on her against the St. Andrew's cross and the spider web, but not across her knees.

Ironically, her mother had never spanked her in this position either. She'd forced Brooke to bend over a chair or couch or table or bed. If Brooke didn't comply, the beating would be longer and worse.

"Relax your body," he ordered softly. With one hand on her lower back, he held her across his knees. His other hand stroked up and down her thighs and butt cheeks.

Her breasts hung over his leg, brushing across the bed with every movement. Her stupid nipples were demanding attention, and she found herself rubbing them intentionally over the comforter.

If he noticed, he said nothing.

She braced herself on her elbows, holding her head up, but the position was strenuous.

"Brooke," he admonished, "lower your arms and set your cheek against the bed. I'm not going to begin until you're relaxed."

Relaxed wasn't a sensation she usually felt when she was being punished, not by her mother or Faith. A nervous tension always stiffened her body. Although, she did recall Faith demanding her to loosen her body also.

More caressing, up and down her thighs. With every stroke, his fingers got closer to her sex. "Spread your legs farther. I want your knees open."

She awkwardly obeyed him over his lap.

"That's a girl. Just like that. It changes your frame of mind when you open your pussy to me. Feel the cool air hitting your clit and those sweet lips of yours."

She moaned before she could stop herself.

"That's it. Let your body do as I say. I want you to be so wet you can't stand it."

He was certainly getting that wish. Arousal leaked onto her thighs.

"That's my good girl. Now, I'm going to spank you, but I'll do it at my pace, and it will be my choice how hard I strike each time. You don't have permission to speak. You may moan or scream or cry out, but no words. If you speak, I'll stop."

She pursed her lips to ensure she didn't break his rule. Even though this arrangement between them was new, she didn't doubt his words for a second.

The first swat that landed took her by surprise. It also pushed her breath out of her lungs. Her skin tingled where his palm landed, but something else happened at the same time. It was as if he'd pushed two fingers into her vagina instead of spanking her.

She gritted her teeth, pressing her forehead into the bed to control her weird reaction.

The second slap resonated louder in the room. It landed lower on her cheeks, right where her butt and her thighs met up. Again, her sex clenched. *Oh. My. God.*

He had said she would come. She had not believed him or understood his plan.

Another two swats landed in succession, leaving her gasping for air. Her arousal went through the roof, her sex pulsing with need.

If he was aware of her body's reaction, he didn't let on. "Your bottom is so gorgeous all pink like this. I can see my fingerprints on your soft cheeks. I wonder how long it will last?" he mused.

"Will I still see the evidence of my spanking on your bottom tomorrow?"

She was glad his questions were rhetorical, keeping her from accidentally speaking out loud.

He rained several more slaps to both cheeks, alternating back and forth, his palm striking the lower part of her butt over and over while she held her breath. All she could think about was the building orgasm he'd elusively promised.

Just when she thought she couldn't take another moment, his hand thrust between her legs, two fingers sliding deep into her channel without warning.

She came instantly, screaming out around her orgasm, her sex pulsing around his now thrusting fingers as they pounded in and out of her, his thumb hitting the bundle of nerves above her sex each time he thrust again.

As her orgasm subsided, she squirmed to get away from his fingers. Too sensitive. An overload of sensation flooded her body.

He didn't let up however, his hand on her back holding her steady as he removed his fingers from her sheath and dragged them up to circle her nub with soaking wet fingertips. He applied more pressure, flicking and circling and tormenting the bundle of nerves until the sensitivity transformed into something else, and she found herself climbing that mountain to the top again.

She gasped at the realization that she was going to come again. He showed no signs of stopping, and the need grew quickly back to a fevered pitch.

"That's my girl. So wet for me. Your little clit is swollen and needy." His fingers worked her hard, relentlessly. She couldn't concentrate on any one feeling because he switched it up too fast. Circling. Pinching. Flicking. Brushing. Rubbing.

She arched into him when she reached the peak and called out his name as she crashed over the precipice. "Carter..."

CHAPTER 18

"That's a good girl. Just relax," he whispered as he eased his fingers away from her sex and then caressed the inside of her thighs. Still holding her down, he marveled at how gorgeous her skin was. He was pretty sure she wouldn't bruise. That would never be his intention. But he did appreciate the warm pink tones.

He felt victorious that he'd made her come. He'd used the spanking to arouse her, hoping she would be able to pull the two needs together into one. And it had paid off as he suspected.

He might be able to give her this on occasion, but only if she allowed him to channel the heat and sting of the blows toward a building arousal. He didn't have it in him to spank, flog, or whip her for the sake of physical release from the punishment. For many people in the lifestyle, it was euphoric. Good for them. He didn't want his submissive to need that sort of thing.

But this...this combination. He could handle this. In fact, his cock was so hard against her thigh, he needed to adjust it.

When she squirmed against him, he winced. "Hold still." He gripped her thigh and then he grabbed her waist and hauled her body farther onto the bed, climbing up beside her. He flipped her onto her back, threw a leg over both of hers, and settled his hand on her chest.

She blinked up at him. "Thank you." Her voice cracked.

"You're welcome. How do you feel?"

"Weird. You made me come with a spanking."

He gave her a wry grin. "That was the plan."

Her face flushed that gorgeous shade that matched her bottom now. "I didn't think it was possible."

"Now you know."

"Will it always be that way?"

"Yes. With me, it will."

"What if I want you to spank me with my clothes on without adding sex?"

"I won't."

"But—"

He set his fingers over her lips and pressed. "Shh. Baby, please. Stop arguing with me for a moment. I'm exhausted."

She grinned, but surprisingly acquiesced.

"Don't move. I'll be right back." He shot her a look of warning as he slid from the bed and left the room. When he got to his own bathroom, he grabbed the lotion with one hand while adjusting his cock with the other. She was going to kill him if he didn't have her soon. But he'd bombarded her with far too many sensations to add penetration with his cock. Not yet.

When he returned, he found her right where he'd left her. "Turn over onto your belly."

She did as he ordered, confusion pulling her brows together.

He popped the lid off the lotion and squeezed some into his hands. After warming it between his palms, he set both hands on her bottom and massaged the skin. It was heated, but he hadn't struck her too hard. It wouldn't be sore for very long.

She squirmed under his touch as he eased his hands up her back to her shoulders, working the lotion into the tight muscles there next. She sighed into the pillow as he continued down one arm and then the other before working back to her bottom and then down her legs next.

She was putty, just as he'd promised.

He kept working until she was fully relaxed, and then he set the lotion aside and climbed up next to her, flattening a palm on her lower back to keep her still. "I'm proud of you. You're a beautiful submissive. It's shocking how deeply you're able to submit to me with so little experience. It's humbling. Thank you for trusting me."

"You're welcome," she murmured. "I feel better now."

"As good as you expect to get without the orgasm added?" he teased.

"Mmm." When he pinched her butt cheek lightly, she squealed. "Hey."

"Answer the question."

"It was amazing. I loved it."

"Good girl." He continued to caress her back, thinking she would fall asleep, but as usual she did the unexpected.

"What do we do now?"

"You mean about your mom?"

"Yes."

"Tomorrow morning, I think we should go visit Mrs. Thurston first thing and see what she knows about you. It will give us more information. And then we'll head to West Palm Beach, if you're ready."

"Do you think my grandparents still live there?"

"I don't know, but it's the best place to start." He wanted to tread carefully. He needed to think things through before they made the drive. There was a reason Laurie Ann Wilson fled her family and her baby's father and hid from them for twenty-two years. That reason could not be pretty.

For one thing, it was clear now that Brooke's mother had been very young when she ran away from home. Perhaps she had already been pregnant when she left.

"I'm nervous."

"I know, baby." He kissed her forehead and then nuzzled her neck, breathing in her scent. He would never get enough of her. "We don't have to track anyone down yet if you'd rather wait. It's up to you."

"No." She blinked. "I want to know. You think you can find my grandparents?"

"Easily. We could go straight to the police station if you want, but I'm betting they know less than us. The case went cold twenty years ago."

She chewed on her bottom lip for a moment. "You can get an address?"

"Yes. If they're still alive, I'll find them. Probably in five minutes."

Brooke pushed on him and wiggled free until she was sitting. She pulled the sheet from the bed up to cover herself.

He tried not to smirk at her sudden modesty. He'd seen, felt, and tasted every inch of her skin. Now she needed to hide? "Where are you going?"

She slid off the bed. "I can't just lie here. Let's find my grandparents." She reached down and grabbed her clothes off the floor, setting them on the bed. The sheet she held was still tucked into the mattress, making it difficult for her to function.

Carter climbed off the opposite side, rounded the bed, and stopped her with a hand to her wrist. "Relax. We'll look up the address. But you don't need to get dressed."

She glared at him as she snagged her panties.

He tugged them out of her hand and put them in his pocket. Spotting the T-shirt he'd given her the first night at the top of the bed, he leaned across her to grab it. "You can wear this. Nothing else."

She flinched. "Carter—"

He stopped her with a finger under her chin. "You pick. The T-shirt or nothing." He had a good reason to keep her in a submissive mind frame. She was stressed as hell, and it was going to get worse before it got better. The only thing that ever calmed her was submitting to him. If he could enforce the role, perhaps he could keep her from losing her mind in the process.

She flushed, which always made his cock jump to attention. Staring at the T-shirt he held out to her, she spoke again. "Carter..."

He could tell by the tone of her voice she was going to argue her point further, so he needed to nip in in the bud. "I didn't say we were done with our scene. Just because I spanked your sweet bottom and you came hard for me doesn't mean you get to break out of the scene and get dressed."

She lowered her gaze.

He kept his voice firm. "Now, you have two choices. I'm going to give you about three seconds to decide, and then I'm going to choose for you. One more word and I'll do more than choose what you won't be wearing. I'll also discipline you for your insubordination in a way you won't enjoy."

After a few seconds' hesitation, she reached for the T-shirt and drew it toward her chest.

"Good decision. I'll meet you in the kitchen." He left her there to put the shirt on and gave her a moment to regroup. If she came out swinging, he'd have to react accordingly. If she came out demure and back in the role, he would pump his fist in his head and reward her.

Five minutes went by before she emerged from the hallway wearing nothing but the T-shirt, her hands folded behind her back.

He pulled out the chair next to him. "Good girl. Come sit. I've already discovered a few things."

Brooke was trembling as she sat next to him. On the one hand, she was out of her mind for obeying him like this. On the other hand, wasn't his dominance exactly what she wanted? She craved it. He'd proven to her this afternoon that she didn't have to be beaten bloody to get release, and she felt an instant calmness flow over her body after he spanked her to orgasm.

If the arrangement was weird, he didn't let on. He'd even explained that many people in the community had similar agreements.

Her heart had pounded and she'd gotten agitated at the prospect of locating her grandparents, but then he'd suddenly stepped in and put a stop to her burgeoning anxiety.

She felt incredibly awkward stepping out of the bedroom in so little clothing, but obeying him also felt...right. "Did you find them already?" she asked tentatively as he scooted her chair in.

"Yes. Looks like your grandmother still lives at the same address she used when your mother disappeared."

Brooke glanced at Carter to find his face pinched. "Where is my grandfather?"

"He died about ten years ago. I found his obituary." He grabbed her hand and drew it to his lips to kiss her knuckles. "I'm sorry."

She frowned. "Not like I knew he existed anyway." It hurt, though. She'd only found out she had grandparents today, and already one of them was dead.

"Your grandmother is only sixty-two, so she wasn't very old when she had your mother either."

"My age," Brooke surmised.

"Yes."

She shuddered. No way in hell could she have a baby at this age, let alone five years ago. She wouldn't even know what to do with a child. Besides, she never wanted to have kids. She feared she wouldn't be able to break the cycle and would treat them the same way her mother had treated her.

"You okay?" Carter asked, leaning to put his face level with hers.

"Yeah."

"The yearbook must be from your mother's junior year of high school. She disappeared near the beginning of her senior year."

"Do you think she ran away?"

He sighed. "Who knows? She could have run away because she was pregnant. Now that we know how young she was, it's a very real possibility. Maybe her parents wouldn't support her."

"But that's not the only option." Several other scenarios could just as easily be true.

"Right. She could have been abducted. She could have run off with your father and then later left him. She could have met your father after she left. All we can do is hope your grandmother knows something."

Brooke nodded. "And Mrs. Thurston. Maybe she can fill in some holes."

"Exactly." He smiled. "Tomorrow we'll at least have answers. They may not be the ones you want, but they will steer us in the right direction."

The idea that her father might have been looking for her hurt. She hated thinking that people spent twenty-two years looking for a child while she'd been sequestered in Miami all this time. Guilt raced through her all of the sudden, and she stiffened.

"What?" Carter asked, twisting to face her again. "What's the matter?" He grabbed her hand again. "You're white."

She licked her lips, her voice shaky when she spoke. "I should have known. I should have told someone. I've probably hurt people with my silence."

He jerked his entire chair around and pulled her out of hers, setting her between his legs, his hands on her arms. "Brooke, that's crazy. This is not your fault. You're the victim. You can't blame yourself for your mother's choices. She might have been selfish, but there's also the possibility she had a good reason for hiding you."

Her voice rose, squeaking. "So she could abuse me?"

He took a deep breath. "Well, that part sucks. It's horrible. No one should be treated that way for any reason. Ever. I'm not excusing your mother's behavior. I'm simply pointing out we don't have all the facts. We don't know her motives. What we do know is that no matter what, you have no blame in this." He gave her a small shake as if he thought it might help her see reason.

She shook her head. "I'm a grown woman. My mother was still beating me at the age of twenty-one. I should have told someone. I should have gotten help. I should have run away. I should have run away years ago. Why would I stay and endure her wrath for all these years? I feel so stupid."

Carter pulled her into his arms as she hiccupped. "Baby, no." He threaded his fingers in her hair and held her tight. "You did the best you could with what you had to work with. You didn't have money. You didn't know who you were. You had no family. No friends. She manipulated you. You played her games the best way you knew how to survive."

"I'm so weak and stupid," she told his chest, her arms hanging loosely between them. She didn't even want to lift them to hold him back. What an idiot.

His lips were on her ear now. "You're the exact opposite of weak and stupid." He pulled her back a few inches, forcing her to look at him. "You're so strong. You lived. You're getting better every day. You're a survivor. I'm in awe of your strength. I don't know how you do it. It tears my heart to shreds every time I think of what you endured. Most people would be broken."

She stared at him, thinking he'd lost his mind for a minute. "I *am* broken," she managed.

He shook his head. "No. You're scratched. There's no blood." He gave her a small smile. "A little therapy to help you let go of the guilt and you'll be so much more confident."

She searched his eyes, finding nothing but faith in her. Faith she didn't share. "I have no education. I'm a grown woman who's never been to school. I can't even get a job because I don't have a social security card."

"You said you were homeschooled, right?"

"Yes, but what does that mean? So, I took yearly exams. I never graduated. I don't even know what I don't know."

"Well, I'm no expert, but I can tell you're educated. I bet if you looked into it and took a few classes, you could pass your GED easily. Then the world will open up to you."

She smirked. "How? Then I could clean houses for people who take pity on me for the rest of my life?"

"No. Unless that's what you enjoy. I mean, you can choose anything you want to be. Go to college if you want. Get a degree." His eyes shot wider. "Hey, you have a driver's license, right?"

"Yes."

"Did your mom go with you to get it?"

"Of course. She wasn't happy about it, but she finally relented when I was eighteen. She needed me to be able to run errands for her, and work." What was his point?

He smiled wider again. "Then you have a social security card somewhere, *and* a birth certificate. We just need to hunt them down."

"Hmm." Was it possible?

"How are we going to do that?"

He shrugged. "I don't know, but we'll figure it out."

CHAPTER 19

Brooke had never been more nervous than she was the next morning as they drove toward West Palm Beach. She kept fidgeting in her seat, unease making her nearly nauseous.

They had first been to visit Mrs. Thurston at the apartment building where Brooke had lived for as long as she could remember. The kind, older woman had been gracious and helpful without asking too many details, thank God.

The most important thing Brooke and Carter had learned was that Brooke's mother had been pregnant when she moved into the building, and she had given birth at the closest local hospital. Mrs. Thurston said a man had never been in the picture as far as she knew.

Carter had reassured Brooke that knowing where she was born would make it incredibly easy to obtain her birth certificate and then her social security card.

Now they were on their way to see her grandmother, having decided not to give the woman the heads-up.

It was eleven in the morning when Carter parked the car in front of the address and turned to face Brooke. "You okay?"

"Not even close," she responded, forcing a smile. "But I never will be." She was, however, eternally grateful to have Carter on her team. The first man she'd ever had a real relationship with. Other than her appointments with Faith, she didn't even have friends. She'd been so lonely since her mother died that it had worn her down.

She was no longer alone. But was it right to get into such an intense relationship with the first man she met? Probably not. Now wasn't the time to worry about Carter, though.

She took a deep breath. "Let's do this."

Carter rounded the car, took her hand, and led her to the front door. He knocked.

She thought she might hyperventilate.

After a few moments, an older woman opened the door. "Can I help you?" Her voice was hesitant, and she looked like she might slam the door in their faces at the least provocation.

Carter spoke, bless him. "Are you Wanda Wilson?"

"Yes." She frowned.

"Did you have a daughter named Laurie Ann Wilson?"

The woman's eyes widened. Her hand flew to her throat, and she looked like she might faint.

"Ma'am?" Carter continued, wrapping an arm around Brooke's shoulders. "I know this is a shock to you, but I believe this is your granddaughter."

For long moments, the older woman stared at Carter without blinking. And then her gaze shot to Brooke. She swallowed. "My Laurie? You're her daughter?"

Brooke nodded, unable to speak. Emotion nearly choked her.

"Can we come inside, ma'am?" Carter encouraged.

Wanda opened the door farther. "Of course." She stepped back enough for Carter and Brooke to pass and then she shut the front door. "Please, have a seat."

If it weren't for Carter, Brooke was pretty sure she would have fainted. He held her up, physically and emotionally. He led her to the worn older sofa across the room and guided her to sit next to him. Keeping her hand in his, he held it in his lap.

Brooke eyed her grandmother carefully. She looked older than she probably was. Life hadn't been kind to her. Her gray hair was pulled back in a tight bun, and her dress and shoes looked like they were over twenty years old. She lowered onto an armchair across from them. "Is it true?" A tear slid down her cheek, and she grabbed a tissue to dab at her eyes.

"I believe so," Carter continued. "We've done all the research we could, but we have so many holes in the story."

"Where...?" Wanda's voice trailed off. She cleared her throat. "I mean, how...?"

Carter squeezed Brooke's hand and glanced at her before continuing, seeming to read her mind. He knew exactly what she needed. "Unfortunately, Brooke's mother passed away about six months ago."

"Brooke?" Wanda's gaze shot to her. "That's your name? What a lovely name." And then she jerked her attention back to Carter. "Did you say my daughter died?" Her lip trembled, and she wiped her eyes again with the tissue.

Carter nodded. "I'm afraid so. She had a stroke. She went quickly. I'm so sorry." Brooke was grateful to him for easing this woman's pain.

More tears fell. Wanda glanced away. "All these years..." She looked back. "Where do you live, dear?" she asked Brooke.

Brooke finally found her voice. "Miami. I've lived there all my life."

Wanda slowly nodded. "So close..."

Brooke cleared her throat. "Can you tell me why my mother left? Or how?"

Her grandmother pursed her lips, her face so sullen it was difficult not to cry with her, but Brooke had cried a river in the last week. She didn't have anything left at the moment.

"Ma'am? Can I get you anything? Some water maybe?" Carter offered.

The older woman shook her head. "No. I'm fine." She stared at her lap for a long time. "How old are you, Brooke?" she asked.

"Twenty-two."

Another slow nod as Wanda probably did the math and processed the reality.

"I assume my mother was pregnant when she left. Did you know?"

"No." The one word was soft. "We weren't...close."

Carter spoke again. "Would she have been afraid to tell you she was pregnant?"

A wry chuckle shocked Brooke. "That would be an understatement. My husband probably would have killed her."

Carter flinched at Brooke's side.

Brooke was taken aback too, but at this point very little would shock her. "Her father?"

"Yes." Wanda nodded. "He was very strict."

Carter interrupted. "Did he abuse her?"

Wanda stared at Carter for a long time before shifting her gaze to Brooke. "I'm so sorry. I should have done something. I should have gone to the police. I should have left him." Her voice trailed off.

Brooke realized the woman was wracked with the same guilt Brooke felt. She had known about the abuse, and she had done nothing. Brooke knew from Carter's intimations and some of the things he said outright that her mother's history had probably included abuse. It was common for abuse victims to carry on the tradition because it was all they knew.

"I understand your husband passed about ten years ago?" Carter asked.

Wanda nodded. "He was in an accident. Died on impact." Brooke noticed her grandmother did not shed a tear for that loss. She shuddered, but she held her head higher and didn't give him that satisfaction. There was a good chance she too had been abused.

"Is there any chance you might know who my father is?" Brooke asked.

Wanda's brow furrowed and she cocked her head, and then her face cleared and she sat up straighter, slowly nodding. "I know exactly who your father is. You look just like him."

Brooke leaned into Carter, relief and excitement and fear consuming her. She grabbed his arm and held on tight as if he could keep her from slipping into another dimension. "Do you think he knows about me?"

"I don't know. Maybe. Maybe not. He never said anything to me, though. Your mother was secretly dating him before she disappeared. He came over every day for weeks wanting to know if she'd called or if the police had any leads. He was distraught, but he never mentioned a pregnancy."

"Would you mind giving us his name and any information you have?" Carter prompted.

"Of course. I remember him well. His name is David Rollings. He still lives in the area. I saw him just a few weeks ago at the grocery store. His parents still live in the same house two blocks over."

Brooke's heart raced with anticipation. She had never imagined a day when she would meet a blood relative, and now she found out she had several. She was still scared out of her mind, but she felt stronger too. "Do you know if he has a family?" She would need to be careful approaching a man who knew nothing about her and possibly upsetting his wife and kids.

Wanda smiled. "He's married, and he has two boys. I think they must be about eight and ten years old." She was crying again, needing to reach for another tissue to wipe her eyes. "I can't believe you're here. And my Laurie…" She dipped her face again. "I never got to say goodbye."

Brooke glanced around the room, trying to picture her mother as a little girl growing up in this house. She had no idea what level of abuse she might have experienced, but she'd had a yard and school and friends and even a boyfriend—all things she had later denied her own daughter.

Carter wrapped his arm around Brooke's shoulders and tipped her chin back. He must have read her mind because his words answered her unspoken questions. "It's no excuse, but she thought she was doing the right thing at the time. Protecting you. Keeping you safe."

Brooke bit her bottom lip to keep the tears at bay and blinked up at the man she owed her life to.

Carter glanced at Wanda and asked another question. "Was your daughter by any chance depressed, or did she suffer from anxiety?"

Wanda nodded, her face so filled with sorrow it hurt to watch her suffering. "We never had her diagnosed, but I always knew she had issues. She would often go from really happy to really angry in an instant. It was hard to judge her, though, since her father was so...unreasonable. The slightest provocation would set him off. It was like he was two different people. Laurie was the same way, but I didn't know if her depression was caused by him or if she was born with the same tendency."

Brooke flattened her hand on Carter's chest and gasped. It all made so much more sense now. Her head started spinning, and she didn't realize she was holding her breath until Carter's fingers squeezed her neck and he leaned her head toward her lap. "Breathe, baby." He pressed her farther. "Brooke." His voice was firm. "Breathe."

She sucked in a rough inhale and blew it out.

He held her steady. "That's it. Again."

Another deep breath. When Brooke was finally able to lift her head, she found Wanda handing Carter a glass of water. And then the woman took a seat on the other side of Brooke. She looked so...tired. Worn down. Defeated. Brooke felt sorry for her.

Wanda spoke softly. "I didn't do right by your mother. I take the blame for that. I have to live with it for the rest of my life. I can never apologize enough for my negligence. I hope you can find it in your heart to visit me from time to time. I can't expect you to forgive me, but I'd love to know how your life is going. It would give me a peace I don't deserve."

Carter set the glass of water on the coffee table. "Ma'am, I don't think Brooke is ready to make any decisions right now. She's still processing her life. The woman who raised her didn't even use her real name. It's confusing. But I do know she was excited to find out she had relatives, and if you give her a chance, I think you'll find Brooke to be a kind, loving woman with a big heart."

Brooke blinked back tears that could no longer be stopped. One slid down her cheek and then another. Maybe Carter had overstepped his bounds, but he was not wrong. She already felt something unique and dear toward her grandmother. They had both endured a similar existence.

Brooke reached out a hand and squeezed Wanda's. "Carter's right. I'm still figuring things out and learning who I am. It's overwhelming, but I want to be a part of your life if you'll have me."

Wanda lurched forward and wrapped her arms around Brooke. Already the woman was nothing like her daughter. Even on her mother's best days, she rarely expressed affection so openly. Of course, there was a good chance Wanda hadn't either while Laurie was growing up or even until after her husband died.

"Do you have pictures I could look at?" Brooke asked.

Wanda's face lit up. "I do." She jumped to her feet and rushed across the room to pull some albums down from the shelves. She seemed younger than she had an hour ago. Before she returned, she paused, her gaze going to a framed picture on the shelf.

Brooke couldn't make out who was in the picture from across the room, but she held her breath again as Wanda returned.

Her grandmother's hand was shaking as she handed Brooke the photo.

Brooke took it, noticing the woman in the picture was her mother. She looked so happy. She was wearing a formal gown and her hair was piled high on her head, hanging in long ringlets. Brooke had never seen her look that happy.

She shifted her gaze to the other person. It must have been a school dance or something. Her date had on a suit and a bow tie that matched her mother's pink dress. He held her hand tight in the picture, looking as carefree and happy as Brooke's mother. "Her father didn't want her to go to that dance, even though Laurie insisted this boy was only a friend. I talked him into it."

Suddenly, she gasped. "This is my father..."

No one spoke.

Oh my God. He looked so much like Brooke. There was no mistaking her identity. They had the exact same hair and eyes and nose. Even their jawline was similar. Brooke clasped the photo to her chest and closed her eyes.

For the first time in her life, she had history. Family. So many people after a lifetime of solitude.

CHAPTER 20

Carter was uncertain about the wisdom of going straight from Wanda's house to Martha and Gentry Rollings's home two blocks away, but Brooke was high on life and wanted to rip off the Band-Aid without hesitation.

To a certain extent, he agreed with her. If it were him, there was no way he could drive away and come back another day, but he was also worried about Brooke's state of mind. She was fragile and stressed.

Again, they had not called ahead, but this couple would be far more blindsided than Wanda Wilson. After seeing pictures of David Rollings, Carter agreed there was little doubt Brooke was his daughter. The resemblance was uncanny. She looked like she belonged to these people.

When a man opened the front door, any lasting doubt fled. He had to be Gentry Rollings, and he was just as taken aback as expected at the appearance of a woman at his door who had to make him do a double take. "Hello? Do I know you?"

Brooke was stronger this time. "Not yet. My name is Brooke Madden. I'm Laurie Wilson's daughter. Unless I'm mistaken, I'm pretty sure I'm your granddaughter."

For a moment, the older man stood there staring at Brooke as if she'd sprouted two heads. And then he opened the door wider and stepped back. "Come inside." He turned his head toward the house and called out, "Martha, honey, can you come to the front room?"

Carter was stunned by this man who looked so much like his son and his granddaughter. They had strong features.

They were all standing just inside the house when a woman appeared, wiping her hands on a dishtowel. She was smiling broadly when she rounded the corner, and then she came to an abrupt stop, her mouth falling open, her eyes widening.

She glanced back and forth between her husband and Brooke, stunned. One hand flew to her chest. "My God." She glanced at her husband again. "You look exactly like my son."

Gentry curved his arm around his wife's shoulders. "This is Brooke Madden. She thinks she might be David's daughter."

Martha's face paled. "My God," she repeated.

Gentry pointed to the living room. "Please, come in. Sit."

Carter reached out a hand. "I'm Carter Ellis." He didn't elaborate. His demeanor with Brooke would speak for itself. She was his. He didn't need to explain that fact.

"Who…?" Martha's voice broke off after the one word.

"My mother was Laurie Wilson," Brooke explained as Carter led her to the sofa and eased her onto it.

Carter realized she was much more relaxed with these people. They'd done nothing wrong. They'd had no culpability in her crazy life.

As soon as they sat, a beautiful tabby cat jumped up onto Brooke's lap and batted at her hand.

"Jasper, get down," Martha commanded.

Brooke reached under the cat's chin and scratched, a smile forming. "He's fine. You're a cutie, aren't you?" she directed toward the cat.

Carter was certain Brooke had never had a pet, and watching her with the orange-striped cat tugged at his heart strings.

"Laurie Wilson…" Gentry began, "She was Joseph and Wanda's daughter. She disappeared when she was seventeen."

Brooke nodded, seeming to wait for it to all sink in.

Martha looked ready to cry. "She was dating David."

Silence took over for several long seconds while everyone processed.

Then Martha spoke again. "Does David know?"

Carter answered. "We aren't sure. We don't think so. We didn't know who Brooke's father was until we went to her grandmother's house this morning. If he knew Laurie was pregnant when she left is anyone's guess."

"I don't think he would keep something like that from us." Martha shook her head. "I mean, he was very distraught when Laurie went missing, but he didn't say anything about her being pregnant. I think he would have had a harder time recovering if he'd known. He would have looked for her harder. He was just a boy at the time, but he wouldn't have let her take off with his child, nor would he have left her to raise a daughter on her own."

Brooke cleared her throat. "Do you think it would upset him to find out about me?"

Gentry nodded. "Of course, but not in a bad way. I think he'll be very sad to know he never met you and hadn't been given the chance."

"How did you come to find us?" Martha asked.

Carter explained the saga as they'd managed to piece it together so far, even adding the abuse that led Laurie to leave with her unborn child. By now it was apparent she had been worried her father would make her life a living hell if she told him, and she probably hadn't wanted Brooke to know the wrath of her grandfather. Ironic since she was destined to repeat history.

When Brooke's second set of grandparents were up to speed, they decided to call their son.

"He's at work," Gentry explained, "but I think he'd want to leave early this afternoon. And it might be easier if he met you alone before he tells his family."

Carter agreed. The plan was reasonable.

Ten minutes later, a younger version of Gentry walked through the front door, his brow furrowed with concern. "Dad? You guys okay? What's the emergency?" His gaze traveled from his father to Carter and Brooke. And then he froze in his spot.

The clock ticked while his face turned white, and then he staggered closer and lowered to his knees on the other side of the coffee table. He planted his hands on the surface, his gaze locked on Brooke. When his lips finally parted, he still didn't speak.

Carter felt sorry for the man, emotions taking over his own system after so many introductions. And they were not even done. He needed to stay strong. For Brooke.

"I always wondered," he whispered.

Brooke smiled sweetly, grasping Carter's fingers tight. Another tear to go with the thousands. She wiped it away. He could feel her pulse pick up as she met her father. It was a precious moment.

Finally, one corner of David's mouth tipped up. "Guess we don't need a paternity test," he joked.

Everyone else gave a nervous chuckle.

Brooke held his gaze while Carter watched her closely. She seemed to be in control. "You didn't know," she confirmed. That question had undoubtedly weighed on her.

David shook his head. "No. But I knew her father was an asshole, and I knew she wanted to get away, and I knew..." he hesitated. "I knew we had unprotected sex."

Another round of explanations followed, this time with everyone talking on top of each other. Eventually, Martha lured them all into the kitchen where she pulled a casserole from the oven as if she made one every day in case company showed up. She even served a fresh pie she'd baked that morning.

Carter's heart was full, watching Brooke come alive. The stress she'd endured meeting her maternal grandmother was not present here. Grief and sorrow for their lost years, yes, but not the remorse and guilt.

David made a few phone calls to his wife and eventually decided he needed to tell her in person and alone. It wouldn't be fair to anyone for Kelly or their sons to be blindsided.

They exchanged phone numbers, and David insisted he would work things out and introduce everyone that weekend. He was eager to have his sons meet their sister.

Brooke was nervous as hell to find out she had two half brothers. The evidence of her stress was taken out on Carter's hand. He doubted she had any idea how much of the day she'd spent clinging to him, but he wouldn't trade it for the world.

It was late when they got back to Carter's house. Brooke had slept most of the trip, her seat lowered, her hand still clutching Carter's. When they got home, he rounded the car, lifted her into his arms, and carried her inside.

She was so worn out, she didn't even comment or argue when he took her to his bedroom, stripped off her clothes, pulled one of his T-shirts over her head, and tucked her into his bed.

Five minutes later, he had the lights all out, the house locked up, and was sliding into bed behind her. He gathered her back to his front and relished the soft sigh as she relaxed into him.

Before today, he had claimed this woman as his own. Now... Now he felt so much love for her that he was bursting. He wanted to tell her how he felt, but he knew it would scare her to death and possibly push her away. So, he kept his mouth closed, kissed her neck, and fell asleep.

Brooke awoke slowly to the feel of a hand on her thigh. She smiled as she registered where she was and who was touching her.

She had come so far in such a short time that she didn't even flinch at being brought to consciousness by a man. In his bed. In his arms.

When his fingers hit her sex, she moaned.

He whispered in her ear, "I was wondering when you might wake up."

"It's hard to sleep with you fondling me."

She felt his grin against her neck. "You've slept enough. Time to play."

She sucked in a breath at his words. They were both gentle and firm at the same time. He meant to dominate her. And her heart pounded at the idea.

His hard shaft pressed against her butt from behind, and he ground it closer as she arched back. "Baby..."

"Please don't tease me anymore. I'm not fragile. Make love to me."

He nibbled across her shoulder until he reached her ear again. His teeth bit into the soft flesh. "How about you let me make the decisions this morning, and you keep that sweet mouth closed unless I ask you a direct question."

She flushed, her sex tingling at his words. Every time he dominated her like this, she came more fully alive. She wanted him inside her more than she'd ever craved anything in her life. She could feel the edge of stress that always took over her body when it needed an outlet.

After everything that happened yesterday, she wasn't surprised, but she needed release, and she craved it in a way that would soothe her soul. Did he know what she needed?

"You're mine, baby."

She groaned, sinking deeper against him, her nipples abrading against his T-shirt.

"Say it."

She licked her lips.

"Say it, Brooke. You're mine."

"I'm yours," she whimpered. She was so totally his. Did he not know it?

"Good girl. Now lips closed."

She pursed them as though that had been the demand.

Carter eased her onto her back, taking her lips in a heated deep kiss that curled her toes. He tipped his head to one side and devoured her as if he were starving and she was his breakfast.

She met him stroke for stroke, her tongue learning the inside of his mouth as she grabbed his biceps and dug her fingers into his muscled arms.

He nudged her knees open and pressed his thigh between hers.

She moaned into his mouth as his leg rubbed against her naked sex. "So wet for me," he murmured against her mouth. "I love the sounds you make." He lifted his face a few inches, breaking the kiss. "I'm going to claim you completely, Brooke. Now. And I won't let you go afterward. I won't be able to."

She stared at him, unsure about a response. On the one hand, she understood him completely. On the other hand, her life was upside-down and she had no idea where it was leading her. It wouldn't be fair to expect him to follow her or wait around while she made life changes and found herself.

One thing she knew for certain, she wanted Carter to be the one to take her virginity. She wanted him to dominate her completely and take her someplace no one would ever be able to emulate. She had no idea what the rest of her life might look like, but this morning was going to involve sex and lots of it.

She wasn't lying. She was his in every sense of the word. But would he be able to take the journey she was on with her? Probably not. She ignored the melancholic thought and concentrated on the way he slid his hand under the hem of her shirt and drew it up her body.

In seconds she was naked under him. He rose up next to her and held her gaze while he stripped off his sleep pants.

Her eyes shot to his groin the moment his penis popped free, bobbing long and stiff in front of him.

He took her hand and brought it to the shaft. "Wrap your fingers around me, baby." His voice was low, earnest, demanding. So many things at once.

She circled his girth eagerly, wanting to know the feel of him. Smoother than expected. Hard and velvety. She watched as she slid her hand up and down. The tip was wider and the slit at the top had white, creamy semen leaking out.

She licked her lips, and he groaned. "One day soon I'll want your lips around my cock, but not today. I'd come too fast inside that sweet mouth of yours." He fell forward, planting his hands at both sides of her head.

She continued to hold his shaft, loving the feel of him in her hand. Powerful. Strong. Urgent.

He wrenched her hand off him seconds later. "That's enough."

She blinked up at him, hoping she hadn't done something wrong.

But he was smiling down at her. "Baby, your hand feels like heaven around my dick, but I don't want to come in your fist." He leaned down and kissed her lips. "I want to come inside your tight pussy."

She squirmed under him, wishing he would lower his body over hers. She even grabbed his hips and tugged, but he didn't budge.

"Don't try to control this," he told her lips. "You'll regret it."

His words made her sex grip, wetness leaking out. How would he punish her for urging him to claim her? She gave another tug to his hips.

He bolted to his knees, grabbed her wrists, and lifted her hands over her head. Grasping both wrists in one hand, he took her jaw in the other. "Remember how I warned you I would punish you if you were deliberately disobedient?"

She tried to remember, digging in her brain.

He lifted a brow, waiting for a response.

"I forgot." All she knew was that she wanted to tempt him to take her. Now. Not later. Now. He seemed to be on a lazy river while she was soaring overhead on the fastest waterslide in the park.

He narrowed his gaze. "It would be best if you recalled on your own, Brooke. If I have to remind you, you'll spend the better part of the morning wishing you had obeyed me."

Her nipples pebbled when he glanced down at them, tightening to the point that she wanted him to suckle them.

"Brooke," he demanded.

She jerked her gaze back to his. "You said you wouldn't give me what I wanted if I was bratty or whiney," she stammered, trying to recall his words before they bit her in the butt.

"What else did I say? How did I tell you I would punish you if you tried to manipulate me into dominating you?"

She closed her eyes, licking her lips as she searched her brain. *Damn.* A rare cuss word filled her head. "You'd ignore me. Put me in a time out."

"You want to spend this morning with my cock in your pussy or standing naked in the corner staring at the paint job?"

She swallowed. "You inside me, please."

"You gonna try to control it?"

"No." No way would she jeopardize this opportunity. His threats made her squirm even more. Would he really stick her in a corner like a child? A shiver raced down her spine.

"Good girl." He kissed her again and then his face lowered to her chest where he sucked one nipple in hard and fast, his teeth pinching the tip enough to make her gasp.

She squirmed against him as he devoured her breast. Any concern she'd had earlier in the week about her body image flew out the window. Carter genuinely liked her. He thought she was sexy. He wanted her.

He's already claimed you.

She tipped her head back and closed her eyes as she succumbed to his touch. His lips were everywhere and nowhere, teasing, tempting. She wanted more. She wanted everything.

She wiggled against the mattress, wishing he would turn her over and spank her before he entered her, but he didn't show signs of intending to give her that play. Part of her was disappointed because she had never been through more stress than yesterday. It was boiling inside her like an overstuffed pressure cooker. It would explode, and there was no telling what the fallout would be.

Now that she'd had a taste of BDSM, she wanted more. She wanted to be able to come home at the end of a long day and know the man waiting on her would take her over his knee or restrain her to his bed, or secure her hands to a cross or a bench or anything in the world. As long as he eased her stress by flogging her or spanking her or even whipping her. She needed to feel the pain to get the relief she craved.

Didn't she? Several times now Carter had given her relief another way—his way. Through sex. Orgasms that scrambled her brain. Was it enough? Part of her still thought she needed to feel the pain. It pushed her deeper, farther, harder. She wasn't sure she could give up the darker aspects of masochism and rely on only the sexual side of the lifestyle.

Carter's hand slid between her legs and stroked through her folds, gathering her wetness and then circling her nub. His fingers chased away her concerns. They always did.

"Your clit is so responsive, baby."

She shuddered at his words. Clit. Pussy. Cock. So foreign. When would they sound less shocking to her?

Her nipples abraded against his chest, their sensitivity almost more than she could bear. Every movement against them sent a wave of tingling across her chest. She arched toward him, but her focus shifted a moment later when he nudged her legs apart and settled a knee between her thighs.

One finger rapidly flicked over her clit, taking her breath away. In seconds she was right there. So close. Two days ago she hadn't known such sensation existed. Now she craved it like a drug addict. The build. The release. The pleasure.

When he thrust his finger into her tight channel, she gasped. "Carter…"

"I love the way you say my name. Desperation in your voice. Sexy as hell."

She would have flushed if all her inhibitions hadn't flown out the window. Instead, she lifted her hips into his touch.

He pulled his finger out and pressed his thigh against her sex. Hard. The pressure was intense, making her *need*. She craved his finger again. She craved his…cock. "Please…Carter…" She wasn't above begging.

He pressed her wrists into the mattress and stared down at her. "I'm going to claim you now. You're so tight." He kissed her lips gently and then nibbled a path to her ear again where he resumed speaking in a whisper. "It will hurt when I thrust into you. I'll hold steady for a while so you can adjust to me. Catch your breath. And then I promise you heaven."

She nodded against his cheek. She wanted this. She was scared, but not as much as she was eager.

"You're sure?" he asked her ear, sending a shudder down her body.

"Yes. Carter, please."

He rose above her again, releasing her hand and reaching across her body to pull the drawer of the nightstand open. She couldn't imagine what he was doing until he rose on his knees and used his teeth to tear open a small square wrapper. A condom. *Right. Duh.*

He added his other leg to the space between hers and nudged her wider as he rolled the rubber down his length, holding her gaze the entire time. And then he was over her again, both hands threading with hers and pressing them into the mattress. He lined his cock up with her entrance and teased her by rocking through the wetness.

She drew her knees up higher, willing him to enter her.

And then he thrust inside, all the way to the hilt.

Her breath left her lungs. Tears stung the corners of her eyes. Her heart beat out of her chest. The stretch was tighter than expected. It hurt.

"Look at me, Brooke."

She couldn't focus as she wildly tried to make eye contact.

"Take a breath for me, baby." He seemed so in control. She was being torn in two from the inside out, and he wanted her to breathe?

She didn't move.

"Brooke," his voice was commanding. "Eyes on me."

She met his gaze, still unsure she would survive this and wondering why anyone would do it more than once.

"Breathe," he demanded.

She sucked in a lungful and let it out.

"That's my girl. Again."

She obeyed him a second time, deciding she might live.

The pressure. So tight. Filling. Maybe not so bad. Maybe even good.

He watched her closely as he slowly eased almost out and then pressed back in. It hurt less that time. He did it again. Something changed. The pain shifted into something almost satisfying.

"That's it. Keep breathing."

She blinked, realizing she was holding her breath again.

The next thrust was deeper—if that was possible. The base of his cock slammed into her clit. She moaned. *Oh God, that felt good.*

Again.

Better. So good.

His fingers held her tighter, clasped around hers as if the two of them might get torn apart if he didn't hold on. His jaw was tight. His eyes glassed over.

She lifted her hips the next time he entered her, moaning.

"Oh, baby. If you don't stop making that noise, I'm going to come too soon." He gritted his teeth, his words disjointed and muffled. Almost before he finished speaking, he picked up the pace, thrusting faster.

Her eyes rolled back as the entire seismic event shifted from painful to bearable to *oh my God, that feels good*. She stopped breathing again for an entirely different reason, concentrating on every nerve ending as her body came alive in a way she never imagined possible.

Every thrust pushed her closer to the edge. Every time the base of his cock hit her clit, she thought she might combust. She wasn't sure if she wanted to reach that peak or stay on the edge of sanity. The edge was very, very nice.

In the end, she didn't have a choice. Carter slammed in deep, set his lips on her ear, and demanded, "Come, baby. Now."

She shattered, her body nearly convulsing with the tremors. She was only vaguely aware of him groaning out his own orgasm on the heels of hers. For long moments, she did nothing but luxuriate in the feeling of being so full and so sated, and then she blinked her eyes open to find him smiling down at her.

Sudden embarrassment crept up her skin. Had she screamed? Yeah, she was pretty sure she had.

He nuzzled her nose with his and then kissed her gently. "Beautiful."

She nodded. He was not wrong.

When he slid out, she winced. "Don't move. I'll be right back."

Move? How could she move? She didn't even close her legs. She was limp and heavy and unable to do more than glance around and catch her breath while he headed toward the bathroom and returned a few minutes later with a wet washcloth.

Her skin flushed as he nudged her legs wider and wiped away the evidence of her virginity. She didn't even look.

And then he was back on the bed, gathering her in his arms

and pulling the covers over her shivering body. He kissed her shoulder, nestling her back to his front on their sides. "You okay?"

"Better than."

"Good. Thank you for giving me that. It was the best gift I've ever received."

She closed her eyes, unable to speak.

For a while, he stroked her skin everywhere—arm, thigh, belly, breasts, neck… And then he wrapped his arm around her and held her even tighter as though she might escape if he gave her the chance.

She didn't want to escape, though. She wanted to do it again. No way would she ask for something like that. She wasn't bold enough. But she thought it. Would it be as good the second time?

"I need to feed you," he whispered.

"Not yet." She snuggled infinitesimally closer.

He chuckled, the movement vibrating against her neck.

"I'll cook. Give me a minute." Maybe if she presented it that way, he wouldn't be so eager to leave her.

"Mmm." The tone of his *mmm* had her stiffening. It suggested he was about to say something important. "You had a rough day yesterday. How about you submit to me today. Let me handle things. I'll tell you when your services are needed." He brushed her hair away from her face as he rolled her onto her back to meet her gaze.

She licked her lips. *All day?*

"It calms you when you let me dominate you. Don't fight it. Let me control things. You'll relax if the decisions are not yours to make."

Two things happened. One, her recently sated body jumped to attention, wanting more. Two, she admitted to herself he was right. Every time she let him dominate her, she found peace. Every time she took control of her life, nervous tension clawed at her.

She had no idea if letting him dominate her so thoroughly for an entire day was the right thing to do. Didn't it imply serious weakness on her part?

She needed to learn to stand on her own. She'd spent twenty-two years under her mother's thumb and then six months floundering like a lost kitten. She was stronger now. No, she didn't have the skills to make it on her own, but she had the will to get them finally.

Carter was responsible for nearly every milestone of her emergence. She owed him her life. Without him, she had no idea when she would have found her family or had the knowledge to get her birth certificate or social security card. Without him, she would be sleeping in her car, homeless, looking for work without success. Without him, she wouldn't be anyone or anything.

He was frowning at her, and she realized she hadn't hidden her emotions. "What's running through that mind of yours? I'm not asking you to go skydiving without a parachute. I'm asking you to submit to me so that your mind can take a day of rest."

She nodded. It would be ridiculous to fight him on this. Even if it was the wrong thing to do, she needed today anyway. She needed to pull herself together and make some decisions. It would be so much easier to take a moment to breathe if she submitted to him. He'd proven that several times.

"Good girl. Clear your mind of everything I see in your eyes. You have one job today, obey me."

She nodded again, the butterflies in her belly fluttering so hard she had to fight not to squirm. She didn't want him to realize how aroused she was again.

Of course, there was another way he could clear her head and soothe her soul. It would be much faster and last longer. Should she dare suggest it?

She opened her mouth to speak, but he stopped her with a finger to her lips. "How about instead of coming up with excuses and trying to control me, you give up the fight and do as your told?"

Another quiver. Her sex felt warm and funny. "Okay." This was good too. This feeling he instilled in her with his words.

"Good. Let's shower, and then I'm going to feed you."

Let's? Did he intend to shower with her?

He gathered her in his arms and carried her to the bathroom. After setting her on her feet, he turned on the shower and closed the door.

She stood in the bathroom feeling awkward. She'd never showered with someone, of course. Like everything else. He knew that.

While the water heated to fill the room with steam, he gathered towels and set them on the white countertop. His bathroom was huge. She grew chilly standing on the gray tile. Finally, he opened the glass door and took her hand, leading her into the spray of warm water.

She sighed at the contact and then closed her eyes as he angled the water over her hair. When she started to lift her hands, he gently rebuked her attempts to help. "Stand still. Let me take care of you."

She was glad she wasn't required to speak because her throat was thick with emotion. No one in her life had ever said "Let me take care of you." No one had cared enough to see to any of her needs. Especially the emotional ones.

She relaxed into his touch as he worked shampoo into her hair, loving the feel of his hands on her scalp and the way he gently ran his fingers through the length over and over. After rinsing and applying conditioner, he washed the rest of her body.

It should have embarrassed her to stand in Carter's shower and let him run his hands all over her naked body, but she couldn't find the will to do anything except enjoy his touch.

When she thought he was finished, she found him flattened to her back, his hands on her breasts, molding them in the slippery soap. "Love your tits," he whispered.

Her head rolled back against his chest.

"Flawless skin. Pink nipples that jump to attention when I touch them. Sexy." He punctuated his words with a pinch to the swollen tips, making it difficult to stand still.

Letting her rinse her hair alone, he quickly washed his own body and then shut off the water and led her to the fluffy white rug on the tile. He patted her body dry and wrapped her in a huge white towel next. And then he led her from the bathroom.

Her belly dipped to a new level when he settled her on the bed and sat behind her to run a comb through her hair.

She held back tears, glad he couldn't see her face. So much kindness. Would life with him always be like this if she agreed to stay and let him dominate her?

Other than insisting she was his, he hadn't specifically mentioned a future with her. She didn't want to bring it up and ruin her bliss because she feared an argument would ensue when she told him she needed time and space.

She couldn't lean on him for everything. It wasn't right. Moving directly from her apartment into his house was a bad idea. She didn't know who she was. She only knew who she wasn't. It would take time to find herself. If he wouldn't give her that time, then things with him would have to come to an end.

He finished and set the comb aside, hauling her body backward against him. His lips were on her neck again. "Stop thinking so hard. Let your brain relax."

How did he know?

CHAPTER 21

Carter eyed her carefully all day. She submitted to him easily, letting him make choices for her so she wouldn't have to. She even kneeled in front of him for a while without complaint. He'd learned it calmed her. Every time he noticed her getting flustered or stressed, he knew he could point between his legs and her entire body would relax.

He also knew she wanted more, and he had no idea how to handle that problem. He was skilled enough to handle a masochist, so he wasn't worried about injuring her physically. But he was seriously concerned about the emotional ramifications of harming her mentally.

She'd been abused. Her entire life. He didn't want to contribute to that. It worried him. He knew her well enough to recognize the times she opened her mouth to say something and held her tongue, struggling not to ask him to spank her, or more. He really needed to call Lincoln and get his advice. Lincoln was a sadist. He understood that aspect of BDSM much better than Carter.

So, when Brooke fell asleep on the couch in the afternoon, Carter stepped out back with his cell phone to call his best friend.

After a few seconds, Lincoln answered. "What's up?" he asked as a greeting.

"Hey, you busy?"

"Nope. You okay?"

"Yeah." Carter sighed, running a hand through his hair as he stared across his backyard without seeing anything. "Need your advice."

"Okay."

"It's Brooke. I keep hoping she'll let go of her obsession with masochism, but she won't let it go."

Lincoln chuckled. "You knew she was a masochist the first day you laid eyes on her."

"Yeah, but I didn't know anything about her then. I was hoping she could get what she needed from a tamer more sexual form of BDSM."

"And she's pushing you," Lincoln stated.

"Yes. I know she gets release doing things my way, but it's never enough. I'm not sure I can be what she needs." He choked out those words, hating the admission. It would kill him to let her go.

"We all suspected she had been abused. Were we correct?"

"Yes. But not by a man, by her mother."

"Wow. Okay, then it's probably a habit. She's used to being struck by something."

"It's more than that. I think she seriously believes she's done things she needs to be punished for. She isn't just role-playing. She wants the atonement she gets from a skewed view of reality." A shudder raced down his spine.

"Makes sense. It's not that uncommon, Carter. She's not alone."

"I know, but it scares me. I never want to harm her."

"She's important to you."

"Yes."

"Then you need to step up to the plate and be what she needs.

You can do it. It's not like you aren't trained. You surely aren't afraid of injuring her physically."

"No. It's not that." He lowered onto a chair on his deck and leaned his elbows against his knees. "I know I'm trained, but I never visualized myself in this position. I'm not a sadist. You're the sadist."

Lincoln laughed. "And look what happened to me? I ended up with a woman who isn't a masochist. The universe sometimes guides us in unexpected directions. All we can do is go with the flow."

"Does it bother you?"

"What? That Sasha isn't into masochism? Not at all. I worried about it at first, but then I got over it. I love her. She's it for me. I wouldn't care if she wanted me to sell the club and leave the lifestyle. I'd do anything for her."

Carter chewed on his lower lip, pondering Lincoln's words. He made sense. Carter would do anything for Brooke. She was totally under his skin as if he'd known her for years. She was his. What was holding him back? "I'm afraid of harming her, emotionally more than anything."

"So take it slow. I'm not suggesting you grab a cat o' nine tails and beat her bloody. Start small. See how she reacts. Work your way up. Negotiate. Keep the lines of communication open."

Carter cringed at the visual.

"Have you struck her at all? Spanked her?"

"Yes."

"And how did she react?"

"I combined it with sex. She thrived."

"Then there's your answer. You like your submissives to get off sexually from the experience. Make sure she does. Every time. Keep her on the edge. Do everything you can to steer her in a sexual direction. Combine the two. I assume whatever her past looks like, her abuse didn't include sex if it only came from her mother?"

"No. Never." Thank God.

"Work your way from spanking to something harder until you finally reach a tool you can both agree on, something that gives her the release she needs without compromising your preferences. Guide her so that every experience gets her off until she connects the pain with sex instead of some misconceived need to redeem herself."

Carter took a deep breath, lifting his head. "What if it's not enough? What if she wants me to draw blood? I could never do that."

"Then you'll know you weren't meant to be together. But I don't think it will come to that. I spend my days with a woman I would never practice sadism with, and I don't miss it. You'll add a little sadism to your life, and I'll bet anything it will stop making you nervous, especially if you combine every scene with sex. If she gets aroused when you land a flogger on her, win-win."

"Maybe." He hoped Lincoln was right.

"If she's as into you as you are her, she'll be willing to compromise also. She'll let go of the need to be beaten harmfully once she gets a taste of what it's like to submit to your way. If not, then it wasn't meant to be."

"Yeah." That might possibly be the worst part. Subconsciously Carter was dragging his feet out of fear that no matter what he did, it would never be enough for Brooke. Lincoln was right. Carter could flog her. He could easily use a lot of different equipment on her without compromising his personal tastes.

The scariest part of all was inching closer and closer to what would inevitably be a hard line for him only to find out it still wasn't enough for her.

The only way to find out would be to take a leap and hope for the best.

"Thanks, man. Appreciate the advice."

"Anytime."

Later that evening, she was once again on the floor at his feet, hands behind her back, head in his lap. He had been stroking her hair for a while, loving the feel of her locks running between his fingers at least as much as she obviously enjoyed feeling his touch.

His heart swelled. She was so perfect for him. He desperately wanted her to see it, but he was afraid to say too much and scare her. It was one thing to claim her during sex, but in a calm moment, it was so much more powerful.

His fingers kept tracing the line of her neck. A few times he even halfway circled it from behind. She sighed at the touch.

Suddenly, he knew he not only wanted to own her, but he would do whatever it took to get there. She had so many things to figure out, but he wanted to be with her through all of it. He wanted her in his life forever. He still wanted her to grow and find herself and be the best she could be, but he wanted her to do all that as his.

Ever since his talk with Lincoln, he'd felt more confident. Determined. He could make this work. He would need to take a few personal risks, but he could do it.

While he continued to stroke the line of her neck, a sudden realization struck him. He wanted her to wear his collar.

The idea had never entered his mind before. Not with any other woman. No one he had dated or dominated had elicited this feeling. This sense of ownership. This desire to claim her.

He knew others who had collared their submissive, but he'd never pondered the idea for himself. Until now.

Until Brooke.

What would she say?

He wouldn't dare broach the subject today. Hell, he hadn't even pointed out in their most lucid moments how much he cared about her. He was falling in love with her.

So, when she lifted her head and licked her lips, meeting his gaze with complete seriousness, he couldn't deny her anything. "Please flog me." Her lip trembled. She was worried he would turn her down, and she'd obviously worked very hard to ask.

He had no idea if it was the right thing to do, but he couldn't disappoint her either. He needed to trust himself. Take Lincoln's advice and work with her. He cupped her face and held her gaze. "You're sure?"

"Yes. I need the release. I know you keep hoping submitting to you is enough, and I don't want you to think I don't like it. I do. I love it. It takes the edge off and helps me relax, but sometimes I need more. And I need to know I can ask for it and not be denied. If you can't, I don't think this will work out."

She was so brave. So strong. So gorgeous.

He nodded. "All right, baby. But I want us to meet with some other people soon and discuss this to make sure it's not doing you more harm than good." If she continued to push for more, he would want Lincoln to step in and provide advice. Not just on the phone but in person.

"Okay." She narrowed her gaze. "It's Saturday night. Shouldn't you be at the club? You didn't go last night either."

He smiled. "Took the weekend off. They'll survive without me. This was more important."

She nodded. "Then you'll do it?"

"Yes. But you'll use your safeword if you need it too, right?"

"Yes. Red. Yellow if I need you to slow down."

He cupped her chin. "Go to the bedroom, remove everything, hands and knees on the bed."

She eagerly stood and padded from the room while he leaned back, stared at the ceiling, and prayed he was doing the right thing. Again.

Gathering up all his strength, he followed her. As he entered the bedroom, he tugged his shirt over his head and dropped it on the floor.

She was already on the bed in the position he'd requested

when he passed by her to grab his bag of toys from the closet. He'd used a flogger on lots of women. It could be soothing like a massage, but that wasn't what Brooke had in mind. She needed him to strike harder.

After taking the time to mold her sweet bottom with his hand, he dragged the tips of the black leather across her skin.

She giggled when he skimmed her waist, squirming to one side. "Tickles."

He smiled and did it again, loving the sound of her laughter.

"I'm gonna start slow and easy and build from there. You will use your safewords if it gets too intense. I won't fault you for needing to slow down. Use yellow freely. We'll regroup and then continue."

"Okay." She lowered her head, her hair falling in long curly locks around her face. He didn't want to pull it back this time, sensing she needed the escape. The partial solitude.

"Lower to your elbows. Forehead on the pillow. Bottom high in the air."

She did as he instructed.

"Part your knees."

She inched them out, her movements so much faster than even a day ago. She was such an amazing submissive. He didn't doubt that for a moment. But a masochist?

He shook doubts from his head, set his hand on her lower back, and lifted the flogger to land it across her butt cheeks. She rocked forward only an inch. He knew he hadn't struck her hard enough to elicit anything but the knowledge about the feel of his flogger.

No two people struck in exactly the same way, and no two floggers had the same impact. Whatever scenes she'd done with Faith wouldn't be the same.

She held herself stiffly until after he'd struck her about a dozen times, and then her shoulders relaxed and she sighed into the pillow.

After climbing between her legs, he held her hip with one hand and continued to rhythmically swat her bottom, back and forth, up and down, hitting her thighs and occasionally her shoulder blades.

Her skin heated, turning a gorgeous shade of pink that made his cock hard and surprised him. He didn't ordinarily get aroused from this sort of domination. He also didn't ordinarily have an emotional connection to his submissive when he did a scene.

Brooke brought something new out of him. Almost scary.

When he was sure she wouldn't rock away from the contact, he released her. "I expect you to remain in this position. Don't lean away from me. Understood?" He didn't want to restrain her. Not tonight.

"Yes." Hopefully she recognized the importance of his request.

He picked up the pace and the force, the sound of every swat filling the air with the soothing tone of dominance.

She moaned finally, sending relief down his spine. He wanted her to get aroused. If he was going to whip, flog, spank, or paddle her regularly, he wanted it to end with sex. Lincoln was right about that. Carter wanted to redirect her release in the form of orgasm, even if it followed a session that left her ass pink from palm prints, leather, or welts.

Since she was clearly in the zone, enjoying every second, he continued, increasing the pressure again while gauging the level of redness covering her thin skin.

The moment she arched her neck, he dropped the flogger and reached between her legs to thrust two fingers into her pussy.

She screamed his name. "*Carter.*" And then she came around his fingers, making him the happiest man on Earth. Thank. You. God.

When she was spent, he expected her to collapse to the bed in exhaustion.

But his little sub had more stamina than he gave her credit for.

CHAPTER 22

Brooke had never felt so amazing in her life. So totally sated and perfect.

Except one thing.

The penetration she'd experienced for the first time that morning had haunted her all day. His fingers simply didn't do the trick. She needed him inside her more than her next breath.

She rose up, spun around, and attacked the button on his jeans as fast as she could.

He let her. In fact, when her shaking fingers fumbled, he brushed them away and unzipped his jeans for her. Without a word, he shoved them down his hips and kicked them off. He wasn't wearing underwear, and he'd already ditched his shirt before he flogged her.

In seconds she had him in her hands and leaned forward without warning to suck him into her mouth.

He grabbed her head, threading his fingers into her hair. "Brooke... Baby..."

She couldn't stop, enjoying the taste of him. Salty on her lips, the precome leaking every time she flicked her tongue over the tip. She wrapped her hand around the base of him and sucked him in deeper.

He groaned loudly and tugged her hair hard enough to pull her off. His face was filled with frustration when she leaned back. Instead of letting him control her any more tonight, she shoved him onto his back and climbed over him.

His mouth hung open as if he intended to say something, but she never gave him a chance. Instead, she straddled his hips and slammed down over his cock.

The stretch was tight, and she was sore from fucking him for the first time that morning, but she settled on his cock, tipped her head back, and took a deep cleansing breath.

When her body acclimated to his girth, she leaned forward, set her palms on his chest, and lifted almost off only to thrust back downward again.

"Jesus, baby." He grabbed her hips. Instead of stopping her, though, he helped her, lifting and lowering her body off him, taking away some of the work.

She closed her eyes and moaned as her arousal rose to a fevered pitch once again. She'd come just one minute ago, and already she was close again. It felt so amazing. Nothing like it. Even better perhaps from on top than it had been underneath him that morning.

Carter slid one hand around to her front and found her clit, rubbing it hard while she continued to stoke the fire. How he managed to keep up with her, she had no idea, but it didn't take long for her to reach the edge.

Her mouth fell open, her breath caught in her throat.

"Come for me, baby. Show me how good it is."

Her pussy gripped his cock, milking him with so much force it had to hurt. But he didn't look like he was in pain when she was finally able to focus on his face. Pure bliss. His eyes were on her, but unseeing. His nostrils flared with desire. His lips were pursed.

And then he thrust his hips up into her, gripped her tight, and stopped her from rising again.

She swore she could feel the pulse of his orgasm against her cervix.

Heaven. Pure heaven.

It was still early when Brooke reached for her cell phone on the bedside table to see what time it was. Her phone was an older version and simple. She'd never used it very often in the past.

But today, for the first time in her life, there were numerous texts she'd missed the day before. Several were from David Rollings, the man she now knew was her father. A few were from his parents and her maternal grandmother too.

Overwhelmed with emotion, she read every text several times before closing the phone and holding it to her chest as if it were a pile of letters saved for years. In a sense, it represented exactly that.

"You okay, baby?" Carter's gravelly voice drew her attention, and she tipped her head his direction to find him frowning at her where he lay only inches away.

"Yeah. I think I am." She smiled.

His brow furrowed. "That sounds serious."

"It is."

He pushed up onto his elbow to look down at her face where she lay on her back. "You want to talk about it?"

She swallowed the lump in her throat before she spoke words she knew would hurt him. "I need to go to West Palm Beach."

"Okay. That's reasonable. Let's shower and eat breakfast and go for the day, yeah?"

She turned to face him more fully. "No. I need to go alone. I need to spend some time there." She reached for his face with one hand, cupping his cheek. "I need to stay. Alone. Get to know my family. Find out who I am."

He didn't move. His expression was too difficult to read. Slowly, his head dipped, and he settled back onto his side, his chin on her shoulder. "I was hoping to walk this path with you, help you through the process."

A tear slid from the corner of her eye. She was hurting him, but it couldn't be helped. She grasped his hand with hers and squeezed. "I know, and I appreciate everything you've done for me. I do. But this is something I need to do on my own. I need to find myself, figure out who Brooke is. I need to explore and think and grow and learn and so many things. Please. This is hard for me. Don't make it harder. Don't make me feel guilty about taking the time to do this."

He drew her fingers to his lips and kissed her knuckles. He wasn't even angry. It would almost be easier if he argued with her or stomped away or even forced her to submit to him and ordered her to stay.

It would be easier if he whipped her so hard that he drew blood. But he wouldn't do any of those things, and she knew with sudden clarity that she had to leave him.

There was no guarantee he would wait for her. Nor was there any guarantee she would be right for him when she found herself. But she had to do this. She couldn't be with him until she knew who she was…alone.

Every person who texted her had offered her a place to stay. She would go to West Palm Beach and figure things out. Think. Clear her mind. It was the right thing to do.

After several minutes of silence, Carter hauled her to his chest and kissed her forehead before he met her gaze dead-on. "You're mine, baby. I know you have to do this. And I totally understand, but I need you to get that you're mine. When you're done finding yourself and getting to know your family, I'll be here. Waiting."

"I can't ask you to do that, Carter," she choked out.

"You didn't ask. It's just a fact. Time and distance won't change things between us."

She nodded. "Thank you."

"No, baby, thank *you*. Thank you for taking a chance on me. Thank you for coming home with me that night instead of stubbornly sleeping in your car. Thank you for submitting to me so beautifully. Thank you for being the exact kind of woman I know fits so perfectly in my life that my soul is calm. I will be here for you. Anytime you need me, you call. If you want to talk, call. Text. Email. If you want me to come visit, just say the word. I won't bug you. I'll give you all the space you need. But Brooke?"

She licked her lips. "Yes."

"Come back to me, baby."

She said nothing, unable to commit to that demand as much as she wished she could. Luckily, he didn't ask for a response. He pulled her face into his chest and held her tight. His chin was on the top of her head, but she would swear he whispered *because I love you*.

He finally let her go, and they said very little while she packed up most of her things in her car, stacking a few unnecessary boxes in the corner of his guest room. He insisted. Perhaps it gave him some peace of mind thinking that if she left some things, she would have to return.

She sent a few texts to each of her family members, and by ten o'clock, she stood beside her car, forehead against Carter's chest, fingers draped in the loops of his jeans.

He gripped her face, kissed the top of her head, and opened her car door. With nothing more than a wave, he let her go.

She held her breath for a long time as she watched him standing in the driveway while she pulled down the street, and then she turned the corner and he was no longer in her line of sight.

For fifteen minutes she wiped tears from her face, but she forced herself to gather her wits. She had so many questions. Needed so many answers. It was time to face her future.

CHAPTER 23

Two weeks later…

Carter was on his knees, lining up a poorly cut piece of tile when he felt the presence of someone in the room. He lifted his gaze to find Rowen standing across the room. Lincoln was next to him. "Shit. What are you guys doing here? You scared me to death."

Lincoln stepped forward, pointing at the floor. "Seems like you were fighting that same piece of tile the last time I came to the house."

Carter shot him a glare. "Nope. That was on the other side of the kitchen. And before you ask why I'm still working on the kitchen after two weeks, the answer is simple: There was a problem with the plumbing, and I had to work in another part of the house for a while until the plumber could straighten things out in the kitchen."

Rowen chuckled.

Lincoln frowned. "When have I ever questioned your judgment or capabilities when it comes to construction issues?"

Carter stood, stretching his legs.

"Have you spoken to her?" Rowen asked.

It was the first time either of them had pointed out the elephant in the room since two hours after she left him. Instead of wallowing in self-pity that Sunday afternoon, Carter had driven to Lincoln's house and met with him and Rowen, telling them about Brooke's decision to spend some time in West Palm Beach.

It might have been cathartic, but it also brought his closest friends up to speed and avoided a constant barrage of questions. Until today.

"No." He wiped his hands on his jeans and turned to grab a bottle of water.

"Texted?" Lincoln asked.

"A few times. What is this, an intervention?"

Lincoln lifted a brow. "Do you *need* an intervention?"

"Nope."

Rowen rocked forward on his feet. "Is your woman sleeping in your bed?"

Carter rolled his eyes.

Rowen continued, "Then, yes. I'd say you need an intervention."

"Don't be so dramatic. She's getting to know her family."

Lincoln's turn. "She's been doing that for two weeks. Don't you think it's time to go visit her?"

Rowen chuckled again. "Or drag her pretty ass home?"

Carter sighed, rubbing his forehead. "I might be a little chicken." There were few people he would admit something like that to, but his two best friends whom he had bonded with over their shared military background and love of BDSM clubs deserved his honesty. Hell, they were business partners. Brothers. Closer than most blood relatives.

"You?" Rowen lifted a brow. "Now, *this* is troubling," he joked.

"At the risk of sounding like a girl, what if she's decided she's not interested in what I have to offer?"

Lincoln responded in kind. "At the risk of sounding like your mother, you've given her enough time. Go get her."

Carter sighed. "And if she won't come back?" His biggest fear.

"You're bigger than her," Lincoln teased. "Carry her out."

Carter smirked. "That will go over well."

Rowen made his way across the precariously placed tile and grabbed a water bottle off the counter. "Did something happen between you two besides her finding her family and all that shit?"

"Not really. Not from my view anyway. We click like no one I've ever met. She's perfect. The only thing I was concerned about was her tendency toward masochism. It worried me." Carter hadn't shared as much with Rowen as he had Lincoln.

"You're qualified to top her without hurting her," Rowen pointed out. "I could have told you that the night you first got together. Faith knows her tendencies well. You shouldn't have been blindsided. What were the issues?"

"She's been abused. By her mother. I don't ever want to do anything to emotionally harm her. Makes me fucking nervous."

"How many times have you complied with her requests?" Rowen asked.

"Twice. Once with my hand and another time with a flogger."

"Did she do okay?"

"She was fine." Carter threw up his hands. "It still makes me nervous. What if one time she slips into a deep subspace and doesn't stop me and has a negative experience? It takes so little suggestion to get her into subspace. You can practically command it."

"Do you think she used that as a coping mechanism when her mother beat her?" Lincoln was finally serious and concerned.

"Probably. I never want to do anything that would set her back to that kind of abuse."

"Understandable. Why don't you scene with her at the club with one or both of us monitoring? I'm sure Faith will be willing to help too," Rowen suggested.

"Yeah, I suggested that, but we never got around to going to the club while she was with me, and shit hit the fan so fast things changed. Both times I gave her what she wanted were kind of urgent. She might have literally lost it if I hadn't taken care of her."

"She needs some counseling, Carter," Lincoln pointed out.

"I know. But we didn't have time to make that happen either. We didn't have time for anything." Carter was frustrated, and his rising tone was surely an indication to both his friends.

"I have a list of lifestyle-sensitive counselors in the area. I'll get you some names." Lincoln set a hand on Carter's shoulder. "Go get her. Take tomorrow off and go get her."

Tomorrow was Tuesday. Carter glanced around.

Lincoln gave his shoulder a shove. "The damn house will still be here when you get your shit sorted. Don't worry about it. Assign someone else to lay this tile. There are more important things in life than flipping houses."

Carter nodded. He stood taller and exhaled fully for the first time in over two weeks. His friends were right. He would go tomorrow.

Brooke was dying. A slow ugly death sent by the devil to zap her energy and send her running to the bathroom every half hour. She had barely made it the last two times, and now she was back in bed, curled in a ball, shivering.

Martha was at her side for the tenth time that morning. "You poor girl. I brought you some orange juice and some Sprite. Which one sounds better? You need to drink something. You've been vomiting for two days."

Brooke moaned as she nodded. She watched Martha's worried expression as she left her alone. Brooke didn't honestly care what she drank or didn't drink at the moment. She felt so badly that she'd even lost the ability to feel embarrassed about being so sick in a stranger's home.

Not that Martha and Gentry were strangers. They were her grandparents, and they had made her feel at home from the moment she arrived. It had made more sense for her to stay with them.

Her other grandmother, Wanda, made her slightly uncomfortable. Eventually, she would get over the unease, but Wanda created most of the tension herself with her constant apologizing for the "sins of her past."

David had been amazing also. He'd brought his wife over the first evening and then his kids the second night after school. The boys were adorable. Both of them had the same red hair as Brooke, and they had accepted her into their lives seamlessly.

David's wife had also. Her name was Kelly, and she never gave any indication she was perturbed by this new development. Maybe she had freaked out when David first told her. But she didn't let on in front of Brooke, which was very much appreciated.

Everyone seemed to understand that the person who had lost the most in this saga was Brooke. The rest of them were adjusting appropriately, but they did not once make light of her situation.

And then there was Carter.

With each passing day, it got more and more difficult to reach out to him. She had treated him badly. There was no reason why she had to leave him just to come to West Palm Beach to meet her family. It would have been easier every step of the way if he'd been by her side.

He would have held her hand and listened to her when she stressed over each new milestone. Instead, she'd shunned him as though he were nothing. And she felt stupid calling him to say she'd made a mistake.

He was probably angry. He hadn't indicated anything of the sort in his three texts, but she hadn't given him much of a choice.

She'd drawn a line and told him not to cross it. She didn't have a right to be frustrated with him for doing as she demanded.

She missed him. Several times she'd pondered what her life would look like without him. The thought of going to another fetish club or submitting to another Dom made her as queasy as whatever illness was currently sucking the life out of her. No way could she submit to another man.

She wanted Carter. In fact, she realized she would take him any way she could get him. Even though he had an aversion to striking her as hard as she'd like, it wasn't a deal breaker. He was kind and generous and caring and loving and so many other things. The list was long. So what if he didn't want to whip her hard enough to really hurt?

Now she was sick. The flu had kicked her butt. And she hadn't even had the energy to let him know.

She should call him. She knew he was probably missing her as badly as she was him. Hell, he hadn't completely let her go either. He'd been thinking about her and helping her get to her future goals because she'd received a certified envelope a few days ago that contained her birth certificate. There was no other information with it, but Carter had obviously been the one to order it, and he'd placed the request on a rush. A quick Google search told her she could easily get her social security card from any local SSA center. That was a relief.

She had silently choked up at his thoughtfulness. She didn't know if anyone could possibly grasp how important it was to have her birth certificate in her hands, but it meant so much to her that she literally stuck it under her pillow the first night. The first piece of paper that confirmed she was a real person with a real identity.

Her birth certificate listed her mother's real name—Laurie Ann Wilson. The space for the father was blank. But at least Brooke Madden was not a fake name. Well, it was fake, but it was legally Brooke's identity.

One day she would see about adding her father formally to her birth certificate, if that was even a thing. She would ask him.

Another package had arrived several days ago also, by courier. Brooke had cried for a long time that night after finding out Carter had retrieved her mother's ashes from the coroner. She spent the next day contemplating what to do with them, and then gave them to Wanda. It hadn't been a tough decision. Brooke didn't need the constant reminder in her face, and Wanda had been beyond grateful to have that little piece of her own daughter returned to her.

Shaking visions of her mother's urn from her head, she closed her eyes. Jasper jumped up at her feet and curled into the curve of her legs. He calmed her every time, and he seemed to have a sense that she needed to be loved.

On the edge of her consciousness, she thought she heard voices in the front room, but she was too exhausted to move a muscle or attempt to listen to who had arrived. Besides, she was not good company, and there was a real fear she might vomit again if she moved.

It took her a moment to realize she was no longer alone. She opened her eyes only enough to see who was in the room, and then she gasped. "Carter?" She started to sit up, but her head was spinning.

He rushed forward, sat on the edge of the bed, and set a hand on her forehead. "Baby, you look like shit. Why didn't you call me?"

Jasper jumped down from the bed and scampered away.

She forced a smile. "I didn't want you to think I was ever unattractive?" she joked. She had never been so happy to see anyone in her life. In fact, she grabbed his hand and pulled it against her chest, snuggling into his warmth. That was all she had energy for.

He felt her face again with his other hand. "You don't feel feverish. How long have you been sick?"

"A few days. I can't keep anything down, and I have no energy."

His brow was furrowed as though she'd just announced she had terminal cancer instead of the flu.

"I'm sure I'll be fine. I just need to get the nausea under control," she reassured him. He looked unreasonably worried.

Seeming to force his face to relax, he climbed up behind her and spooned her body against his, smoothing her hair from her face.

She felt one hundred times better already. His touch calmed her in a way nothing else could. It suddenly occurred to her how stubborn she'd been. A stupid tear escaped her eye at the same time. "I'm sorry," she whispered.

"Baby, for what? For being sick? People get sick. You'll be fine." He stroked her cheek with the back of his knuckles.

She shook her head slightly, stopping herself when she realized it was a bad idea to move. "For leaving you like that. For insisting I needed to find myself."

"Nothing to apologize for. You had every right. I told you I understood. You found out your entire family lives here, and you wanted to get to know them. I get it, baby. It's not crazy at all."

"But I didn't have to cut you off to do it. I thought..." She wasn't sure how to explain herself. "I was afraid maybe I wasn't who I thought I was and I would figure out I needed something else."

"And?"

"I was wrong." She gripped his fingers so tight against her chest it hurt. "I'm just me. No matter who I meet or how many family members I have or where I go or what my birth certificate says, I'm still me." She sucked in a breath and finished on a whisper. "I'm still the same person who fell in love with you."

He flinched. "Oh, baby. You don't know how much those words mean to me. I'm so crazy in love with you I can't function. I don't even know what I did to fill my time before you came into my life, but now I sit and stare at the ceiling for hours in the evenings, hoping you'll call."

"Why didn't you say something?"

"You needed space. I wanted to respect that."

"But now you're here," she pointed out.

He laughed. "I was done respecting that. I missed you. I need you back. I need you in my bed. It's empty without you. The house is quiet."

She let the tears fall freely, still worried she might throw up if she got too emotional or moved. "You tracked down my birth certificate and my mom's ashes."

"I did. I guess they arrived?"

"Yes. Thank you." She squeezed his hand. "No one's ever gone out of their way for me like that."

"Baby, you're my life. I'll go out of my way for the rest of time for you. I'll remind you of that daily until you die. Nothing that pertains to you feels like going out of my way. I did it because I love you. Because I knew it would mean the world to you to have your birth certificate."

She smiled. "I slept with it under my pillow the first night."

He chuckled behind her. "Not surprising."

"And my mother's ashes," she murmured. "I can't believe you did that."

His fingers threading in her hair felt so damn good. "I hope I didn't overstep. I thought they might give you closure."

"Thank you. They did. I gave them to Wanda. She was very grateful."

"I'm glad."

She sobered. "My family is amazing. Even Wanda is coming around. She's nervous all the time, but she'll get there."

"I'm sure guilt eats her alive."

"Yes. It's hard to watch."

For several moments they simply lay there. She felt...home. Loved. Secure. Relaxed for the first time in two weeks. It had been wonderful getting to know her family, but Carter was her life. He was her future.

Finally he cleared his throat as though he had something important to say. "You choose. I can stay here with you, or you can come home with me. I know you don't feel well, so if you'd rather me stay here until you're on your feet, that's fine, but I'd like you back at home under my roof in my bed as soon as you feel like you can make the trip. I'm not going back without you. It's your home too now. It feels wrong without you there. It's not alive when I'm alone. It was just a house before you came. Now it's a home. Our home."

For a long time she couldn't speak. Did he have any idea how his words made her feel? Finally, she tipped her head his direction to see his eyes. "Take me home."

CHAPTER 24

Brooke lay in the back seat of Carter's truck, incredibly glad he'd driven it instead of the sports car. There was no way she could have driven her own car. Carter insisted they would retrieve it another day.

It would only take a little over an hour to get to his house, but she knew she would feel so much better sleeping in his bed tonight instead of the guest room at her grandparents' house.

Crazy, since she had actually slept only two nights in Carter's room and a week in his guest room. She'd spent more days and nights with her newfound family than she had with Carter.

And yet, he was her world. She felt complete when she was with him. She felt at home in his house. Like she belonged there. She had felt like a guest in her grandparents' home. No fault of their own. It just happened.

They had been sorry to see her go, and she had asked them to explain the situation to David, but their expressions made it clear they were relieved to see her on speaking terms with Carter—a man her grandmother said clearly adored her and thought she walked on water.

Gentry had spoken to Carter for a while in the living room

251

while Martha gathered Brooke's belongings and packed her stuff. "Don't you worry, dear. I'm sure you'll feel much better when you climb into your own bed tonight and get a full night's sleep."

Martha knew the gist of how long Brooke had been with Carter, but she also knew how solid the relationship was and how much Brooke loved him. There was no hiding it. She winked when she pointed that fact out.

Brooke thanked her profusely and hugged her tight.

Brooke hadn't spoken for a while when Carter pulled the truck in the driveway. And for a good reason. Her stomach was threatening revolt. She sat up slowly, let Carter help her out of the car and into the house, and then she shrugged him off and bolted for the guest bathroom in the hall because it was the closest.

Luckily she made it just in time. To her dismay and slight horror, Carter was behind her in an instant, holding her hair and stroking her back.

When she finished, setting her forehead against her arm, he released her. She listened to the water running and then a cool cloth landed on the back of her neck. "Sit up, baby. Let me wipe your face."

She felt ridiculous having to be coddled like this, but not nearly as uncomfortable as she had in Martha's home. Crazy?

Carter lifted her off the floor, cradled her in his arms, and made his way to the master bedroom. After setting her gently on the mattress, he removed her shoes and then helped her out of her jeans.

She should have felt at least a twinge of modesty again as he pulled her shirt over her head, took off her bra, and then tugged one of his T-shirts into place. Instead, she felt nothing but loved.

He helped her lie down, pulled the covers over her shoulders, and kissed her cheek. "Rest. I'm going to order some groceries for delivery. You have any requests?"

She shook her head. Nothing sounded good to her.

He kissed her again and padded from the room, leaving the

door open. So damn thoughtful. If she needed him, she could call out his name easily.

If she hadn't been so tired, she might have cried again, but she closed her eyes and fell asleep in minutes, relaxed. Home.

She had no idea how much time passed before she felt a hand on her shoulder, but her eyes shot open to find Carter leaning over her, brow furrowed. "You've been asleep for hours, baby. I was worried. You need to drink something. Can you sit up?" He cupped her arm to help her.

She struggled to sit, and suddenly felt incredibly thirsty. She drank the contents of the glass he handed her completely without stopping. Lemon-lime soda. Not too cold. Slightly flat. Perfect.

Taking a breath, she decided she might live.

"Feel better?"

"Yes. I think so." Maybe she had simply needed sleep and Carter. Her bladder screamed for release, though. "I need to use the bathroom." She waited for him to stand and give her space to swing her legs around, but when he didn't budge, she lifted her gaze. "Carter? Can I get up?"

"Yeah." He seemed reluctant, but then he stood slowly, held out a hand, and helped her to her feet. "You steady?"

"Yes. I can make it to the bathroom. I'm fine." She took a step, but he was in her space, not budging.

He tucked a finger under her chin and lifted her face. "Humor me?"

She frowned. "About what? The bathroom? You want to hold my hand while I pee?" She shook her head. "No way. I'm fine. Much better. See?" She stood taller, gathering strength. He was not going to the toilet with her. She drew the line at that intimacy. Maybe after ten years with a man she could lighten up in that area, but not this soon.

His expression didn't change. "I don't mean about the bathroom. I'm sure you can pee alone. But I want you to do something." He took her hand slowly and led her to the bathroom.

When they got there, he grabbed a box off the counter and held it out.

She stared at it, confused. And then she read the words on the front and froze. She backed up a step, tugging her hand to free herself from him, but he held her tight.

"Don't freak out," he said calmly. "It's not the end of the world. If it's positive, we'll deal with it. I love you. I'll love every one of our kids. You might not have planned on having them this fast, but life throws curve balls."

She stared at him as though he had two heads. He had. She was sure of it. She jerked her hand free and backed up. This couldn't be happening.

She shook her head as she hit the wall at her back. "No. No no no." She rubbed her temples with her fingers. *No fucking way.* She was not a cusser, but it was totally warranted in this case. At least in her head.

"Brooke, calm down," he said as he approached slowly.

"Calm down?" Her voice pitched. "Calm *down*?" she shouted. "You think I might be pregnant, and you want me to calm down?" She was in shock. Without a doubt. She couldn't fully process this development, and why hadn't it occurred to her? She didn't even have a fever. All she had was this never-ending nausea.

It made perfect sense, if the universe thought she was playing a joke.

Carter was in her space now, but he didn't touch her, thank God. She didn't think she could handle touching him at that moment. "When was your last period?"

She rubbed her forehead. "I don't know. I've never been regular." Fear gripped her stomach, threatening to revolt again.

"Look, it's unlikely. It's only been a few weeks since we were together. I don't think women get morning sickness this early. But it's a possibility. Let's just make sure. We'll handle it no matter what the results are. Together, baby."

"Handle it? A baby? Are you insane? I can't have a *baby*," she screamed, crossing her arms as a shudder wracked her body. *No fucking way,* she repeated in her head.

"Why not?" He was smiling. "They're cute. I want some. It's not like we're too young."

She shook her head, fighting renewed nausea, though she couldn't know the cause this time. "You're not too young. But I am. I'm only twenty-two, and besides, I'm not having kids. Ever."

He flinched. "That's a little dramatic, don't you think?"

"No. Don't tell me how to feel. I never want to have kids."

"Why not?" The concern on his face was palpable.

Perhaps she should have mentioned this fact sooner, before she came home with him and essentially agreed to move in with him. But, Lord, they hadn't known each other long enough to have had such a serious discussion. "I'm not fit to be a mother. I come from bad blood. I'm broken. I can't raise a child, Carter. That's *insane.*" She was trembling now. Freaked out like never before. She would rather die of kidney failure than pee again in her life.

And that was a real possibility if she didn't empty her bladder soon. But she sure wasn't going to pee on that stick. In fact, she slapped the box out of his hand, sending it skidding across the floor.

When he stepped closer, she looked away. But he took her hands in his, pressed them to the wall at her sides, and flattened his chest against her. "Okay, I don't even know where to begin, so I'm not going to try right now. Let's make a deal. You pee on the test strip and leave it in the bathroom. Then we go in the family room and talk. It won't change anything."

She started to cry, unable to stop not just tears but actual ugly sobbing. "How did this happen?" she asked rhetorically.

He slid his hands up her sides, cupped her head, and pressed her cheek against his chest. "We had sex. We didn't use protection."

"We had sex two times," she told his chest.

"And we didn't use a condom that second time. I'm so sorry. I didn't think. It's no excuse. I should have protected you. I accept responsibility. But it's done now. And we need to know one way or the other."

She flattened her fists on his chest. "It's not fair. I've only had sex two times in my life. I can't be pregnant."

He kissed the top of her head. "No matter what, we'll handle it. Together. I love you."

She tipped her head back and looked at him. "I love you too, but I'm not having kids."

He looked concerned, but he released her, grabbed the box from the floor, and ripped it open.

She flinched several times as she waited. And then he held out the stupid test. "Pee on this part. Set it on the back of the toilet. Then we'll go sit in the family room."

"I'm gonna need to do tequila shots. I hope you have some," she muttered as she took the test from him in two fingers as if it would give her a disease.

"You like tequila?" he asked.

"No idea. Never tried it. I'm just guessing it might come in handy."

He was still laughing as she shut the bathroom door. As badly as she needed to pee, it took a few minutes to calm down enough to convince her bladder to focus. And then it took a few minutes to have the guts to leave the bathroom and face Carter the Optimist again. How could he be so calm?

He was leaning against the counter, arms crossed, face worried. "Okay?"

She nodded, looking in the mirror as she washed her hands. She might have looked like death before this new development, but now she was literally green.

He led her to the family room, sat in the corner of the couch, and pulled her back against his front. For a while, he simply held her, one arm under her chest, one hand stroking her arm. "It's going to be okay, baby," he finally said.

"Not even close."

"You're not your mother," he hedged.

She winced. "And my grandfather? It's obviously hereditary. Abuse must run in the family. I don't ever want to be in a position to injure a child, Carter. You shouldn't want to take that risk either."

"It isn't in your genes, baby. It's learned behavior. Yes, some people repeat the mistakes of their parents because they don't know any different, but not always. And you'll have help. You'll have me. You'll get therapy. You'll learn to cope with what happened to you. You're way too kind to ever hurt anyone, baby. I know it."

She shook her head and dug her feet in. "It's not that simple. It scares me to death. I would always be nervous around a child, afraid. You would worry all the time too, wondering if you could really leave me alone with a baby. Wondering if you could trust me not to lose my temper. It would destroy us. I won't do it."

"You might not have a choice," he calmly pointed out.

She stiffened and jerked to get away from him.

He held her tight, clutching her to his chest with the arm under her breasts. "Brooke, stop."

"No." She struggled. "Don't you dare tell me what to do with my body. I'm not having a kid, Carter. Ever. Not today and not next year. I can't." She tugged, but he was stronger than her.

When she reached back to swing at him with her arm, he grabbed her wrist mid-air and pulled it down to her side. He held it with the arm across her chest and grabbed the other one right before she managed to take an awkward swing at his chin.

He even threw a leg over both of hers. And then he kissed her neck. "Calm down."

"*No*," she screamed, furious with him for being so calm and so...big.

"Brooke." His voice was filled with a familiar tone this time. Commanding. It stopped her in her tracks.

No. Not now. Don't let him dominate you right now. She squirmed, ignoring his tone, fighting for freedom.

He picked her up and manhandled her until she was on her knees between his legs.

Immediately she stopped struggling. It was indescribable how that simple move changed her. It frustrated her and pissed her off, but she stopped fighting and tipped her head to the floor.

"Clasp your hands behind you," he demanded. "Now, Brooke."

She obeyed him instantly, shivering as if she were cold.

"Shoulders back."

She straightened her spine. Surreal after her struggle. Part of her was furious with him for his ability to dominate her so thoroughly.

He set a hand on her head and stroked her hair. "Good girl. Deep breaths."

She inhaled slowly and exhaled just as long.

"Again."

She repeated the process, shocked to find her heart rate relaxing. Some of her insanity left her body.

"That's my girl." He soothed with his words, while his hands stroked up and down her bare arms. She was still wearing nothing but his T-shirt. "Now, I want you to listen to me without interrupting. When I'm done, you may speak."

"Okay." She would at least give him that. He deserved it.

"First of all, I never meant to imply I would stop you from controlling your body. If you truly didn't want to have a baby right now, I would let you terminate it. I wouldn't like it, but I would get over myself. I would even take you and hold your hand, so let that concern go."

Her shoulders relaxed.

"Second of all, you're wrong about your strength. You're the strongest woman I have ever met. It takes an incredibly strong woman to be submissive. And you are so very submissive when I take control."

She knew that was the truth. It scared her to death. Would she be this way with other Doms? She would never know. Right?

He stroked the skin at her neck and shoulder. "I know it's scary, this deep submission you have. It scares the hell out of me sometimes too. But luckily I'm trained and I know my weaknesses. I know how to recognize when you need to submit, and I know how to ensure you're safe during those times.

"I'm also clear you need something from me I've been uncomfortable with, and I'm working on it. I've been talking to Lincoln. He's an amazing sadist. He's helped me realize I can give you what you need. Lincoln and Rowen both agreed to work with us to get me to understand your needs and help make sure I can take care of those needs without harming you emotionally."

She swayed toward him. He would do that for her?

"Meanwhile, we'll get a counselor to help you deal with your past. You're strong. I know you can do it. Lincoln knows several in the area who are trained to work with people in the lifestyle. We'll try a few until you find someone you like."

She pursed her lips. How did she get so lucky?

He cupped her cheek and tipped her face back. "Look at me."

She obeyed him, unable to stop herself.

"We need a game plan. A loose, temporary one. We need to go look at that test, and we need to face reality and deal with it. No decisions need to be made tonight. But we can't even face those choices without all the facts."

She nodded. "Okay." She felt stronger now. He did this to her. Empowered her when she needed it. Perhaps their arrangement was unconventional, but it worked for them. It worked for her. He seemed to be on board. "But not yet. Give me a few more minutes."

He nodded, smiling.

A few more minutes of ignorance before you turn my world upside-

down. What if she was pregnant? Was he right? Could she handle a baby? She trembled at the thought. It had never occurred to her she'd ever be in a position to make this decision. She hadn't imagined even having sex or going on a date before a few weeks ago, so pondering the concept of kids had not been in the forefront of her mind.

If the test showed she was pregnant, could she terminate it?

She tipped her head back down, not wanting him to watch her display of emotions.

He seemed to understand, and pulled her forward so her cheek rested on his inner thigh, his hand threaded in her hair.

The idea of getting an abortion brought bile to her throat. She didn't think she could go through with it. It wasn't the baby's fault she'd been so consumed with the selfish desire to fuck that she'd forgotten to take precautions.

So, no. Abortion was not an option. Not for her.

What about adoption? She considered that for a moment. But the thought of spending nine months carrying a child that also belonged to Carter while he watched made her realize she would never be able to go through with it.

Images of the two of them leaning over a crib and smiling down at a sleeping infant filled her heart with something uninvited. Love. Unconditional love.

No matter what, she wasn't ready to be a mom. She had so many things to do. She wanted to get her GED. Maybe she really could go to college or at least get a job. She had only begun to ponder her future a few weeks ago. Being pregnant at this stage in her life would change everything once again.

And then, as she sat there thinking through all the what-ifs, the answer to the biggest question became clear. She didn't need to worry about continuing the cycle of abuse from her mother. She would never hurt another living being. She didn't have it in her. She wouldn't even spank her own child. Ironic since she liked Carter to spank her. Before she could stop herself, she asked him the question on the tip of her tongue. "How do people in the lifestyle raise kids and continue to practice BDSM?" She blinked, tipping her face toward him.

He smiled. "They manage." He stroked her hair. "They get creative. Lock the bedroom door. Make lunch plans while kids are at school. Get a sitter when they want to go to the club. Lots of ways." He looked less concerned, his shoulders relaxing, and she realized the implications of her question.

She glanced back at his lap, gathering her thoughts. So many of them running amok in her mind. Loose strings of concepts normal women would have considered. But she was not normal.

"We're going to be fine, Brooke," he promised, gently nudging her to face him again.

She needed to know something before they looked at the test. "Would you stay with me if I never wanted to have kids?"

"Yes." He didn't hesitate. "I mean, I'd like kids, but it's not as important to me as you are. If it meant that much to you, I'd live a long and happy life by your side without sticky fingers, dirty diapers, and college tuition payments."

She thought she might cry, again. "What if *I* want to go to college?" she joked.

"Except yours. That's already in the budget, though."

She widened her eyes. "What?"

He shrugged. "I moved some money around while you were gone. It's all worked out."

"You would put me through college?" Shock didn't begin to describe her emotions.

He narrowed his eyes. "Of course. When you figure out what you want to study, we'll make it happen."

Her heart was overflowing. If this amazing man could find it in his heart to keep her as his own and arrange for her to have everything in the world her heart desired, surely she could make room for one tiny baby. Or two. Maybe two.

She smiled. "I love you."

"I love you too, baby." He gripped her shoulders. "You ready?"

"Yes."

"Don't move." He left her there on her knees, shaking, but not nearly as distraught as she had been earlier. She could handle this. She was strong. And she had the best man in the world at her side.

CHAPTER 25

Three nights later…

"You okay?"

Brooke lifted her gaze to find Faith staring at her, concern written all over her face. She had never been so happy to see someone in her life—except maybe Tuesday morning when Carter showed up at her grandparents'. But she'd never had a real girlfriend before she met Faith, and she hoped the two of them could be friends. After all, their men were as close as brothers.

"Great. Thanks." Brooke set a hand on the padded leather bench she stood next to in the middle of Zodiac's main floor. The leather was supple and somehow calming.

"Rowen said you had a stomach bug."

"I did. Food allergy, they think. I went to the doctor on Wednesday finally. No idea what caused it. Any number of things are possible. My body isn't accustomed to most of the food I've eaten in the last few weeks." Brooke patted her stomach, glad the nausea had passed.

She wasn't sure if she was relieved or disappointed about the negative pregnancy test. By the time she was willing to read it, she'd convinced herself she could handle being a mother. She smiled at her private thoughts, not saying anything to Faith.

"I'm glad you're feeling better."

"I wasn't expecting to see you here this afternoon," Brooke continued. She had come early with Carter, insisting she was completely healed and ready to try some new scenes. He'd invited Rowen and Lincoln, which wasn't strange since they also owned the club and were knowledgeable about the dilemma she and Carter were facing.

Of course Faith was with Rowen, and she too knew her craft well. Brooke trusted her.

Faith smiled. "Thought I could help."

"I'm glad you're here." Brooke did something she had rarely done in her life until the last few weeks. She leaned forward and gave Faith a tight hug. "I appreciate your help."

"Sasha is here too. Have you met her?"

Brooke shook her head. "Not yet, but I've heard a lot about her." She was Lincoln's girlfriend. She was also Rowen's sister.

"I hope you don't mind. I invited her. I thought it might be nice if you had a stranger in the room too. It adds to the atmosphere of a real club scene, but at the same time, you'll have the knowledge that Sasha is someone you can trust. You'll be fast friends eventually. I can feel it. You have similarities."

Brooke tipped her head to one side. "Like what?"

Faith chuckled. "You're both very submissive. And strong."

"You're not?"

Faith laughed. "Oh I am too. It's just different somehow."

Footsteps behind Brooke alerted her to the arrival of the men. They had been upstairs while Brooke wandered around in the main room of the club for a few minutes.

When Brooke turned around, she found all three men and a woman approaching. The brunette would be Sasha.

Sasha was almost as small as Faith, but her personality was

vibrant, exploding from her eyes in an inviting way that told Brooke she was going to love her. With springy brown curls hanging down her back and green eyes that stood out even more than Brooke's, she was incredibly attractive. "Hey. I'm Sasha. Nice to finally meet you." She stuck out a hand.

Brooke took it, shocked by her grip and warmth. "Brooke."

"Hope you don't mind if I watch? Carter thought it might be a good addition."

Carter came up behind Brooke and wrapped an arm possessively around her middle, tugging her against his chest. He kissed the top of her head. "It seemed awkward to leave Sasha out of our scene since the rest of us are all here."

Brooke smiled, tipping her head back to look at him. "I'm glad you invited her." She was as nervous as she'd ever been, but adding Sasha had nothing to do with it.

"Love your dress," Sasha added, her gaze roaming down Brooke's body and back up.

"Thank you." Brooke blushed, feeling the heat creep up her cheeks at the compliment. She wasn't used to being admired. Nor was she accustomed to wearing a dress.

Carter had bought it for her and surprised her that afternoon before they left the house, laying it out on the bed with a delicate set of matching bra and panties. All three items were black.

Brooke's book of firsts was going to have a long list tonight. She'd never worn lingerie that wasn't purely utilitarian before. She'd never owned a little black dress. She'd never exposed her skin in public—and she knew from several negotiations with Carter in the last few days that he expected her to expose herself in this intimate setting to a certain degree.

Ever since she'd put the lacy bra and thong on, she'd been preparing herself mentally for the eventuality that everyone else was going to see her in nothing but the set.

Carter's hand slid up between her breasts to cup her face, angling her head back and exposing her neck. He spoke to the room at large, but his gaze never left hers. "She's beautiful all the time, but it's very gratifying to watch her move in this dress because she feels pretty in it too."

He wasn't wrong. She felt like a model. "Thank you," she mouthed even though she'd already thanked him about two hundred times.

He leaned down and kissed her lips gently. "As sexy as this dress is, I'm about to take it off. You ready for that?"

She swallowed. *Already? Now? I guess that's what we're all gathered here for...*

Carter lifted a brow as he spun her around to face him. He cupped her cheeks in his usual way, essentially blocking her off from everyone else to keep her focused strictly on him. "I know it's a big step for you, and we don't have to do this today. We don't have to do it ever. It's up to you."

She bit her bottom lip, trying to drag forth the courage to participate in this scene. They had a deal. If she wanted him to strike her with any significance, he needed to be able to see her bare skin to ensure he wasn't hitting too hard or breaking her skin.

She understood his perspective, and she desperately wanted to take this next step, but it was going to be huge for her to expose so much of her body to other people. Friends. Close friends in the lifestyle. No one would judge her. Ever.

She could do this. "I'm ready."

Carter kissed her forehead and then turned her to face the bench she'd been staring at before everyone came in the room. "Lift your arms, baby," he whispered in her ear.

She took a deep breath and let him slide the silky material of the dress over her head. In less than a heartbeat, she stood in the main room wearing nothing but the black, lacy bra and thong that suddenly seemed skimpier than they had earlier.

Her butt was totally exposed, which was intentional because

Carter intended to devote most of his attention to that area of her backside.

He set a hand on her lower back and smoothed it down over one cheek and then her thigh. His lips were inches from her ear as he spoke to her in a voice everyone else would have to strain to hear. "I'm going to lift you onto the bench now. You know where to put your knees and elbows."

She nodded.

He gripped her waist and lifted her into position.

She bit down on her lower lip, trying to calm herself. Four other people were in the room. All were silent. She could feel them positioned around her at different angles. Their presence was intentional—ensuring her physical and mental safety.

"I'm not going to secure you to the bench, but I want you to keep your hands and knees where they are. If you wiggle too much, I'll not only bind your ankles and wrists, but your waist too."

She nodded, unable to say a word. *My waist?*

"Safewords?"

"Yellow and red," she murmured, settling her cheek on the cool leather, eyes closed. If she didn't look directly at anyone, she might be able to pretend they weren't there.

"Good girl." He shifted her slightly with his fingers on her hips from behind, and then he molded them to her butt cheeks, gripping the flesh, warming her. When his palms slid down to her thighs, his thumbs super close to her sex, she felt the first twinge of arousal.

It still shocked her that she could get so turned on by his dominance. Nothing like that had ever happened with Faith, but then again Brooke hadn't been interested in Faith in that way. She'd simply enjoyed the release.

Shocking her further was the fact that she liked what Carter did to her even more. The addition of a new kind of release she'd never dreamed of still surprised her every time he touched her.

When he worked his magic to bring her to orgasm at the same time he struck her with his hand or one of his tools, she reached a level of euphoria she'd never thought possible.

As his hands smoothed up her body, he leaned over her and set his lips on her ear again. "Are you aroused?"

She could only hope he heard her whispered "Yes."

"I'm going to spank you first to get your mind in the right place and warm up your skin, and then I'm going to use a crop on you. Understood?"

"Yes." She more than understood. She couldn't wait. No one had used a crop on her yet. She was anxious to experience the sting. He'd warned her it would be intense. Faith had used a whip on her but not with enough force to leave lasting welts, and Brooke had never exposed her skin for any of her scenes with Faith.

His first swat landed without warning, making her flinch. He soothed the skin for a second and then repeated the action on her other butt cheek. She might have jerked a bit but not as forcefully as the first time.

A series of rapid spanks then landed all over her bottom, up and down, some of them halfway on her thighs. Those were the ones that made her horny. She started to panic a bit at the prospect of coming in front of all these people.

She hadn't anticipated the ability to get aroused with an audience. It snuck up on her. She had no way to stop it.

"Trust me, baby," he whispered in her ear. "Nothing will happen we didn't discuss."

They had not discussed orgasm, but he couldn't control her body's reaction to his touch.

Several more swats landed on first one cheek and then the other, and then Carter was behind her again, massaging her bottom. "You ready for the crop?"

"Yes." She'd been ready for days. If it hadn't been for the stupid foodborne illness, she would have insisted he dominate her like this sooner. "Please." She said the word in a respectful tone, not allowing it to come off as pleading.

"Good girl." With a hand on her lower back, he used his other hand to set the folded leather end of the crop against her heated butt, dragging the cool leather over her skin. Moments later, he tapped her flesh in one spot, each tap growing in intensity. Finally, he lifted it a few inches and *thwack*.

It stung. It took her breath away. It also felt amazing.

She moaned, letting her head loll back and forth against the padding of the bench. That first strike of the crop sent a tingling straight to her clit. She wouldn't be able to avoid an orgasm. Would anyone notice?

Gripping her pussy, she forced herself to concentrate on Carter's touch and the sting of the crop as he slapped her with it again in another spot. "Okay?"

"Yes." *Perfect.*

He stepped closer to her side, dragged the crop across her skin several times, and then swatted her harder than before.

Yes. God, yes. It felt so good.

"More?"

"Yes." Her voice was breathy, broken, tight. She didn't care. She would never apologize for this kink. It was so exactly right for her.

Picking up the pace, he let the crop strike her in a row of sharp stings up and down her butt and thighs.

She moaned every time he got close to her sex, flinching several times, focusing on the pain. She wondered what her butt looked like and couldn't wait to see the evidence of his cropping later. It would serve as a reminder of his dominance and her submission for the next several hours, every time anything grazed her skin.

He paused, rubbing her heated skin with his palm again while she caught her breath. When he spoke into her ear again, she was in a zone. "Talk to me, baby. I need to know you're okay."

"Better than. Please, Carter. Don't stop."

"Okay."

She trusted him thoroughly. He'd explained to her on numerous occasions that he would not draw blood and he would stop when he thought she had slid too far into subspace or was disassociating too much. She knew that was why he kept checking in with her.

She loved him so much it gripped at her heart. This was out of his comfort zone. He'd made that clear, and yet he was doing this for her. For *her*. Someone cared enough to do something for her. It meant the world to her.

Another string of slaps hit her butt, covering every inch of skin, harder. The sting was welcome. She craved it. It calmed her soul while it amped up her arousal at the same time.

When the tip of leather suddenly swatted the sensitive flesh of her inner thighs, flicking back and forth between them, she cried out, not in pain, but in shock. The contact went straight to her pussy.

It didn't last long, though. After a few moments, he moved around to the backs of her thighs, alternating back and forth between them. He landed two stronger slaps to her butt cheeks next, both directly aimed at the base of her cheeks where she would sit. And then he stopped.

The sound of footsteps seeped into her conscience. She'd nearly forgotten she had an audience. A moment later, Carter's lips were at her ear. "Everyone went upstairs, baby. They could see we're fine without them. We're alone. I want you to let go for me."

She moaned at his words.

And then the leather stroked between her legs again, teasing, tempting. Instead of another volley against her inner thighs, he tapped her pussy.

She nearly came undone as she screamed out. The desire to come was so close. She gritted her teeth against this craving.

Wickedly delicious. A month ago, she never would have believed in this combination of pain and pleasure, and now she was living proof.

Several more swats again to her inner thighs, higher, so close...

Another quick flick across her sex...

And then the final tap landed right on her clit.

She came so hard she arched her chest off the bench, lifting her head as the pulsing orgasm took over her entire body. Wave after wave of release. Before she could catch her breath, something thrust into her channel.

She nearly died when she realized it had to be the handle of his crop. Fucking her fast and hard. Soooo good. She should have been embarrassed. Carter was watching her come completely undone, but she didn't have the energy to care at the moment.

Fingers landed on her clit, the bundle of nerves supersensitive from the slap of the crop. He pinched the nub hard and then spanked it with the tips of his fingers.

She came again, the second orgasm washing over her with even more power than the first. So intense. The best experience of her life.

When she finally started to return from wherever she floated, he eased his fingers from her and pulled the crop out of her tight channel. Before she managed to open her eyes, he was in front of her. He had her face in his hands, steadying her head, and something smooth touched her mouth.

She moaned as she realized it was his cock.

"Swallow me, baby." His grip was firm. His voice demanding.

She'd never wanted anything more. Opening her mouth, she sucked his length as deep as she could.

He groaned into the silence of the room, pumping in and out of her mouth so that her only job was to keep her lips parted and breathe through her nose.

Her limited experience with blowjobs should have bothered

her, but the noises coming from Carter combined with his firm grip on her face and his rough thrusting was enough to assure her he enjoyed every second.

Empowered, she managed to draw her cheeks in and suck harder.

He panted, his thrusting coming faster, deeper, nearly choking her. She had to open her throat and take every inch of him or risk gagging, which wasn't an option.

She was peripherally aware of three things at once—the stinging of her ass, the pulsing of her pussy, and the powerful weight of Carter's dominance. It was heady and would have brought her to her knees if she weren't already in a position of submission.

The way he controlled her made her body melt. She was his in every possible way, and he knew it.

On that revelation, her lips tightened, and he came. She swallowed every pulse of his come as it hit the back of her throat, luxuriating in the power she had over him even though this was his scene.

When he finally pulled out slowly, her mouth was sore, the perfect kind of sore that would remind her who her Dom was. He gently angled her face to one side to rest against the leather. Next, he squatted in front of her face and kissed her reverently. "Open your eyes, baby."

She hated to break the scene and return to reality, but she forced herself to look at him.

He was so perfect. Gently, he lifted her off the bench and cradled her to his chest as if she were an injured animal. Careful to avoid touching her butt more than necessary, he carried her to a couch and sat, arranging her against his chest, her heated cheeks exposed.

He grabbed a blanket and tossed it over her, but left her stinging skin open to the air. So thoughtful. She closed her eyes and snuggled into him. "Thank you."

He held her tighter. "You were so beautiful. Was it everything you wanted it to be?"

She lifted her face and smiled. "Beyond my dreams. Were you okay?" She had reached a turning point in her life. She knew she craved the powerful experience that came from masochism, but she also loved this man with all her heart. If he couldn't stomach the idea of dominating her in that manner, she would find a way to let it go.

He grinned back. "Perfect. I admit I was concerned, but watching you come undone like that was heavenly. It's stressful because I worry constantly that I'm going to harm you in some way, but clearly Lincoln, Rowen, Faith, and Sasha weren't worried. They gave their approval. I'll get more comfortable with it every time I do it as I'm more reassured you're strong enough to take the blows and even channel them into something stunning to watch."

She smiled broader. "I can't even describe the feeling. It's like my body is purged of whatever crap builds up in my mind and I can let it go for a while."

He nodded. "I can't imagine what that feels like, but you aren't the only submissive to describe it that way, so I get it. And I'll do my best to make sure you have what you need from me." As he spoke, he circled the back of her neck with his fingers, pressing her closer.

The weight soothed her, and she sighed.

"You like my fingers on your neck, don't you?"

"Yes. It centers me. Reminds me I'm yours."

"Mmm. What if it were permanent?"

She giggled against him. "You going to follow me around gripping the back of my neck."

"No, but I'd love to collar you."

She hesitated, trying to remember if she'd heard that term and coming up short. Finally, she lifted her gaze again. "Collar?"

He ran a finger around her throat, tracing an imaginary line like a necklace. "Sometimes people use a collar as an outward symbol of their commitment. It can be a literal collar that's heavy and constant or a chain like a necklace that serves as a symbolic collar."

"People wear them in public?" She'd occasionally seen something like that on younger people and assumed it was a style. She didn't think it suited her.

He shook his head. "Some people do, but most people in the lifestyle reserve actual collars for private or when they're at a club. When they're in regular society, they wear a thin chain with a small symbol of their commitment that most people wouldn't understand."

"You'd like me to have one?" Her heart rate picked up at the idea that he wanted to make that kind of commitment to her. She couldn't fully wrap her head around how it might feel to wear something like that, but she did know it seemed important to him, and she liked to please him above all else.

"It would be a dream come true."

She smiled. "Then you shall have your wish."

Eyes closing, he drew her closer to his chest and slid one hand to her heated bottom. It reminded her of his dominance and warmed her heart.

She swallowed back tears, tucking her face against his chest again. "I love you."

"Baby, I love you so much it hurts."

CHAPTER 26

For the next month Brooke settled into a routine with Carter. He had taken so much time off work to help her adjust that he needed to get back to his real life, and she insisted he do so.

So, he worked most days, leaving the house early and returning mid-afternoon, while she learned the ins and outs of his computer and spent her time studying for her GED. Until she got that piece of paper, she couldn't move on with her life.

She was motivated by the fact that she wasn't making any money. However, her desire to get a job was repeatedly met with a frown and a lecture, so she was gradually learning to accept that she could and would rely on him while she went to college. The prospect was exciting.

Every day she spent some time looking at local universities and scanning through the hundreds of degrees. She had no idea what she wanted to study yet, but knowing she would one day walk through the halls of a college campus made her so happy she could hardly contain her excitement.

It pleased Carter to see her that way, and he let her know every day.

When he was at work or the club, she often spoke to her new

family members on the phone. She and Carter had gone to visit several times, and her father had come to see her twice.

Two weeks ago, Carter had come home carrying a precarious box in his arms. He set it gently on the kitchen floor as if the contents were glass. She was eyeing him suspiciously from the sink as he approached.

The twinkle in his eye made her pause. "I got you something."

She dried her hands on the towel and turned to fully face him. "Why?" She couldn't begin to imagine what was in the box.

He shrugged. "Because I love you."

She glanced around him as a scratching noise caught her attention. What the hell? And then her eyes bugged out as a tiny white furry face peeked out of the top of the box. Shoving him out of her way, she rushed across the room to kneel in front of the kitten. In an instant, she had it in her arms and it was pawing at her face.

She giggled, glancing back at Carter. "You got me a kitten? I can't believe it." It was adorable, its little body covered with splotches of browns. When she scratched its neck, it purred.

"I guess you like it," he teased as he leaned over, kissed the top of her head, and headed back to the garage. A minute later, while she sat on the floor playing with the fur ball, he returned with several more boxes, holding them up. "Litter box. Food. Toys. I didn't know what all to get. The guy at the pet store helped me."

She smiled, love making her choke up as tears ran down her cheeks. No one had ever done something so thoughtful for her. "Thank you," she finally managed.

Over the past two weeks, the kitten had taken to following Brooke everywhere she went. Carter wasn't superfond of it jumping up in bed with them, but he humored her most of the time. When the plans involved sleeping.

Carter worked at the club Wednesdays, Fridays, and Saturdays. She stayed home a few of the nights, but she liked to go with him and either perch on a bench near the entrance where he was the bouncer or hang out upstairs in his office.

Sometimes Sasha or Faith kept her company when she was upstairs, but she preferred to watch his broad sexy body by being near him on the main floor.

He often caught her staring at him and sent her a warning look that made her giggle. Sometimes he kissed her hard and fast or pinched her butt or cupped her breasts. Every touch made her arousal grow throughout the evening.

He hadn't mentioned the collar again since their conversation after the cropping scene, but she had begun to pay attention to every member of Zodiac as they came and went from the club. Many of them had collars. Some were subtle. Some were obvious. Some even had chains attached to them—either dangling or held by their Masters.

Brooke wasn't sure how she felt about the actual leashes, but the collars themselves were often intricate and specially chosen. They meant something to both the submissive and their Dom.

She wanted one.

Did he catch her staring at them sometimes? She thought so. Few things got by him. Sometimes his expression held a slight smirk, and then she would yank her gaze to something else. She never brought the subject up, though. It felt like something that needed to come from him.

It was a Sunday. She wouldn't forget because Sundays were her favorite day of the week. Carter didn't work at either job, and he insisted she take the day off from studying to spend quality time with him every week also.

The morning routine wasn't anything out of the ordinary. He woke her early with his mouth on her pussy, pressing her legs wide. After she came so hard she was left limp and breathing heavily, he made breakfast.

But when she joined him in the kitchen, she knew something was different. He was quiet. Nervous. Not his usual self.

She stressed over whatever might be on his mind while forcing eggs and bacon down her throat. He'd never faltered from his regular calm personality in all the time they'd been together, so this awkward vibe made her imagine all sorts of scenarios that brought bile to her throat.

She'd never considered what might happen if he got tired of her or broke things off. She would be lost.

On the flip side, there was no way he would use his mouth to send her soaring in the clouds if he intended to dump her an hour later. On that thought, she tried to relax.

After breakfast, he led her to the family room, sat on the couch, and guided her to her knees in front of him. Also not out of the ordinary. He was too quiet, but she forced herself to wait to hear what he had to say.

For a long time, he ran his fingers through her hair, keeping her face tipped to the floor and occasionally correcting her posture with a nudge to her shoulders or a tap to her inner thighs.

She was nearly out of her mind with worry when he finally spoke. "I got you something."

She held her breath.

"It took a while. I had it made."

Her heart filled. She was pretty sure he reached behind him to pull something out from between the cushions.

Moments later, he held a long narrow box in front of her. "Open it."

She lifted her face to his and then released her hands from behind her back. Her fingers were shaking as she opened the box. And then she gasped.

The thick leather collar took her breath away. It was the lightest pink she'd ever seen, almost white. It was about two inches wide and adorned with several jewels as well as a few rings. She reached out with trembling fingers to touch it as Carter lifted it out of the box. "Do you like it?"

She sucked in a breath, meeting his gaze. "I love it."

He smiled as he wrapped it around her neck, tipped her head forward, and brushed her hair out of the way to clasp it at the top of her spine.

When she lifted her head, the weight of the collar had an immediate effect. It spoke volumes, centering her, putting her in a submissive frame of mind, giving her a sense of belonging, making her feel loved and cherished. Owned.

She grabbed Carter's thighs and squeezed them with her fingers to keep from toppling over as she became almost faint. "Thank you, Sir."

His body jerked. He grabbed her face and tipped her head back. His eyes were wide. A slow smile spread across his face. "Say that again."

"Thank you...Sir." She had no idea that one word would have such an impact on him. They had never discussed it. Not once. She wasn't sure if he wasn't fond of the specific sign of respect or if he hadn't wanted to pressure her to use it. In any case, she felt an overwhelming sense of ownership the moment the collar's weight pulled on her neck. The word slid out naturally.

Apparently he was not displeased.

He stroked her cheek. "Again."

"Sir."

He smiled again. "Beautiful."

She leaned her head into his touch.

"You're mine."

"I'm yours, Sir."

That was the end of the talking portion of the day. Thirty seconds after that, she was in his arms.

Thirty seconds after that, she was in his bed.

Thirty seconds after that, she was naked and on her knees. The only thing she wore was the collar. It was all she needed. The constant reminder would be a powerful declaration of her love and submission.

Forever.

AUTHOR'S NOTE

I hope you enjoyed this third book in the Club Zodiac series. Please enjoy the following excerpt from the fourth book in the series, Mastering Rayne.

.

MASTERING RAYNE

CLUB ZODIAC (BOOK FOUR)

Prologue

Fourteen years ago…

"Dad?"

"Yeah, honey?"

"Would it be okay for my friend Stella to come over this weekend?" Rayne bit her lower lip as she waited for her father to respond. She'd never once asked him if she could have a friend over. She'd also never had so much as a playdate in all of her twelve years. Not at the house at least.

Warren Bryant lifted his gaze from the newspaper he was reading at the breakfast table and frowned. "You know that's not possible, honey. Your mom isn't well."

Of course.

Rayne stood taller and adjusted her plaid uniform skirt. She cleared her throat, willing herself not to whine. Her father hated it when she whined. "I know, but Mom is *never* well. And she doesn't ever come out of her room. Stella won't even know she's here." The house was enormous. Rayne was probably right.

There was the off chance she would not be right. But, who cared? She didn't understand why her mother's illness had to be such a secret.

Warren narrowed his gaze. "Rayne, you're too old for this conversation. You know better. We don't air our dirty laundry. It's unseemly. Please tell me you haven't been talking to your friends about your mother's situation."

Rayne shook her head, her thick braids swinging back and forth. "Of course not, Dad. But, Stella's parents are getting a divorce. Her parents are always yelling at each other. She's going through a hard time. She needs a friend. I thought it would be neighborly to offer her a weekend someplace else."

Rayne hoped she sounded gracious and helpful. She tried so hard to sound grown up. Wasn't she supposed to be hospitable?

Her father sighed, lowering his paper. "You see, that's exactly the kind of thing I'm talking about. You kids should not be gossiping about the state of anyone's parents' marriages. If Stella's parents are getting a divorce, I'm sure they don't want their daughter yapping about it to her friends."

Rayne's shoulders fell. Half the time she felt jealous of Stella, though she would never say so out loud. If her own parents would get a divorce, maybe Rayne wouldn't have to keep so many secrets.

Ever since she was a small child, her mother had been sick. Rayne couldn't even remember a time when MaryAnn was well. Some months she was better and would come out of her room and join Rayne and her father in the living room. But most of the time Rayne never saw her.

Rayne swallowed as she looked at her father, wishing she could understand better, while knowing it wasn't possible to ask questions. He would say she wasn't old enough or that he didn't want her to worry about adult issues.

Blah blah blah.

Warren was an older father. He was in his sixties, while her mother was forty-five. Sometimes he seemed more like a grandfather than a father. Even though he was fit and healthy and went to work at his consulting firm every day, he had old-fashioned ideas that sometimes embarrassed her in front of other people. Like this one.

Rayne knew she wasn't like other kids. She had spent most of her life in the care of the staff and her father. He had never treated her like a child. She'd been expected to behave far older than her years since she'd been born. While other kids would have found themselves eating pizza in the kitchen and kept out of sight when adults were over, Warren Bryant had expected Rayne to attend with him and behave older than her years.

She had honored his wishes for all of her twelve years. Never once had she gossiped about her mother. Usually when kids spoke of their mothers, Rayne would smile and agree with them so she wouldn't stand out.

Other mothers made cookies and helped their kids with homework.

Other mothers came to school plays and orchestra performances.

Other mothers nagged their kids to clean their rooms or take a bath.

Not Rayne's mother. She'd give anything to have a nagging mother. She'd never experienced it. And her father was not the nagging sort. He was serious most of the time, and busy. It was usually the housekeeper who ensured Rayne's needs were met.

In a last-ditch effort, Rayne tried again. "Everyone knows when the other kids have parents divorcing. It's not the sort of thing people can keep to themselves."

Divorce wasn't a word she'd ever heard mentioned in her home. She knew from her classmates that it was common and messy and destroyed homes. Sometimes other girls in her school moved away when their parents split up. Sometimes they cried and had to go to the counselor. Rayne had no idea why adults would behave in such a childish manner, but clearly they did. Often.

Her father shoved from the table. "Well, that's unacceptable, Rayne, and if I find out you're gossiping with other girls, I will pull you from that school and get you a home tutor."

Rayne trembled. That was the last thing she wanted. This was totally backfiring on her. She felt tears well up in her eyes and she choked them back, not wanting to appear weak in front of her father.

He turned around and headed for the sink to set his coffee mug in the basin. "Gather your things. You need to leave for school soon."

Rayne turned and fled the room, grateful for the dismissal. She hadn't won this battle, but she did know one thing for sure. People led very twisted lives, and most of them hid their private lives from the world. It made her sad.

When she grew up, she wanted to find a way to help people so they wouldn't have to go through so much stress alone.

Chapter One

Fourteen years later…

As Colin Wynne arrived at the door on the twelfth floor of the downtown Denver office building, he glanced at the gold plaque that declared he was in the right place—Rayne Bryant, Divorce Attorney. Colin glanced at his sister, London, who was wringing her hands. He smiled, hoping to convey some level of support. Lord knew, she needed support.

The moment he opened the door, he heard shouting. Male shouting. Angry male shouting. "There isn't going to be a divorce, so you can shred those goddamn papers now and move on with messing up someone else's life. If my wife contacts you again, tell her you won't be available to help her."

"Sir—" Rayne's voice began. Colin couldn't see her yet, but he recognized her soft tone.

The man interrupted. "You listen to me, bitch. No fucking divorce."

Colin's spine stiffened as he stepped into the outer office, London behind him. In his peripheral vision, he briefly took in the brown leather sofa and matching armchair, the abstract artwork in warm colors, and the plants. All this was on his left. On his right was a receptionist's desk with a woman he presumed was Rayne's receptionist on her feet, her lips pursed, her eyes wide. Behind her was a full wall of windows.

None of this was nearly as important as the man who stood between Colin and Rayne, his large frame nearly filling the open doorway to Rayne's office as he continued to shout. He was approximately five-nine and built. Not as built as Colin, but the man worked out. His dark hair was slicked back, and he was dressed in an expensive suit, tailor-made to fit him.

Colin couldn't see his face, but he assumed it was probably red. It was going to get a whole lot redder if he didn't lower the finger he was shaking and stop yelling at Rayne.

Leaving London just inside the waiting room, Colin rushed forward until he arrived at the man's side. "I advise you to calm down and lower your arm right now."

The man's face was indeed red with rage as he glanced at Colin. "Fuck you. Who the fuck do you think you are? Stay the fuck out of my business."

Colin pulled his shoulders back and stepped closer, his brow furrowing as his tension increased. "I don't know what your deal is, but I think you need to leave. Now."

The asshole glanced up and down Colin's frame as if finding him lacking. "I'll leave when I'm goddamn ready." He jerked his gaze back toward Rayne. "Are you following me?"

Rayne licked her lips and swallowed. She didn't meet Colin's gaze, but at least he could see her partially now. She stood tall, her shoulders back. She was about five-eight, but in her heels, she stood closer to six feet. She wasn't outwardly intimidated by this guy. Her gray pencil skirt was perfectly straight. Her pale green blouse that brought out the green of her eyes had not one wrinkle. Her smooth, silky brown hair was slicked back in a long ponytail at the base of her neck.

With perfect makeup and nails, Rayne was as professional as she could possibly be, and formidable as always. Colin sucked in a quick breath, remembering how she could affect him every time he'd seen her. It had been a year, but nothing had changed. "Sir, I'm not following you anywhere. And you're not my client. Get out of my office before I call the police."

Colin pulled his phone out of his pocket, liking the direction her mind was running. "I'll do the honors," he stated loud enough for the angry motherfucker to jerk his gaze toward Colin.

"Put that damn thing away, asshole. This is not your business."

Colin held up the phone and lifted a brow. "In five seconds, it's going to be my business. I hope your suit doesn't get too messed up while you spend the night in the county jail."

The fucker had the audacity to fully turn toward Colin, hands fisted at his sides, eyes narrowed, face dark red, teeth gritted. He growled. And then he turned his head back toward Rayne. "I'm leaving, but you better heed my advice. Shred the contract. You have no idea who you're dealing with." Luckily, the man turned around and stomped from the office.

As the door slammed, Colin flinched at the same moment he realized London was nowhere in sight. *Shit.*

Rayne stepped forward, but Colin turned around and headed toward the door.

"She said something about the bathroom," the receptionist offered in a kind voice.

"Colin?" Rayne asked.

He opened the door and glanced at her. "Be right back."

"I'll help you." Rayne dashed forward.

Colin opened the door to the hallway, and Rayne ducked under his arm to step out first.

"Bathroom's right over here," she began. "Let me check." She opened the door to the women's room and disappeared inside. "London?" she called out as the door slowly closed behind her.

Colin couldn't hear anything else, but a few minutes later, Rayne returned. "She's fine."

Colin blew out a breath, leaned against the opposite wall, and ran a hand through his short brown hair. "It was difficult to get her to come here at all. I'm sure she's about to bolt after that scene."

Rayne cringed. "I'm so sorry."

Colin frowned. "*You're* sorry? You don't have anything to be sorry about. How often do you get a client screaming at you like that? What a dick."

"Yeah. He wasn't the most pleasant sort, was he?" She shot him a teasing grin.

"Pleasant? That guy is probably going to kill his wife with his bare hands when he gets home."

"Yeah, I'm sure my receptionist is warning her right now. Shelly's amazing."

"Good."

Rayne's gaze wandered up and down Colin's frame. "You look good. Colorado must be working for you."

"You're looking well yourself. How do you maintain that Miami tan in Denver?" he teased, noticing how her skin glowed. She'd moved to Colorado a year ago. Colin had only arrived two months ago.

He'd known her for a few years. They'd frequented the same fetish clubs in Miami. At one point she'd dated one of the owners of the Miami branch of Club Zodiac, Rowen Easton. Colin had been a member of another Miami club, Breeze, before transferring his membership to Zodiac. He'd seen Rayne in both clubs at one time or another.

She scrunched up her face. "Fake tan. Don't tell anyone."

He chuckled. "You're going to get cancer." She looked hot as sin, but no way would he let her fake tan if she were his. What the hell was he thinking? Rayne was most certainly not his.

She shot him a tilted grin, and set him straight. "I don't bake it on. It's a lotion." She nodded toward the door. "You think she's going to come out?"

"Honestly? No. Not without coaxing." Colin sighed. Now was not the time to think of Rayne the way his mind was wandering. He was here to help his sister get her life straightened out and divorce her husband once and for all.

It was sheer coincidence that Rayne happened to have finished her law degree in Miami and then moved to Denver to set up her practice ten months before Colin arrived to open a second location of Club Zodiac. A convenient coincidence, since Colin didn't have to hunt down a divorce attorney with no recommendation.

Besides, it hadn't exactly been a tough decision. Ever since his sister had shown up on his doorstep, bruised and beaten, he'd known in his mind her situation might land him right where he was standing now. Next to Rayne Bryant. Not a hardship. In fact, she was intriguing. She always had been. After watching her hold her own with that asshole today, he was even more impressed with her.

Though he'd known her for several years and had spoken to her on many occasions, he'd never done a scene with her. He'd also never asked her on a date.

Colin had known for a long time that he was attracted to Rayne. However, she had been in a relationship with Rowen for most of the time Colin had known her. By the time the two of them broke up, Colin too had been in an ill-fated relationship. He shuddered at the memory.

"I'll go back in and speak to her," Rayne suggested, nodding toward the bathroom. "Anything I should know?" She kept her voice low. "When you made the appointment with Shelly, you didn't give her many details."

"I'm hoping after you meet with her, you'll know more than me, actually." He wasn't kidding. The details of his sister's fucked-up marriage were largely a mystery to him. She'd arrived at his home a week ago, battered and broken, emotionally and physically. She'd spent most of her time in the guest room and hadn't said much to him yet.

Rayne nodded. "That's what I get paid to do."

Ten minutes later, Rayne had convinced a reluctant London to exit the bathroom and return to her office. Rayne would have met with the woman alone normally, but London had insisted on having her brother present, so here they were.

It was all Rayne could do to keep from wincing every time she met London's gaze. The petite woman was about five-five, and she didn't weigh enough. Her thick, gorgeous, brown curls were pulled back from her face with a clip, but there wasn't much she could do to tame them. Not that she needed to. Most women would give anything to have hair that amazing.

What stood out to distract from her huge brown eyes was the fading purple and yellow circle around the left one and the angry, red scratches down the other side of her face.

It was a warm day in Denver. Midsummer. But London wore a long-sleeved T-shirt and jeans. Probably to hide other injuries.

Colin sat in the chair next to his sister, across the desk from Rayne. He looked amazing. Blue dress shirt, khaki pants. Loafers. In the past, she'd most often seen him dressed in black inside Club Zodiac. Today, he was not a Dom.

He kept rubbing his fists as if he might punch the next person who pissed him off, and Rayne couldn't blame him. Between the guy who'd just left her office and the man who'd undoubtedly used London as a punching bag recently, Colin had earned the right to have his blood boiling.

"I understand you'd like to file for divorce," Rayne began.

London shrugged. "I'm not sure. I mean, I certainly don't want my husband crashing into your office and threatening you like that last guy."

"And you think he would do that?" Rayne asked, hoping to coax her to spill as much information as possible.

She shrugged again. "He's unpredictable. There's no telling what he might do."

"Is he the one who gave you that black eye?"

"Yes." Her voice was soft.

"Do you have any other injuries I can't see?" Rayne asked.

"Yes," London whispered. A tear escaped her eye, and she reached up to swipe it away.

Every time she met another battered woman, Rayne wanted to scream. It never got easier. She'd seen more than her share, both in the last year working with them and during her internship in law school as a legal advocate for a women's shelter. Not that every marriage ended in abuse. Most did not. But she'd learned the signs early on. She'd always been the sort of person who kept her ears open and her mouth closed. "Did you file a report with the police?"

"Yes."

"You did?" Colin asked.

Rayne glanced at Colin who looked pale. His shoulders were slouched, which was uncharacteristic. Granted, the times Rayne had seen him in the past had all been at Zodiac or Breeze in Miami. On every occasion he'd been in full Dom mode while she'd been in her half-assed sub mode. In fact, this was the most dressed she'd ever been in his presence. That thought made her flush as she jerked her attention back to London.

London nodded. "Before I came to your house." More tears fell.

Rayne handed her several tissues from the box on the desk. "When was this?"

"Saturday night. Louis came home late, or early Sunday morning, I guess you could say. He was drunk, as usual, and he started screaming at me to fix him something to eat. I was asleep when he got there, but I scrambled out of bed and hurried to the kitchen, knowing it would be easier to comply than argue."

Rayne noticed Colin gripping the arms of the chair. He hadn't been kidding. His sister hadn't filled him in on these details yet. "Go on," Rayne encouraged.

"I had bacon frying when he stomped back into the kitchen. He grabbed the pan off the stove and slammed it through the wall. He said if he'd wanted breakfast, he would have asked for breakfast. He wanted a meal. Spaghetti or lasagna."

In the middle of the night?

"I was so tired." London glanced down, making herself smaller in the chair. "And emotional." Her voice was so low, it was hard to hear her. "And then my stomach roiled as it had every morning for a week. I raced toward the bathroom, but Louis grabbed my arm. He started screaming at me not to walk away from him. Rambling on and on about his dinner. My stomach revolted, and I couldn't stop myself from vomiting. Right in the hallway. It splashed all over the front of Louis, running down his shirt and jeans and shoes."

There was a long silence, during which Rayne feared she might have to stop Colin from punching a hole in the wall. She stared at him, willing him to calm down. "Are you pregnant?" she finally asked in a soft voice.

London let out a long sob and wiped her eyes again. "I don't think so. Not anymore."

"Not anymore?" Rayne asked, her own stomach clenching in a manner that threatened a revolt. She knew she wasn't going to like London's next words.

London's voice rose as she rushed to explain, leaving her face lowered to her lap. "He was so pissed. He grabbed my hair and yanked me to the floor. And then he started kicking me. Hard. All over. Worse than he'd ever done before. I curled up in a ball, but he didn't stop. He just kept kicking me and calling me names.

"And then he left me there in the hallway while he took a shower and changed clothes. I didn't move. I couldn't. I was too scared. In shock, I think. When he returned, he told me I was lucky he didn't own a gun, but he was going to fix that and he would be back."

Rayne rarely permitted herself to react outwardly to her clients. She'd heard so many stories in the past year, she could write a book about assault. Besides owning this law office, she also worked pro-bono for the local women's shelter. Those women had stories that would make anyone's skin crawl. But London...Jesus.

Rayne sucked in a sharp breath before she could stop herself. She also stood and rounded the desk to set a calming hand on Colin's shoulder, hoping to soothe him enough that he might stop white-knuckling the arms of the chair.

"Fuck," he muttered.

"Did he come back?" Rayne asked as she squatted down between Colin and his sister.

London shrugged. "I don't know. I called the police as soon as he left. They took a report, and then I took a taxi to Colin's apartment before Louis returned." She dipped her head and spoke in a whisper. "I was...bleeding. A lot. For several days."

Damn. He'd probably caused a miscarriage. Some days Rayne really hated dealing with so much abuse. "Was that the first time you'd reported him?" she asked in the calmest voice she could manage.

London nodded as another sob escaped. And then she suddenly sat up straighter and met Rayne's gaze. "I'll never, ever go back to him. But I'm scared out of my mind that he won't let me go peacefully."

Rayne nodded. "That's understandable. But you've come to the right place. I have a lot of experience with abuse. I promise I'll do my best to ensure you're safe and can go on with the rest of your life."

"Thank you." London smiled for the first time since she'd arrived. It was weak, but it was a start.

Rayne felt Colin's hand on her back, a gentle squeeze. A silent thank you.

A welcome touch that soothed Rayne as much as it probably did Colin. Rayne had never subbed for Colin, but she'd seen him in action, and she knew he could calm a sub with his touch.

It was incredibly inappropriate for butterflies to take flight in her belly at this moment, but it happened anyway. It had been a long time since she'd been to a club. Not since she'd moved to Denver. She'd had way too much on her plate to contemplate extracurricular activities.

But Colin's hand touched something deep inside her, dragging a need to the surface she'd ignored for too long. Perhaps it was time to check out the local scene.

As she stared at Colin's sister, Rayne pondered, not for the first time, at the logic of someone like her finding solace in the arms of a Dom. Someone who spent her days working so hard to help people out of abusive situations attending fetish clubs by night.

She had studied law and abuse for many years. She was also well-educated about the nuances of D/s. It was clear to her that there was no connection between abusive relationships and consensual submission. The two were eons apart.

Besides the constraints on her time, Rayne had held off visiting a local club on the off chance she might run into someone in her profession. Or worse—an abusive spouse she might have encountered along the way who fancied himself a Dom.

The chances of either happening were slim, however, and after seeing Colin today, she felt a renewed need to venture back out into the scene. It was time. Perhaps she should even inquire with Colin about the local clubs. She knew he had moved to Denver to open up a new Zodiac, but he undoubtedly had the scoop on other clubs that were already operational.

She could call him and ask a few questions. Or, she reminded herself with a shake of her head, she could google and keep her relationship with Colin professional.

ALSO BY BECCA JAMESON

Project DEEP:

Reviving Emily

Reviving Trish

Reviving Dade

Reviving Zeke

Reviving Graham

Reviving Bianca

Reviving Olivia

SEALs in Paradise:

Hot SEAL, Red Wine

Hot SEAL, Australian Nights

Dark Falls:

Dark Nightmares

Club Zodiac:

Training Sasha

Obeying Rowen

Collaring Brooke

Mastering Rayne

Trusting Aaron

Claiming London

The Art of Kink:

Pose

Paint

Sculpt

Arcadian Bears:

Grizzly Mountain

Grizzly Beginning

Grizzly Secret

Grizzly Promise

Grizzly Survival

Grizzly Perfection

Sleeper SEALs:

Saving Zola

Spring Training:

Catching Zia

Catching Lily

Catching Ava

The Underground series:

Force

Clinch

Guard

Submit

Thrust

Torque

Saving Sofia (Kindle World)

Wolf Masters series:

Kara's Wolves

Lindsey's Wolves

Jessica's Wolves

Alyssa's Wolves

Tessa's Wolf

Rebecca's Wolves

Melinda's Wolves

Laurie's Wolves

Amanda's Wolves

Sharon's Wolves

Claiming Her series:

The Rules

The Game

The Prize

Emergence series:

Bound to be Taken

Bound to be Tamed

Bound to be Tested

Bound to be Tempted

The Fight Club series:

Come

Perv

Need

Hers

Want

Lust

Wolf Gatherings series:

Tarnished

Dominated

Completed

Redeemed

Abandoned

Betrayed

Durham Wolves series:

Rescue in the Smokies

Fire in the Smokies

Freedom in the Smokies

Stand Alone Books:

Blind with Love

Guarding the Truth

Out of the Smoke

Abducting His Mate

Three's a Cruise

Wolf Trinity

Frostbitten

A Princess for Cale/A Princess for Cain

ABOUT THE AUTHOR

Becca Jameson is a USA Today best-selling author of over 80 books. She is most well-known for her Wolf Masters series and her Fight Club series. She currently lives in Atlanta, Georgia, with her husband, two grown kids, and the various pets that wander through. She is loving this journey and has dabbled in a variety of genres, including paranormal, sports romance, military, and BDSM.

A total night owl, Becca writes late at night, sequestering herself in her office with a glass of red wine and a bar of dark chocolate, her fingers flying across the keyboard as her characters weave their own stories.

During the day--which never starts before ten in the morning!--she can be found jogging, floating in the pool, or reading in her favorite hammock chair!

...where Alphas dominate...

Becca's Newsletter Sign-up

Contact Becca:
www.beccajameson.com
beccajameson4@aol.com

facebook.com/becca.jameson.18

twitter.com/beccajameson

instagram.com/becca.jameson

bookbub.com/authors/becca-jameson

goodreads.com/beccajameson

amazon.com/author/beccajameson

Printed in Great Britain
by Amazon